REVENGE
AIN'T SWEET

Colin Mardell

APS BOOKS

Yorkshire

APS Books,
The Stables Field Lane,
Aberford,
West Yorkshire,
LS25 3AE

APS Books is a subsidiary of the APS Publications imprint

www.andrewsparke.com

First published worldwide by APS Books in 2023

PROLOGUE

23:35 hours, Mid-March - Omsk, Siberia

It was minus twenty degrees Celsius, and biting wind threatened to cut right through the old man's barely adequate clothing as he trudged the four kilometres to his tiny apartment. It hadn't snowed since the previous night, but he could feel that it wouldn't be long. The last snowfall had been compacted into a glass-like sheet by hundreds of trampling feet throughout the day, but like all Russians, he'd schooled himself to stay upright.

Dmitri Turgenev was sixty-eight and didn't know if he would survive this winter let alone the following one. He'd been born in a small village on the Baltic Coast in Leningrad Oblast where the climate was much warmer. At the time, his father, an active and loyal member of the Communist Party, was mayor of the small nearby town of Sosnovy Bor. The town, which otherwise would have been a non-entity on the Russian map, only earned recognition by virtue of the nearby nuclear plant that provided much of its employment.

Encouraged by his parents, as a single child Dmitri worked hard at school and eventually earned a first-class degree in political science at Saint Petersburg University at the time when it was still known as Leningrad State. His work ethic earned him a place in the St Petersburg administration under Anatoly Sobchak, a co-author of the Constitution of the Russian Federation, and an early influence upon Vladimir Putin.

Dmitri, recruited by Putin acolytes before the fall of the Soviet Union, rode the wave that swept the ruthless man to power, becoming a close ally during his first premiership. Like all those that had remained loyal, Dmitri was rewarded with a position of power and the wealth that went with it.

The advantages that went with Putin's sponsorship included access to huge wealth but carried with it all the dangers of holding a tiger by its tail. As long as you were able to produce results - in other words enrich the Russian state - your position was secure. However, if performance slipped, everything you thought was yours was at risk of being taken away. In Dmitri's case his success in creating foreign currency for the Russian State was better than most; the prestige and rewards he'd received reflected that.

Seven months earlier Dmitri Turgenev had been a dollar billionaire, one of Russia's elite. He'd wielded the power to demand subservience or issue punishment which he exercised without compassion or conscience at the slightest provocation. With three homes inside the country and two in Europe, a yacht, a property portfolio which included chains of department stores, supermarkets, luxury hotels and interests in shipbuilding, his wealth was quite literally beyond the dreams of almost every Russian citizen.

Several years earlier however, someone in whom he'd placed a great deal of faith, had proposed a scheme that, had it succeeded, would have gained the country a huge military advantage and potentially massive financial gain. The ambitious long-term plan involved an enormous investment in time and money, requiring the personal approval of the president himself. It had taken a great deal of persuasion on Dmitri's behalf, but in the end his friend Vladimir had grantehis approval for the plan to go ahead.

After a significant setback there was little hope of salvaging the scheme but the friend had persuaded Turgenev to double down and seek permission to try again. Putin had granted permission, but made it clear what the consequences for Dmitri would be, should there be any further significant losses. Already at risk of losing much of his wealth, he gambled that the potential for profit and prestige were too great to be ignored.

Four years later the plan had spectacularly failed, effectively losing the whole investment of well over a billion dollars and leaving the Russian state open to ridicule. Putin's response had been to strip Dmitri of everything, banish him to Omsk and give him the post of Ticket Office Manager at one of the city's Railway stations. His long-term friendship and loyalty to President spared him the *fall from a balcony*. Instead the oligarch's fate was arguably something worse, something which to all intents and purposes was still a death sentence. At his age, with no other means of support than a pitiful salary, a poor diet and with little suitable clothing beyond what he could steal or buy second-hand, the likelihood of long-term survival was slim.

With another two kilometres to traipse to his meagre home, a pickup truck pulled up beside him. The passenger door opened, and the driver shouted, "Get in Turgenev."

He didn't know the man who looked menacing.

"No, I don't want to." Turgenev quickly turned attempting to hurry away. At his age and in these conditions, running wasn't an option. The worn tread of his second-hand boots skidded from under him on the frozen ground and he fell onto his hip. The pain when he landed was excruciating, and he feared he might have broken a pelvic bone. At his age in this part of the world that would mean the start of a long painful end to his life.

The driver didn't get out of the vehicle. He just pointed a gun and impatiently said, "Stop fucking around and get in the car you stupid old bastard, or I'll put a bullet in your knee and leave you here; you'll be dead before breakfast."

Knowing the man was right, Dmitri struggled to his knees, crawled to the car and with great difficulty, painfully climbed inside.

When the man ordered him to shut the door, it was a struggle to obey, but he eventually succeeded. Seconds later the man did a U-turn and drove back the way he'd come.

"Where are you taking me?"

"Somewhere we can have a very long talk."

"I have to be back at work by six o'clock in the morning or I'll lose my job."

"You're not going back to work; you're going to help me, and if I'm happy with your help I'll let you live and reward you with one hundred thousand US dollars. If not I'll kill you."

"I work in a ticket office, what help can I be?"

"I'm not interested in a train ride to Vladivostok. You know things from your former life that can help me get my hands on millions of dollars."

The heater of the fifteen-year-old UAZ pickup bravely struggled against the external temperature but barely held its own. At least it was above freezing inside the cab, and Turgenev was grateful for that.

"Who're you?" the old man asked.

"You don't recognise me? I must have come into your office giving you copies of reports once a month for at least eleven years, and yet you don't know who I am? You arrogant asshole, I'm Miron Sokolov. I was Chief Accountant for your chain of department stores."

"I know your name. Didn't you stand in after Zaitsev was arrested?"

"That's right and uncovered the size of his fraudulent activities over the previous eleven years, for which you rewarded me by sending

3

me back to work in the poxy little office in Nekrasovka and installing that cock-sucking asshole Gurin."

"You did good work. I don't know why I don't recognise your face."

"Probably because when I came into the room, you rarely bothered to look up. Most of the time you wouldn't even bother to say thank you."

"What is it you think I know that can help you. They stripped me of everything I owned?"

"I know you've got money stashed away that the authorities know nothing about for just this eventuality."

"If I did, why would I still be in Omsk?"

"Because you know that if you made a run for it they'd know you still had reserves and would then kill you for concealing them."

"There'd be no point in having this alleged stash then, would there?"

"You've been stealing things and selling them so you can gather enough to make a break and grab the cash. I've watched you. That will take years, and I bet you've no plan of what to do when you get it."

"So your plan is to force me to tell you where this supposed secret hoard is and take it?"

"Only if you don't help me find where the real money is. All I need from you is enough to get me out of the country, and the information to help me locate the mother lode."

"I don't know what you mean."

"Stamelis; I need to find him."

"He's almost certainly dead. If not, he will be as soon as he reveals himself."

Sokolov took his eyes off the road and turned to his hostage. "It won't matter if he's dead; you know things about him that will help me find his money."

"Putin's people will have taken all he had left, like they did mine."

Sokolov sneered. "And we both know that he didn't get all of yours."

"How can you get out of the country?"

"Unlike you, I've made some preparations and I know someone. Now shut the fuck up and let me drive."

"Where are we headed?"

"Kingisepp."

"That'll take days."

"No more than three if we're lucky with the weather, and you can do your share of the driving."

"What if I refuse?"

"By the time I need to take a break your chances of getting back to your job will be zero, so you'll be as good as a dead man anyway, and you'd be pretty stupid not to stay with me. Your days as a railway employee are over; your only chance of survival now is to stick to me like a second skin."

Turgenev lapsed into silence, exhausted from the sixteen hour shift he'd not long finished, and ten minutes later he was fast asleep. When he next woke it was already daylight. He glanced at the dashboard cloc. It was almost 10am; he'd slept for nearly ten hours. He wasn't surprised. It was the warmest he'd been since October, and he'd been working twelve and sixteen hour shifts six days a week for six months.

He was stiff and his neck hurt where he'd slept awkwardly. When he tried to move a sharp pain shot through his left hip joint making him cry out.

"Awake at last; about time. I'm going to stop and fuel up at the next gas station then you can take over while I sleep."

"Where are we?"

"Approaching Suksan."

"Won't they miss you at work today?"

"I was sacked over a month ago. They told me that I should have known that Stamelis' scheme could never have succeeded. Fucking ridiculous; I'd no idea that Stamelis even had a scheme, I still don't, although I could have taken a wild guess. I wasn't even supposed to have anything to do with your business with that Greek bastard, but then there were a lot of things I wasn't supposed to have anything to do with. I learnt a lot during my time as Zaitsev's stand in.

"I expect all you Putin ass-licking bastards have been lining your pockets in case stealing from the state like you've all been doing becomes unfashionable and your benefactor in the Kremlin dies or you run out of luck. What I did know about was your little trick of milking off small amounts of money at a time from defaulting accounts after the bailiffs had been in. That was very clever by the way. My guess is you were doing the same thing with all the other businesses, so wherever that nest egg is now, it's probably quite big."

"Why didn't you report me?"

"Because they would have sent me to somewhere like Omsk for not spotting it earlier or reporting my suspicions. You know how they work."

"How can I trust you not to take it all?"

"You can't, but Stamelis has been operating outside Russia, so it's my guess that his stash is massively bigger than yours, and if you want any of it you're going to need me."

"Unless you agree to take me with you, I won't cooperate."

"I was planning to take you with me anyway unless you fuck me around. I need you to help me find my way through that Greek bastard's web of deceit."

They topped up the fuel tank at Suksan and agreed to six hour shifts in driving. The boredom and need for sleep prevented any meaningful conversation over the following two days. The weather had been kind to them, but it was 19:30 on Wednesday when they arrived at the Miranda Aparthotel in Kingisepp. Sokolov had been driving and he shook his fellow traveller awake.

"This will do, for the next night or two anyway."

Turgenev stirred and looked up at the dull featureless building. "I hope you've got some money to pay for this because all I've got is about a hundred roubles."

"I've got plenty, about twenty thousand if I counted it correctly. You should know; I took it from your apartment."

"What?! You bastard!"

"I shouldn't complain if I were you; if I'd left it there you were never going to get access to it again anyway. Stop moaning, grab your bag out of the back and let's go get us a room."

"Bag?"

"I put a few of those pathetic rags from your apartment in a bag."

They were soon alone in their twin bedroom.

"First things first, get yourself in the shower; you stink like a horse with diarrhoea. So do I, but you're worse."

Once they were both clean, they set about finding somewhere to eat and found that Burger King was the only place open.

At first light, Sokolov chased Turgenev out of bed. "Come on you lazy old bastard. We've got work to do. Repack your bag in case we decide not to come back.

Over the last six months Dmitri had become accustomed to taking orders and silently obeyed.

After breakfasting in a café, Sokolov hustled Turgenev into the car.

"Where are we going?"

"We're going to pay your old friend Killip a visit. He won't be expecting you, but if we hurry we can catch him before he leaves for work at the glass factory."

"How did you know about Killip?"

"You've been writing to each other every month since you were exiled."

"But how do you know that?"

"You didn't think that Sunday was my first visit to your apartment did you? I've looked in about five times; you've been saving his letters. Don't worry; I've destroyed them."

"Does that mean that you've been exiled too?"

"No, I was lucky enough to just be dismissed. Like you though, I've salted bits away over the years and it's been enough to last me until now, and they won't be looking for me yet. Let's go."

They dragged themselves up interminable flights of stairs to the top floor of the apartment block where Killip lived. There was a lift, but nobody would trust lifts in residential buildings in a rural town, even if they did work.

Severely out of breath, and in pain, Turgenev knocked on the door.

It opened and an elderly man opened it. "Dmitri, what on earth are you doing here? Are you alright, you look awful, and you've lost so much weight. Come in."

"Killip, this is my friend Miron," Turgenev said after he'd caught his breath, and searched in his coat for glucose tablets.

They were soon all seated with cups of black tea and glasses of vodka.

Over the next hour Sokolov learnt that Killip had been holding a bank account on behalf of his second cousin Dmitri for fifteen years, on the understanding that Killip could retain half of all deposits for himself. An astonishing act of loyalty, in a country where loyalty to anything other than the state normally came at a very high price. It was also an extraordinary risk by both Killip and Turgenev. From a quick look around Killip's apartment, it didn't look as if he'd been spending much of it.

The system they'd devised was that as soon as deposits accumulated to the market equivalent of 200 Euros, Killip would withdraw it and exchange it on the black market for Euros, split the proceeds and then hide them in an agreed place. The net result for Dmitri was he had a nest egg of four hundred thousand Euros, equivalent to about half a million US dollars. Killip had about the same. Deposits had ceased after Dmitri's exile but the pair of them had done well out of it.

"What are you going to do now, Dmitri?" Killip asked.

"We're going to leave the country."

"How?"

"I don't know. Miron has a plan. Don't you?"

"Yes but I don't want to speak about the detail just yet. Killip, you do realise that your position here in Russia is now untenable don't you?"

"What do you mean?"

"If I've discovered Dmitri's secret bank account, and his cousin who lives in Kingisepp; now that he's disappeared it won't be long before the police find their way here too. You need to disappear as well, and soon."

"But my job..."

"You've got half a million dollars hidden away somewhere; what's keeping you in Russia? You're a widower, you've got no children. You've got a crappy job working shit hours for not much more than minimum wages. Unless you've got a girlfriend..."

"Are you saying I should go with you?"

"That's exactly what I'm suggesting, yes."

Killip looked perplexed. "I'm an old man, how can I start again in a new country?"

"A lot easier if you're alive than if you stayed here to be relentlessly tortured by the FSB to get you to tell what happened to Dmitri, before being thrown into the Lubyanka jail for treason."

"You're saying that I don't have a choice."

"None at all from where I sit. So you need to get a move on and pack a bag. Just the essentials you understand."

"Now?"

"Yes, now. Dmitri has been missing for three days; it won't be long before the police start looking, and they'll begin by searching his apartment in Omsk. They may find something that leads them directly to you or they may not; I cleared out most of it, but I can't be sure. Either way they'll get here sooner or later."

Within two hours the three of them were in the car and Miron turned to the others; "Right, where's the money?"

The others looked at each other and hesitated.

"Okay, if that's the way you're going to play it, let me make an educated guess. Is the word Kolgompya familiar to you?"

"How did you know about that?"

"Because I didn't just decide to start this on the spur of the moment. I've been researching this for months. I learned about your father's dacha in December, Dmitri. You allegedly sold it after his death, but the person you supposedly sold it to doesn't exist, and it's now let out to senior Communist Party members for summer fishing trips. What I don't know is where on the site you've cached your stash. Am I on the right track?"

"Yes," he admitted.

Sokolov set the GPS, started the car, and headed toward Kolgompya, a small village on the Gulf of Finland. They'd been driving for less than fifteen minutes when Killip's cell phone rang.

"Hello Yulia. Is something wrong?...Oh God I wonder what's that all about?...I'm not at work, I'm on my way to Petersburg to see my nephew...I'll be back tomorrow about five o'clock. Thank you for letting me know." He hung up. "That was my neighbour; the police have been to my apartment."

"Turn the phone off, remove the SIM card and throw them both out of the window, but not in the same place. You haven't got a cell phone have you Dmitri?"

"No, I'm not allowed. Not that I could afford one anyway."

They'd only driven another ten minutes when Miron turned off the small country road they'd been following and onto an unmade forest track. When they were out of sight of the road he stopped.

"Why have you stopped?"

"We can't go to the dacha in daylight; we don't want to draw attention to ourselves."

"So we have to sit here until seven o'clock?" Dmitri complained.

"More like ten o'clock. The tides need to be right, and we don't want to arouse suspicion of locals who might be out and about. But don't worry, in the intervening time you can tell me everything you remember about Manos Stamelis. Sorry if this gets boring for you Killip, but it's kind of essential to what comes next for us."

In the event it was closer to eleven before they pulled onto the drive of the beach front holiday home. Within minutes Dmitri and Killip had located their stashes in the crawlspace beneath the house. They shovelled long frozen snow away from the access hatch with a shovel that Miron had brought in the back of his truck. Then retrieved the two matching metal lined wooden trunks marked 'D' and 'K' that the money that had been stored in.

"What now?" Dmitri wanted to know.

"Help me with the boat."

"Where is it?" Killip asked.

"Behind those trees. I put it there a week ago. It's heavy so it'll take all three of us to drag it to the jetty."

The Gemini Rib had lost none of its rigidity since Miron had inflated it and put it there with the assistance of a teenaged neighbour whom he'd paid off with a thousand Roubles.

"Are we supposed to paddle the 60 kilometres across the Estonian border?" Dmitri complained. The effort of dragging the heavy boat across the sandy beach had obviously taken it out of him. Although the pain in his hip had receded, it was clearly still troubling him.

"No, if you'll let me reverse the truck up to it, we can attach the outboard I've brought. It's heavy but between us we should be able to manhandle it into place."

"I need to eat something soon; all this exertion will give me a hypo."

"There are some more energy bars in the truck. Will they be enough?"

"I expect so. How long will it take to get across the border?"

"No more than two hours I'm told. The tide should be favourable if we leave within the next hour, but it'll depend on the wind, or if we hear a patrol boat and have to temporarily shut the engine down."

In the event they were at sea in fifty minutes and were once again lucky with wind and sea. There was a waxing crescent moon and intermittent cloud, so in the dark, the safest way to make the journey by boat would have been by hugging the coast. Doing that though, would add more than an hour to the journey and Miron didn't know if the fuel in the small tank would last that long, so he decided to risk cutting across inlets and bays using the app on his phone to navigate.

The exertion had been almost too much for Dmitri and soon after they left the jetty he started to become hypoglycemic. Fortunately,

Killip spotted his cousin's lack of response to his shouts. Rummaging in Dmitri's pockets by the light from Miron's cell phone, the cousin found his glucose tablets. The old man hadn't quite lapsed into a diabetic coma and was conscious enough to chew them.

The air temperature was minus two but with the wind chill and spray it felt much colder. Miron had provided second-hand waterproof fishermen's clothes that he'd bought from charity stores over the previous weeks. There were jackets, bib and brace trousers, and boots, but he had expected them to rely on their own ushanka headwear and glove; every Russian knew to provide those for themselves.

They were an hour and a half into their journey when Dmitri asked, "How much further?"

"We can't be far from Estonian waters now, but FSB Coastguards won't worry too much about territorial waters this close to a European Union country, so we won't be entirely safe until we're on land."

Almost as soon as he'd spoken, Killip spotted a momentary flash of light off their starboard bow. Miron killed the engine and they all ducked as low as they could and waited. The throbbing sound of a powerful patrol boat engine grew louder and louder as it slowly moved past them heading eastwards. Although they couldn't see it, the vessel sounded as if it could be less than fifty metres away. It seemed impossible they hadn't been spotted.

Then suddenly a shout; "There, one hundred metres, five points off the port bow."

The powerful engine suddenly accelerated. The three fugitives cowered in the bottom of the boat as they heard three bursts of machine gun fire. Astonishingly none of the bullets penetrated the skin of their boat and when Miron peeped over the side he saw a small fishing boat lit up in the patrol boat's floodlights. It was towing a semi-inflatable similar to their own that had about six people in it.

"Stay down and keep quiet. They've caught others trying to do the same thing."

It was nearly another hour before the fishing boat and inflatable had been taken in tow by the patrol boat, during which time they'd drifted westwards on the tide for almost a mile. Although they were definitely inside Estonian waters they were probably still more than two miles offshore. They waited until they could no longer see the bridge lights of the patrol boat before restarting the engine and heading south toward the coast. The tide continued to push them westwards, so by the time they could see the white surf of waves breaking on the shore, they'd passed the place that Miron had arranged to be met.

By four-fifteen it was slack water and Miron was able to steer directly toward their pre-planned landing place, a beach no more than five hundred metres long.

The relief they all felt when the bow scrunched on the stony beach was immeasurable.

Separated from the narrow coastal road by a thin strip of trees, the beach was only three metres deep in places.

As he fumbled trying to change the SIM card in his phone with his cold hands, Miron told them, "Okay you two, get these trunks on land while I contact my friend."

"We're here," he simply told whoever answered his call, then replying to whatever had been said, "Okay that's' fantastic."

"They'll be here in a few minutes," Miron announced.

When he turned back to the others, the first of the two trunks was already on the beach well above the surf and only six feet from the trees that separated the beach from the road. The second box was still in the boat and Dmitri was slumped on the side with his head in his hands. "I can't do any more, you'll have to help Killip with the other one."

Anxious to get off the beach Miron didn't argue and climbed into the boat. Killip was already gripping the front lifting handle, so Miron clambered toward the stern and reached for the second strap. As he bent to lift the heavy trunk, a shot rang out and he dropped to the bottom board for cover.

"You're safe now Miron, you can stand up," a woman's voice announced.

"What the fuck?"

"This bastard was about to shoot you." The speaker was an elderly woman gripping a modern rifle as she approached from the trees, lifting night vision glasses from her eyes. She pointed at Killip's body, and the pistol swinging from his trigger finger.

"Iliya, thank god."

"How are you, Miron. It's been far too long?"

"A lot better now thanks, but we'd better get these things loaded into your car in case anybody heard that shot."

"We're over a kilometre from the nearest house, and people like me are always shooting at night around here, lamping for wild boar and the like. Nobody will think twice."

Miron turned to Dmitri. "Did you know he was going to do that, you bastard?"

"I knew he had a gun. I thought he was only going to use it if you threatened us."

"If I detect any attempt on my life by you, I'll kill you without drawing breath."

"I'm not going to kill you; you've saved my life, and I've no idea where Stamelis might have cached any money, but I hope we can find it if we work together."

Miron decided to take him at his word, if only because he had little choice. Between them, they pushed the inflatable afloat again, started the motor, and released it to sail Killip's body out to sea.

It took twenty minutes to drag the boxes through the trees to Iliya's ten-year-old VW Amarok, then an hour and a half to her home on the outskirts of Tallinn. They unloaded the boxes into her garage, before going inside the centrally heated home to get themselves properly warm for the first time in months.

ONE

The ten-year-old BMW X7 pulled up next to the front steps at, Pangbourne Grange, and a tall, lithe, seventeen-year-old girl stepped out to be enveloped in the arms of Jason Anstruther who had been housekeeper to the Parker-West family since she'd been a small child.

"Cassie, you're home at last. For a few months we get to see you for more than two days at a time. How are you?"

"I'm fine; glad the exams are over though. What time will Mummy and Daddy be home, do you know?"

"Anna won't be home until about six I think. She says she's expecting some shenanigans at a board meeting. Drew is due back any moment though. His plane landed early and he's going to take a cab."

"Can I help bring your bags in, Cassie?" the driver asked.

"Would you, Toby, thank you. There's so much more this time because I'm not going back."

"If we all pitch in we can do it in a single trip," Jason suggested.

When all the paraphernalia that went with a teenager permanently returning home from boarding school had been deposited in her room they all returned to the ground floor.

"Thank you so much for coming to collect me, Toby. I could have waited until tomorrow, but all my best friends had already gone home, and I was so desperate to see everybody."

"It was no problem, Cassie. Will you be riding much now you're back?" Toby was the groom and sometime driver for the family.

"Gosh, I hadn't thought about it. I haven't been on horseback since Christmas. That's terrible isn't it?"

"You've been too busy, so I'm not surprised. You're getting a bit tall for Ginger now. Perhaps you should move up to Rocky or Jilly."

"That's a good thought. We should get a horse big enough for Daddy."

"I suggested that, but he said, it wouldn't get enough use to make it worthwhile."

"Do you want tea, Cassie?" Jason asked.

"Oh yes please, I'll make it though. Do you want one Toby?"

"No thanks, I need to finish off in the stable."

Cassie settled at the kitchen table with Jason.

14

"So what've you decided; which uni and which course?"

"It's too soon; my applications went in with everybody else's, my interviews went okay, and I've had some offers, but you already know about them. I'm just going to wait for my results."

"We all know the results are a formality. It'll be 'A-star' across the board.

"Nothing is certain, I want to do History and English Lit. but I had a bit of a blip in history at the beginning of the last school year."

"Nonsense, we all know why that was, it's all behind you now, and to misquote a well-known novelist, it is a truth universally acknowledged that you are a genius."

"Stop it," she said. Jason was always far too effusive in his praise of her.

The security system sounded an alert that someone had just come through the pedestrian gate. They both looked up to the screen.

"Daddy!"

Jason smiled as he watched the girl rush to the front door and run down the drive to greet her adoptive father, wrapping her arms around his neck and smothering his face with kisses.

Drew Parker accepted his daughter's welcome with his normal apparent indifference, but everyone knew that he worshipped her, as much as he did her mother.

"We weren't expecting you back until tomorrow, sweetheart. I was going to collect you."

"I couldn't wait. I had my last paper this morning, I was already packed up to go so I couldn't see the point in waiting. I rang Jason, but he told me that you and Mummy weren't here, so he asked Toby to come and collect me. Aren't you pleased to see me?"

"You know I am. Always pleased to see you, sweetheart."

"Where have you been?"

"Only France, nowhere exotic. I've no plans to go away again, not for a few weeks at least."

"Are you too tired to go for a run? I haven't had chance to properly stretch myself since the weekend before last."

"Give me a few minutes to change," he told her.

Their joint exercise routines had been a big element in helping them bond after Drew had come into their lives when she was eleven. At school she'd been in a small minority that almost religiously began the day with a tough exercise routine, but that had all had to take a back seat to exam prep over the last few weeks.

They ran silently for the first five laps of the mile long Grange property perimeter. He was taller than her and with his long legs and extraordinary stamina he could outrun her over long distances with ease, in spite of a difference of twenty-two years in their age, but he enjoyed her company.

He was a quiet person. Cassie recognised that, and never pressed him for idle conversation. When they talked it was usually for a purpose. Often she sought his opinion, occasionally his advice, more often his reassurance.

She slowed and stopped at the old oak tree which he recognised as a signal that she wanted to talk.

"How were the exams?" he asked.

"Not terrible. Had a bit of a wobble in my second English Lit paper, but I think I did enough."

"So what next?"

"Reading I hope."

"Not Cambridge? Most people would choose that if it were an option."

"I want to live at home, at least for a while. After what happened in Canada I'm not ready to go out into the world on my own."

"Nothing wrong with that, except we'll need to get you a driving licence maybe."

"Can I start driving lessons right away?"

"Sure, I'll try to find someone suitable in the next day or two."

"Can't you teach me?"

"The generally accepted wisdom is that it's not a good idea to learn to drive from a family member."

"I know but you're different."

"Different, how?"

"You're patient with everybody. And you already showed me how to drive."

"I showed you how to operate the controls; that's not the same thing. Not only that; I'm a Yank. It would be better to learn from a Brit."

"I suppose you're right. As usual."

"Another lap or two, then skip the gym fore a few laps in the pool eh?" he suggested.

"Okay."

They hadn't gone more than another twenty yards when she pulled up again and announced, "I've got a boyfriend."

He stopped and turned to see her looking worried.

"That's nice. Have you known him long?"

"About six weeks."

"If I ask you about him, will it upset you?"

"What do you mean?"

"Well you've just announced that you've got a boyfriend for the first time. In normal circumstances that wouldn't be a big deal, even if a load of dads, especially American ones, would think it was. But given who you are, and what with recent history it sort of ups the ante, doesn't it?"

"I suppose."

"Most girls would get upset if their dad started asking searching questions."

"I could ask you not to check him out, but I know you're going to anyway. And I guess it's the right thing to do and best that I tell you what I do know. His name is Robert. He goes to Padbury College which is quite near Downley. Our two schools sometimes have joint events, and we go to see each other's plays and concerts and stuff. He came to our production of Lysistrata, and we got chatting afterwards."

"How old is he?"

"Eighteen. He's starting at Reading College in September studying art and design."

"That's a good area to work in. Does he treat you well?"

"We haven't done anything yet, if that's what you mean."

"That's not what I meant, and unless you'd rather not, I think it might be better if you have that half of the conversation with your mom. What I was talking about was, is he considerate? Does he try to boss you around or get you to do things you'd prefer not to?"

"No. Actually he's really a bit shy, but I don't mind that."

"What do you do together? I mean, what with school and coming home at weekends you can't have much time."

"We go to the cinema or theatre on Thursday evenings. He picks me up after school; we go to somewhere like Nando's or KFC first."

"So he can drive already."

"Yes, he's got an old hatchback, but I think it's in quite good condition."

"Are they allowed to have cars at Padbury?"

"He's not a boarder."

"Why did you choose to talk to me about this rather than your mom?"

"Because Mummy will panic, and I thought if you checked him out first I could tell her there's nothing to worry about."

"What does he know about you?"

"Nothing very much as far as I know. He knows my mum and dad are quite well off, and he knows you're in the security industry. That's all I think. We don't really talk about our parents."

"So what do you talk about?"

"He talks about cricket, I talk about literature. He's not very knowledgeable about it but he makes a lot of intelligent remarks. I pretend I'm interested in cricket, and he laughs when I say something silly because I don't know enough about the rules. I suppose we don't have much in common, but we enjoy each other's company."

"I'm not sure that matters. On the face of things, me and your mom don't have much in common and that seems to work okay."

"Should I go on the pill do you think?"

"You should speak to your mom about that."

"I will, but I don't mean the medical aspect of it. I mean is it a good idea?"

"I don't remember much about my life when I was your age; nothing good anyway. I do remember the first few occasions I went with a girl that way, I was younger then than you are now, and the subject of contraception never came up. I didn't use a condom, the girls never mentioned being on the pill, so I guess either they were, or we just got lucky. My guess is that in the heat of the moment nothing has changed in that regard, but there are other considerations. We're straying into territory that's better discussed with your mom."

"But you're not telling me not to have sex?"

"Sweetheart, if I told you not to; like millions of dads before me have, it wouldn't make a blind bit of difference if that's what you've decided to do. You're a clever girl. You already know the pitfalls of not taking precautions, and I know you're not going to just fall into that sort of relationship just because you think it's expected."

"You're such a great Daddy. I love you so much. My friends say they can't talk to their dads like this."

"You need to talk about it with your mom as well though."

"I know, but can I leave it until you've checked him out?"

"Tell me where he lives."

"I don't know exactly, somewhere in Newbury."

"Then just give me his cell phone number and email address. That should be enough for my purpose. I promise not to read any of your emails or texts."

They did three more laps, then spent half an hour in the pool.

Later, Jason looked up as the lady of the house entered the kitchen from the coach house entrance, the scowl on her face painting a picture.

"Bad day?"

"I hate people whose only motive in life is to make money."

"I thought that was the purpose of big business," Drew said coming into the kitchen.

"It is I suppose, but it shouldn't be to the exclusion of everything else. Nor should it be seen as some sort of weakness or failure if personal gain isn't your raison d'etre. Those assholes were trying to convince me to get the trust to sell their NorArm/Silico shares and invest in other things." *Asshole* was a new addition to her vocabulary since marrying Drew. "They told me it didn't look good that so much of the company was owned by a charitable trust. I told them that as my personal holdings together with the trust holdings had a controlling interest and they would need to live with it, because I wasn't going to budge."

"You knew they weren't going to be happy when you created the trust."

"I know, but it doesn't affect the working model or the share price. They're only trying to get an opportunity to buy up additional shares to give them a bigger slice of the pie, giving them greater control, and enabling them to club together and vote me out of the chair."

"Hasn't Percy still got a big chunk?"

"Yes, and he'll always vote with me, but he's no longer a director and his health isn't so good these days. What's worrying too, is that he's on the board of trustees, so when he retires, whoever takes over won't necessarily vote the same way."

"Who's making the most noise?"

"The ringleader is Steve Boardman."

"Is he that smarmy bastard with Brioni suits, gelled hair, and ten-thousand-dollar teeth?"

"That's him. He's holding the seat for his hedge fund which has a 15% holding."

"What happened in the end?"

"I told the three troublemakers that if they were that unhappy I'd buy them out."

"Could you still do that?"

"Just about I think. It would mean selling a few things, and juggling a few others. It's not what I want. I don't want any more people calling me *Madam Munitions*, like that tabloid paper did. Then the same three wanted to drop 'Silico' from the name of the company. I told them that NorArm is the subordinate part of the company in revenue terms and if there were going to be changes it would be that name to be dropped. It'll be over my dead body, that they'd launder the last remnants of Henry's memory from that company." Henry was her first husband, with whom she'd set up the company.

As she was speaking Cassie joined them. "Mummy!"

Anna's face instantly lit up. "Cassie, sweetheart, what are you doing back? We were going to collect you tomorrow."

"I was impatient to get home, and Toby collected me."

"It's wonderful to see you. A lovely end to a horrible day."

The rest of the day passed without Drew revealing the conversation he'd had with Cassie, and the next day began with her asking him to confirm that he hadn't.

TWO

"I'm going to be out for an hour or two this morning, sweetheart," Drew announced over breakfast.

"Now we don't have to pick Cassie up, I thought you'd be free."

"Sorry, but something came up. It's nothing big so I thought I'd get it out of the way while things are quiet."

"Okay, I suppose I can use the time to be putting a few things to bed from yesterday's meeting. What've you got planned, Cassie?"

"Nothing much. I think I might take up Toby's suggestion and take Rocky out."

"Don't book anything for any mornings next week or the week after," Drew told her.

"Why not?"

"You've got driving lessons starting nine-thirty Monday."

"You booked them already!? You're the best Daddy a girl could wish for."

"You've got a licence and you've passed the theory test, so you might as well get on with lessons. Y

ou don't know how long it will take you to learn, or to book a test.

Anna groaned. "Oh God, I've been dreading this moment."

*****

The young teenager anxiously waited at the bus stop on the outskirts of Newbury. He was worried that the next one wouldn't get him to the middle of town in time for his interview at the government job centre. If he was even a minute late he'd lose his job seekers allowance, and without work it was something he relied on. His parents ran a small dry cleaning and garment repair shop in the town and weren't in a position to completely subsidise him. Looking at his phone for the umpteenth time, he saw that the bus was already late.

He'd have had plenty of time, but when he came out of the house his car wouldn't start. He knew nothing about the internal workings of cars and wouldn't have had time to fix it even if he did, so he ran to the bus stop.

Another glance at his phone told him it was five past ten already. It would take at least an hour to walk, so even if the bus arrived now, it would take half an hour. His shoulders slumped as he realised that there was now no chance of getting there in time.

That was when a big SUV stopped beside him, and the passenger window rolled down. "Can I offer you a ride into town son?" the driver asked in an American accent.

"Are you going into the town centre?"

"Oxford Street, is that any use to you?"

"That would be amazing, thank you so much."

He climbed in, and the vehicle was moving in seconds.

"You've saved my life; I can't tell you."

"An important appointment?" the huge man in the driving seat asked.

"Job centre. They cancel your benefits, if you're even moments late," he said. "Bloody car wouldn't start."

"I'd better get a move on then. What time is your appointment?"

"Ten-thirty-five."

"I'm going to be coming back this way again in half an hour or so, I'll look out for you if you need a ride back."

"There's no need but thank you."

"It won't be a problem."

"I'm not gay."

"Neither am I."

Robert couldn't think of anything else to say, but when they stopped almost opposite the government building, he opened the door to get out, and thanked the driver.

"I'll see you in a few then."

"I don't know how long..."

"It won't matter. Don't be late for your interview, Robert; we can chat after."

As he crossed the road with only five minutes to spare, he looked back and watched the man drive away, asking himself, 'How did he know my name?'

Twenty-five minutes later he stepped outside the government building hoping, that the strange man wouldn't be there. But there he was. Standing in the open space, the man appeared bigger than ever.

"How was the interview," he asked? "I hope it went okay."

"Fine thanks. You really didn't need to wait," Robert nervously answered.

"I thought it would be the best way we could have our little chat. There's a pub a few doors that way. Let me treat you to a sandwich and a beer."

"Why do we need to talk?"

"If it helps you to know, it's in both our interests. You won't have to sign anything, pay for anything, or agree to anything that I'm quite sure you wouldn't be happy to anyway."

"Okay, but I can't be long. I've got to get back and try to fix my car."

In the pub they found a table and took their seats. Almost as soon as they sat down a girl with a crisp, clean, maroon apron and white blouse placed a small glass of beer and an elaborate sandwich in front of each of them.

"I ordered for both of us. I hope that's okay. Please say if you'd prefer something else."

"N-no, this is fine, thank you."

"So Robert, what school did you attend until recently?"

"St Bartholomews."

"Is it a good school?"

"I guess."

"So you're not ashamed that you went there?"

"Ashamed? No of course not."

"How well do you think your A-levels went?"

"Could have been better, but I think I've done enough to get the course I want."

"That's art and design at Reading College isn't it?"

"H-how did you know?"

"I know quite a lot about you Robert, and most of it is very good, but there are one or two little things that still trouble me."

"Who are you?"

"Just call me Parker, until we know each other better."

"I think I'd better go. Thank you for the sandwich."

"You haven't eaten any of it yet, and it would be a shame to let it go to waste."

"I'm going out tonight, and I've got to fix my car."

"You don't need to worry about your car. It's in the workshop. We can go and pick it up after."

"What!"

"We'll talk about it in a minute. First tell me; if you're not ashamed of your school, why have you been telling people that you go to Padbury College?"

"H-how...?"

"Don't be bashful, just tell me."

"A friend of mine from cricket goes to Padbury, and they go to concerts and plays at a posh girls' school. He said if I went with him I might be able to meet a nice girl. I'm not very good with girls, and all the ones at my school think I'm a nerd."

"And did you? Meet a nice girl, I mean."

"Yes."

"Have you told her which school you go to?"

"Not yet, I'm scared she might break it off if she finds out I've been lying."

"Do you think it'll be easier if you leave it a bit longer?"

"No, probably not.

"I think you're right. Let's move on. Three weeks or so ago you received an email asking you to find out more about someone. Tell me about that."

"How do you know these things?"

"I know a lot more than that. Just answer my question, I'll explain in a moment."

"It was from a weird address something like *yournewbestfriend.org.gr* They said if I was able to befriend one of the pupils at Downley School then they'd pay me for information about her family."

"Did they say what girl?"

"No. I didn't reply. I thought it sounded creepy, and it was written really badly. Like, *If Robert find interesting things about girlfriend, then big money possible.* It was signed by someone with a Greek name, supposedly the editor of *EU Inside Story Magazine.*"

"And you didn't reply?"

"It was obviously spam, so I deleted it."

The man's phone had buzzed several times during the conversation, and each time he'd typed brief replies.

"Was that the first time you'd heard from them?"

"I expect so, unless others went into my spam folder, but I got a similar one last week, from a slightly different address."

"Did you reply?"

"No, I blocked it and deleted the email. How do you know all this? Are you some sort of policeman?"

"Do UK cops normally take kids to the pub for a meal?"

"No. What's going on?"

"Nothing to be concerned about. You've put my mind at rest. Finish your sandwich and tell me about cricket while we're waiting for your car to be fixed."

"What was wrong with it?"

"It needed an air filter, three new tires, front disc pads, wiper blades, a windscreen repair, a stop light bulb, and a new exhaust. It'll be an hour or two yet."

"I can't afford any of that."

"It doesn't matter. I paid."

"Why though?"

"Because I don't want you driving my daughter around in a death-trap?"

"Your daughter... Are you Cassie's dad?"

"That's right. Anyway, when are you playing cricket again. I'd like to watch?"

"Sunday, if the weather's okay. If you've never watched it you might find it boring. It's nothing like baseball."

"I can stand a bit of boredom now and then. Sometimes life can get a bit too exciting for me."

"What do you do? Cassie told me you were a security officer or something."

"If she keeps you around, she'll probably tell you a bit more about me. You're her first boyfriend, so it's up to you to set the bar high if you don't want competition. But beware, she's had some really tough times in the past and she won't put up with any bullshit."

It was nearly four-thirty before the garage rang to tell him the car was ready. "Okay, it's all fixed let's go collect it."

Then as he dropped him off to collect the car he said, "Is seven o'clock okay for dinner tonight?"

"What?"

"I'll text you the address. If you really want to surprise Cassie, you won't tell her we had this conversation until later. There's no need to dress up. And bring flowers. I'm told British women like that sort of thing. Here's a twenty in case you're short. Don't tell her where you got it."

"Thank you, Mr. Parker. I don't know what to say."

"Don't say anything; just make sure you treat my daughter well."

When he got home, he was immediately admonished by Cassie for being away longer than he'd said.

"Sorry about that, sweetheart. It took longer than I hoped, but it's all sorted now."

"I don't suppose you had time to look at that other thing we spoke about did you?" she tentatively asked her father.

"Yeah, I set some wheels in motion. I hope to have it sorted by later this evening."

"Thank you, Daddy. Do you want to do some weights before dinner?"

"Good idea, where's your mom?"

"She's in the library. She just had a big row with one of the shareholders."

"I need to speak to her before I change. I'll see you in the gym."

He kissed his wife as she turned to greet him.

"About time. Where have you been?"

"A knotty little thing that needed ironing out. All sorted now. I've invited someone for dinner tonight. Hope that's okay."

"Who is it? Does it need to be special?"

"Just someone I met today, seemed like a nice guy and he didn't have anything on tonight, so I asked if he wanted to spend the evening with us."

"Do we need to dress up?"

"Absolutely not. Cassie and I are going to spend a bit of time in the gym and do a few laps of the pool before dinner if that's okay. The guy's not coming until seven."

"Go ahead," his wife said. "I'm cooking tonight, but I'll ask Jason to help if there's another person to feed. We really do need to find a replacement for Shyla."

It was six forty-five when Drew pressed the button to open the gates. Jason raised his eyebrows but didn't say anything; something was going on; he just hadn't figured out what it was.

Five minutes later Cassie joined the rest of them in the kitchen.

"Why have you laid the table for five?"

"Apparently we've got a guest tonight. Didn't Drew tell you?" the housekeeper asked.

"No. Who is it, Daddy?"

His reply was interrupted by the gate alarm alerting them to a car passing through. Jason wiped his hands on a cloth to go to the door, but Drew discreetly put out his hand to stop him.

"Get that would you, Cassie, sweetheart, it's probably our guest."

She went out to the hall without looking at the security screen. When she opened the door she was silent for a few seconds, before exclaiming, "Robert, what're you doing here?!"

"What's going on?" Anna asked.

"Our guest has arrived," Drew casually announced.

"Does Cassie know him?"

"It looks like it."

Anna and Jason both went to the security screen. "He's kissing her," Anna said.

"From where I sit, it looks more like they're kissing each other," Drew corrected her.

The two observers watched the teenagers turn to walk inside, then they rushed back to their previous positions to feign disinterest.

"Mummy, Jason, this is my boyfriend Robert and look he's brought me these lovely flowers."

"Come in, Robert. This is a lovely surprise; Cassie has kept you a secret from us. I'm Anna by the way. This is Jason, and I'm guessing you've already met my husband," she said, glaring at Drew.

"Nice to meet you Mrs. West, and you Jason. Good evening, Mr. Parker."

"It's all first names here, Robert. I'm Drew."

At the end of the meal, once they'd all got to know each other, Robert thanked Drew for the work he'd had done on his car. "I don't know how to thank you. They did all those things you told me, and they filled the tank, valeted it, gave it a full service and MOT test."

"They told me that it's a nice little car; just needed a bit of care and attention."

That was when Drew's mobile rang. He answered but, because everybody was talking, he put it on speaker.

"Hello."

"Mr. Parker?"

"Yes."

"This is Ariana Georgiou."

Anna was halfway through a sentence, and froze, as did Cassie and Jason moments later when Drew replied.

"What can I do for you Miss Georgiou?"

"I need your help?"

"Why?"

"My children have been kidnapped."

"It's not my help you need; it's the police."

"You don't understand. They're holding Xenia and Elektra until I tell them where my father hid his secret cache of money. I don't know where my father is; you're the only one who knows that."

"Your father is dead, Miss Georgiou."

"How do you know that; did you kill him?"

"I didn't need to kill him, Ariana; his pals in the Kremlin saved me the trouble."

Robert was listening to the conversation in astonishment.

"How do you know?"

"I monitored him for a year. He was alive until mid-August; that's when he disappeared from where he'd been looked after for three months. His body was washed ashore two weeks later. I suspect he made too much noise telling people who he was, and someone believed him. Once his Russian friends discovered where he was they would have had him disposed of. As an unidentified migrant with no papers, he was cremated the following week."

"My God, you're a heartless bastard Parker."

"You and your father exhausted my capacity for compassion for you and your family when you conspired to kidnap my daughter and colluded in the rape and murder of her schoolfriend."

"Does your compassion deficit extend to my eight and ten-year-old daughters as well?"

"What do you think I can do about it?"

"You probably know a great deal more about my father's business than I do, and you are the person that found your daughter when nobody else could."

"What do you know about the people who took your kids?"

"I think they're Russian."

"No surprises there. Where were they taken from, and when?"

"My London house, earlier today."

"Have you called the police?"

"Yes."

"Didn't the kidnappers tell you not to?"

"No. They left a weird ransom note, but there was no mention of the police."

"Okay, I'll be with you in the morning as early as I can. I warn you though, if I discover that you are using your children as bait for some sort of revenge on me, I'll find a way to make sure the authorities permanently remove them from you."

"I'm not. I promise on my mother's grave."

"I'll see you tomorrow."

"Don't you want to know my address?"

"I already do."

"What time?"

"When I'm ready." He ended the call.

Robert was looking from one face to another wondering if he'd wandered onto a film set.

"Are you going to help her, Daddy?"

"No, but I'll try to help her daughters."

Anna was crying. "Is that bloody family going to haunt me for the rest of my life."

"Not if I can help it, but in this case I'm not sure if there's anything I can do to help. Cassie, can you bring Robert through to the study for a chat in a minute. I just need to make a couple of quick calls first."

In his professional life as a security consultant to high-risk VIPs he had many useful contacts. His calls were to two of them.

"Come in Robert, and you Cassie, and take a seat both of you. Robert, after hearing that conversation just now I imagine you're a little confused. I confess I allowed you to hear more than I probably should have, so let me try to put it into context if I can. You're not the victim of an elaborate practical joke. I'm not a spy or secret agent, and I'm not a crook. I run a security consultancy that provides close body protection to high-risk people such as politicians, movie stars, bankers, and wealthy industrialists all over the world. That may explain some of what was said in there earlier. To supplement that, you need to understand that attempts to extort money and actions from Cassie's mother have in the past led to Cassie being kidnapped and held for ransom on one occasion, and four other attempts, including once which resulted in the death of Cassie's sister, and another the rape and murder of her close friend.

"Anna is an extremely wealthy woman and as such she attracts attention from some very nasty people. I hope that that explains why

I put you through that undignified vetting procedure before I gave my approval to you and her being an item. Not that it would have mattered a damn if I'd said otherwise. I apologise for that, but having said it, we're trusting you never to talk about anything that happens inside this house or about any of our family, because a word or two to the wrong people could have very serious consequences for us all. Do you understand?"

"Yes, Sir."

"It's not sir; it's Drew. There's quite a bit on the Internet about our family. Some of it is true, but there's a bucketload of bullshit as well, so I should wait around before you make your mind up about us.. Cassie may want to tell you more but that's up to her. You seem like a nice guy so, I'm pleased to know you."

THREE

06:30 hours, First Friday - Pangbourne Grange

"Does any of this represent a threat to us, Drew?" Anna asked her husband as he dressed in his training gear.

"At the moment, I can't see how, but we won't take any chances. We've got a great alarm system, everybody is well-schooled in our security procedures, and as long as we all adhere to them, there shouldn't be a problem. I've arranged a few additional precautions, and they should all be in place by lunchtime."

"I don't understand why she'd come to you of all people though."

"Neither do I. There are one or two other reputable private hostage negotiators in the UK who could do the job, and it isn't my specialty. When I last looked at her financial situation she had more than enough of her own money to keep most kidnappers happy.

"What do you mean? *When you last looked?* Are you monitoring her?"

"I keep an eye out, yes."

"But what's this about Manos's hidden wealth. I thought that you'd stripped him of everything."

"I didn't strip him of anything. I forced him to compensate us for all the cost and distress he'd caused us to the tune of five million dollars. That was chicken feed compared with what he had access to, I left it to his Russian handlers to take the rest. If there's something the Kremlin didn't know about, I've no idea how I'm supposed to help with that."

"Just be careful this isn't some kind of trap."

Cassie met him on the landing just as she usually did when they were both at home. "Thank you for doing that last night, Daddy, it was so sweet."

"He seems like a nice guy. Any boy wanting a relationship with you has a lot of demotivating practical obstacles to overcome; it seemed to me his financial issues put him at an unfair disadvantage."

"He told me about those emails."

"Possibly a phishing attempt by a gossip magazine, but I've got Digits looking into it. If it turns out to be anything else we'll hit them with a digital storm of biblical proportions."

"I don't think they had cyber wars in biblical times, Daddy."

"Very funny. I'm going for ten laps of the grounds today; you up for it?"

"I think so, but I'm still stiff from that session in the gym last night."

"We'll take it easy for the first few and see how it goes then."

"What time are you seeing that woman?"

"Twelve o'clock at the earliest. I've arranged for some people to gather some evidence before I go."

It was 10:45 before Drew eventually got into the driving seat of the BMW for his journey to the Hampstead address that was Ariana Georgiou's second home. He spent most of the journey talking to associates who had been gathering information, but he started with a brief call to his daughter's boyfriend.

"Robert, this is Drew Parker."

"Er hello. Did I do something wrong?"

"Not at all; you did very well. Are you going to be busy this morning and for the next hour or two?"

"No."

"And you're at home at the moment?"

"Yes."

"You'll be getting a visitor in the next hour. One of my associates will come to install some security software on your computers and phones. It won't affect the performance in any significant way, but we need to ensure that if there are any more attempts to either recruit you or implant spyware it is stopped at source. While they're with you they'll also do deep scans to ensure that there's nothing already there. Are you okay with that?"

"Er, I guess so."

"We won't be prying into your activity, so if you're concerned about any history of viewing porn sites then don't be, I already know about that. If I was concerned about anything you'd been doing up until now, you wouldn't be allowed anywhere near Cassie, and we wouldn't be having this conversation."

"Okay..."

"The lady will also install the software on your parents' computer, if they have one. If you don't want to tell them, they'll never know it's there."

"We all use the same one."

"Okay, speak soon. Have a good day."

The London traffic was abysmal as usual, and it was almost one o'clock before he pulled alongside an Audi A1 in the short driveway of the huge house. The front door opened before he had the opportunity to knock.

"Why are you so late?" Ariana asked.

"I don't remember giving a time; and I had things to do."

"My daughters are missing, and I'm scared. Don't you care?"

"I already know these things. As to whether I care or not, I'll decide that when I know more about what's been going on. Are you going to let me in, or are we going to stand out here all day wasting more of the precious time you seem to be so worried about?"

She stood aside to allow him in before shouting to someone called Carla to make coffee and then leading him up steps into a huge living space. He'd looked at the property details online from when it had been sold the year before for £25 million, he assumed to her. If she'd been the purchaser, she clearly hadn't been impoverished by the death of her father.

"Is this where you live now?"

"Sometimes, when I'm not on Mykonos."

"Tell me about the kidnap."

"It was the day before yesterday, in the morning - the girls were home with the nanny and Carla - they think about ten thirty. I was out shopping and can't have been gone long. Carla was upstairs cleaning, and the girls were preparing for their morning swim with Natalie, she's the nanny. One of them held Natalie at gunpoint while the other went upstairs and restrained Carla using zip ties and tape. When he returned he tied Natalie up the same way, and then took the girls out through the garage."

"How did they get in?"

"Through there." She pointed at the trifold doors into the garden. "It was a beautiful day, and they were open, just as they are now."

"Were there only two of them?"

"The police believe there was a third in the car."

"Do you have CCTV?"

"Yes, but it had somehow been disabled the night before."

"How?"

"I don't know, the police are looking into it."

"It was broad daylight. Why weren't they seen in the garden do you think?"

"The police said that they'd climbed into the garden from the school at the back during the night and hid out behind the garden room where Carla lives."

"Can I speak to Carla?"

"You can try, but she speaks very little English, and her accent is unintelligible. She's Brazilian and speaks a strange mixture of Portuguese and an indigenous language."

"What about Natalie?"

"She was so upset she resigned and flew home to France yesterday evening."

"Tell me more about her."

"French, of course. She's been with me since just after my father disappeared. Her full name is Natalie Laurent; comes from somewhere near Orleans."

"I'll need her details."

"I'll email them."

"Did any of these abductors say anything?"

"They only spoke to give orders."

"What were they wearing?"

"Natalie said that they both wore T-shirts, denim pants, sneakers, and their faces were covered by ski masks."

"What nationality and how old?"

"Natalie thought that one might have been Russian or East European in his late sixties. The second one didn't speak but she thought younger. The police said they made their escape in a maroon Land Rover with false number plates - they were caught on the CCTV of one of the houses opposite. They think that the driver might have been a woman."

"How did you first find out the girls had been taken?"

"I was in Harrods, and they called me using Natalie's cell phone and made her say that two men had got Xenia and Electra. Then one of the kidnappers said they were going to take the girls, and if I wanted them back alive I needed to comply with the instructions they were leaving in the house. I caught a cab, got back as soon as possible, and called the police on the way. The police were here before me."

"What about the instructions?"

"There was an envelope on the coffee table, the cops told me not to touch it, so I didn't until the detectives arrived. They've since given me a photocopy; I scanned a copy for you." She handed him a folded piece of paper.

Your daughters being looked after nothing bad happen to them if you do what we say.

Russian government take all your fathers properties when he disappear, but we know that he had big holdings in property and money that they not take. We want to know where all fathers other money is. When we know we will know how to deal with it.

When you ready to give information make new Twitter account @ManosIsHere with photo of father as profile picture and make name El Stam, with the password Revenge15sw33t. Then we be in touch with how to deliver information to us. When information confirmed we return daughters.

We are patient people and not expect answer in one day, but we not wait forever. If we don't have information we need by 31 July, you not see daughters again.

Do svidaniya,

"Did they take anything?"

"Not as far as I know?"

"Did the police scan for bugs?"

"I don't know."

"I'll send someone tomorrow. I guess the police haven't returned your phone."

"No; nor my laptop."

"Give me a list of any cell phone numbers, and email addresses you use."

She scribbled the information on a notepad and tore off the page.

Taking it from her, he asked, "Have you told the police about me?"

"I told them I'd employ a private hostage negotiator, but I didn't give your name. They asked me not to."

"The thing is Ariana I'm not sure what you want me to do, I'm not a private investigator nor a specialist hostage negotiator. There are plenty of both around. I can recommend some if you want."

"No, I want you. If these people are Russian, they'll be ruthless, I want someone equally cold-blooded on my side. The way you dealt with my father proved how merciless you can be, and to have separated my father from his money as successfully as you did, you must have learnt a lot about how and where he kept his money. I don't have any idea."

"What about all this? You could offer to buy them off with some of your own money."

"I already did. I created the Twitter account they suggested, and they replied saying that I didn't have enough."

"How much did you offer them?"

"Ten million dollars."

"You haven't asked how much I'm going to charge yet, because I won't be cheap. I've already spent close to a hundred thousand pounds, and I offer no guarantee of success."

"Do you want an advance?"

"Not necessary. f you don't pay, I can arrange to take whatever my fee is from one of your accounts any time I need to."

"So, can I assume you're going to help me?"

"If that's what you want. I'll email a contract; you need to accept it within 24 hours. A word of warning though, if any of this puts my family at risk, and I discover that you had any part in it, my ruthlessness will be redirected at you."

"I understand. Do you want to know the name of the officer in charge of the investigation?"

"I already know that, and by now he probably already knows that I'm involved."

"How?"

"His men will have seen me come in."

He left her alone without telling her that his own observers were watching as well.

FOUR

16:30 hours, Friday - Wandsworth London SW11

The top floor of the three-storey terraced house in Mallinson Road looked like the control centre for a moon-shot. It was the home of one of Drew's most useful contacts. His real name was Michael Glover, known in the special forces fraternity as Digits. Glover had been a communications expert with the UK Strategic Command Defence Intelligence, specialising in signals and bizarrely made redundant in the government cutbacks of 2012 after which he went private, providing clandestine intelligence-gathering services for people like Drew, as well as often for the people he used to work for.

"What've you learned so far, Digits?"

"The cell phone numbers that you've given me - that's the one she called you with yesterday and her personal one that she gave to the police - show no indication of unusual activity. I haven't had time to analyse all the numbers in her call logs yet but there were none that didn't fit into the pattern of the previous two months."

"Okay that's good."

"I take it that she didn't mention the other three cellphones that have been making calls via her Wi-Fi then."

"No."

"Difficult to know who's been using them, could be the maid, the nanny, or her or one each. I haven't had time to look at those call logs."

"What about emails?"

"Here's where it gets difficult. The cops have taken her laptop so hacking into it is off the agenda for the moment. Who've you got looking into her finances?"

"I was going to get the same guy I got to do Stamelis' last time, but he had a heart attack and he's out of the game now. Do you know anybody with the appropriate know-how?"

"There's a guy I've used a couple of times who I think could do the job. He's a forensic accountant with high-level IT skills, recently gone freelance. He was with the Financial Conduct Authority in Stratford, until two months ago. Walked out in a huff when his subordinate was promoted over him. He'd bend the rules as much as it takes to unearth wrongdoing, but I doubt he'd be up for stripping people of their assets. If that becomes necessary, I can do that if I have the information to work with."

"What's the guy's name?"

"Dennis Hargreaves; he's fifty-eight and lives near you in Reading."

"Is he geared up with the necessary kit?"

"Oh yes. Do you want me to get him to call you?"

"That would be great; as soon as possible if he's free."

"By the way, Those emails to Robert Taylor purporting to come from Greece originated in Tallinn."

"Estonia; right on Russia's doorstep."

"This is going to be very expensive."

"There could be two young kids whose lives are in danger so the cost is irrelevant, but the Georgiou woman will be paying anyway."

"There's a good chance it'll go international."

"I'm anticipating that it will."

By the time they'd finished deciding what needed to be done and talking through strategies it was past eight pm when he set out for home. He'd called Anna earlier and told her he was going to be late. Not having eaten since breakfast, he considered stopping for a drive-through McDonalds but dismissed the idea after seeing the queue at the only one he passed. He was traveling westward on the M4 when the digital gantry signs began telling people that there had been an incident causing lane closures beyond Junction 8. That would normally result in long tailbacks, so he decided to divert. He'd had to make the same decision in the past, so he knew he'd need to use the Bath Road and turned off at Junction 6.

Fortunately, in spite of other cars using the same diversion, the traffic wasn't too heavy, and was moving at a comfortable speed. When he reached an area where there were fields on both sides of the single carriageway, an old maroon-coloured Land Rover Defender overtook him at speed and immediately braked sharply. Seemingly the driver was attempting to avoid running into the back of a small hatchback.

Drew also braked but the offending vehicle continued to slow sharply, forcing Drew to fiercely brake again. His car began to fishtail, and was rammed from behind by a minibus. Drew succeeded in bringing the car under control enough to prevent it swerving into oncoming traffic, but when the minibus rammed him a second time he was forced off the road onto the grass verge. As hard as he tried he couldn't control the steering over the rough ground and when the nearside front wheel dropped into a deep dip the car flipped, rolled sideways three times, half on and half off the carriageway, the rear clipping the front of the minibus in passing.

Drew was only vaguely conscious of his vehicle's acrobatics before it finished the right way up but facing in the opposite direction to the way he'd been travelling. He was dazed and several parts of his body hurt, but the airbags and seatbelt had saved him from serious injury. After releasing the seatbelt he began to survey the damage to his legs, but as he bent to test a bruised ankle he heard gunshots and the thud of bullets striking the car. Nanoseconds later he heard the blast of a car horn and the squeal of tyres locking on tarmac, followed by another loud thump; then silence.

He lay still across the passenger seats waiting for another volley of shots that never came. It may be that he lost consciousness for a minute or two. He'd never know. The next thing he heard was a voice asking if he was okay. He levered himself upright in the seat to see three or four people gathered around his battered car. The man who'd spoken, attempted to open the door. Drew tried himself with the same lack of result. Then others were trying to prise open the passenger door.

"Where's the gunman?"

"He's dead. He stepped in front of a car."

The windscreen was missing so he asked the men to help him out across the hood.

"You're bleeding."

"I don't care, if this thing starts to burn, I'd rather be out there than in here. I don't think anything's broken."

It took three men to ease Drew's huge frame through the glassless windshield. As his feet touched the ground a police car pulled up. It was the first of four, interspersed with two fire appliances and an ambulance.

Drew was practically ordered into the back of the ambulance by the police. All he was able to find out before he left was that when the minibus behind rammed him the second time and was clipped by the rear of his own car, it was forced into a head-on collision with a delivery van coming from the opposite direction killing the minibus driver instantly.

The driver of the car that had braked in front of him had stopped and got out, before firing a gun only to be hit by another car. Whether the driver that hit him had deliberately targeted the gunman he didn't know, but both he and the van driver escaped with minor injuries.

At the hospital, they put three stitches in his head where he'd hit it as the car overturned, and others in his upper thigh where a bullet had grazed him.

The police interviewed him at the hospital, and he was about to call a cab to take him home when he turned to find Anna and Cassie waiting for him.

"Hi, sweetheart; you didn't have to come. I could have caught a cab."

"Drew Parker, did it not occur to you that when the police call a woman to tell her that her husband has been involved in a serious accident and has been taken to hospital, it might be a good idea for him to call her and tell her that he's not dead?"

"Sorry, I didn't know they'd called you."

"Also what they didn't tell me, but I heard on the radio on my way here was that two people are dead and someone was firing guns."

"Bloody crazy bastards. I've no idea what all that was about."

"I don't know, just a stab in the dark, but maybe it's about you getting involved with that Georgiou woman again. What do you think?"

"It's possible. I need to look into that. Can we go home, I'm starving; I haven't eaten since breakfast."

"What happened, Daddy?"

"A couple of bat shit crazy assholes tried to drive me off the road and when that didn't work one of them tried to shoot me, but he stepped in front of a moving car and got himself killed. The best news is that all the crazies ended up dead, and nobody else got seriously hurt."

"It's no good you trying to make light of it, you could have been one of those dead bodies," Anna told him, in tears.

"But I'm not, so let's go home. I could really do with one of those full English breakfasts you're so good at, Cassie."

They were halfway home in Anna's A class Mercedes when Drew light-heartedly said, "I guess nobody will complain if I replace the X7 now. I'd get cramp driving this for very long, so not all bad eh?"

"That isn't funny," Anna said, trying not to smile.

"I saw Robert this afternoon, Daddy. He said you gave him a new computer."

"Actually it's a refurbished one, and it wasn't the original plan. The one he was using was so out of date that the security software couldn't be installed on it."

"Was it necessary?"

"Maybe not, but better safe than sorry eh?"

When they were home, Cassie set about producing the meal he'd asked for while he showered, thankful for the invention of waterproof dressings. When he returned to the kitchen Cassie kissed him good night and went to bed leaving Anna to talk seriously about what was happening.

"This isn't going to be just a simple case of looking at Manos' finances, locating a hidden cache and paying off the kidnappers is it?"

"Not even that would have been simple, but you may be right. Until I find out who the two dead guys were I can't be sure. Do you want me to get Megan in again to put your mind at rest?"

"Would you, if she's free?"

"I don't think she's working at the moment, not for me anyway. I'll speak to her in the morning."

"What are you doing about the kidnapping?"

"At the moment there's very little I can do, I've nothing to go on. No phone calls, no CCTV, not even any substantive demands except to provide information about something that may or may not exist. This is the weirdest kidnapping I've ever heard of, but then it's not supposed to be my area of expertise. Ariana is right about one thing though; outside of Russia I probably know more about Stamelis and his wealth than anybody else on the planet."

"Surely if there were anything to find, you'd already have found it."

"Maybe not. There was so much Russian linked money, we didn't need to go looking for anything more. All I needed to do was to deny him access to it. Putting him in a migrant facility without ID and no money meant he just got lost in the wretched tide of humanity searching for some sort of safe existence. Nobody would have been interested in his claims that he was a multi-millionaire who hadn't even been reported missing."

"If this hoard of wealth exists, what would it look like? Piles of cash like those South American drug cartels, gold bars or what?"

"I doubt that much of it would be in a physical form. I imagine it's invested in some sort of trust that can operate autonomously. If that's the case, and whoever is controlling it has got wind of Stamelis' death, they may have assumed ownership and are congratulating themselves on their good fortune."

"So you've got two parallel investigations going on at the same time; the missing girls as well as the missing millions, if they exist."

"That's right. Not bad for someone who doesn't even have a private investigator licence."

"You should apply for one. It should be straightforward; you already have an SIA licence for security management."

"Great idea. I'll get Pat onto that in the morning." He was referring to Patricia Spenser his solicitor at Ruskin and Firth.

"If you're going to be laying out a lot of money you'd better let Gerry know as well," Anna reminded him.

"That's true." Gerald Hennessy was Drew's bookkeeper. Parker Personal Security had only one full-time employee and the number of sales transactions per year was tiny; even though they involved very large sums, he only needed a bookkeeper part-time.

FIVE

06:30 hours, Saturday – Pangbourne Grange

"You're surely not going to run this morning?" Anna asked.

"No, just swim, loosen the muscles a bit. I've quite a few bruises."

"Yesterday Cassie asked me if she could go on the pill."

"Good idea."

"You're not worried?"

"Not really; are you?"

"I suppose not, but it's such a milestone. Everything's happening at once, leaving school, driving lessons, first boyfriend, and now the pill."

Drew shrugged. "I wouldn't be surprised if she were the last in her school year to go on the pill."

"You're right, I know, but my lovely baby daughter seems to be becoming a woman overnight."

"I think the events of two years ago took most of what remained of her childhood away. You've been a great mother; you should be proud."

"I am proud; not so much of me, but of her. Your contribution to who she is now has made all the difference."

"She's an easy kid to be stepdad to."

"Are you going to be busy again today?"

"Yes, but at the moment I'm not sure of my timetable."

He was already in the pool when Cassie joined him. They swam silently for half an hour before Drew hauled himself out of the water revealing the extent of his bruising.

"I was so scared when the police called last night."

"They should have asked me before they called. Then you wouldn't have known about it until it was all over and there was nothing to be scared about."

"That bruising is terrible."

"But that's all it is, apart from some minor scratches. The safety measures fitted to modern cars are very effective."

"I know that, but they're not designed to stop bullets, and that injury on your right leg isn't a bruise, is it?"

"No but it's nothing major."

"I wish you didn't have to do dangerous things."

"I spent twelve years in the army, and ten of those in Delta, but when you were kidnapped in Canada, it was the most terrifying thing that ever happened in my entire life. I'd like to have put a team of ten trained bodyguards on you to stop anything like it happening to you again, but you wouldn't have thanked me for that. It's the same with me; we carry on with our lives taking sensible precautions."

"I know, most dads in your position would have stopped me from seeing Robert because he doesn't come from a wealthy family and wouldn't be used to taking the kind of precautions we have to, but you didn't for the same reason."

"He's a lucky guy."

"He wants me to meet his mum and dad."

"That's okay, isn't it?"

"Yes, I just don't want him to think that I've committed myself to a life partnership or anything. It's too soon."

"He may be wishing for something long term, as do most guys when they meet a real nice girl, but it rarely works out like that. When one of them ends it, the other gets upset, but mostly they both eventually move on. If that's what happens with you and Robert, I expect it'll be the same."

"Was it like that for you."

"Not quite, because I was the wrong type of boy for most nice girls, and the girls I went with were mostly the wrong type of girls. I never had a regular girlfriend until your mom."

"What about... intimate things, you know what I mean?"

"I was a soldier; what do you think?"

"Do you want me to cook you breakfast again?"

"No thanks, sweetheart. I need to get started."

His first task was to call Megan Palmer, one of the close protection officers on his books. She'd stayed with them once before, during the debacle involving Ariana's father, Manos Stamelis. Megan knew the family, and they all got on well. Megan was glad of the work, happy to oblige and agreed to be with them later in the day.

Next on his call list was an ex-Detective Chief Inspector, a Scotsman called Angus Finlay. As a constable he'd served in the Parliamentary and Diplomatic Protection branch of the Met Police but transferred to CID and ended up heading a Major Investigation Team. He'd resigned when he was demoted after a murder investigation went tragically wrong as the result of an intervention by an incompetent superior. He was tough and clever and a popular CPO with his clients. Drew had never used Angus in an investigative capacity before, but after hearing an explanation of what was happening, he was keen to be involved.

Soon after ending the call with Finlay, he got a voicemail from Dennis Hargreaves. Drew called him back immediately.

"Dennis, this is Drew Parker. Thanks for getting in touch. Did my pal Digits give you a flavor of what's going on?"

"Digits? Oh you mean Mr. Glover, yes, kind of. It sounds fascinating. I'll need to look closer at the information you've already got before I could commit though."

"I gather you're quite close to me. Would it be okay if I dropped it round later today."

"No problem at all, Mr. Parker. If you can avoid between twelve and one, and between three and four, that's when I take mother to her book club on Saturday. I can't come to you, I'm afraid; I don't drive." He gave Drew the address.

"Thank you, Dennis, I'll see you later."

Not wanting to bother Digits again, Drew called another contact, a friend of Megan's who went by the handle Lightfoot. Drew hadn't wanted to pile too much work onto Glover and as Lightfoot provided similar services he asked him to find out who the two dead ambushers from the night before were and learn as much as he could about them.

He spent the next hour or two collating information to give to Dennis. When he'd finished he went to the kitchen for coffee, where he found Robert sitting with Anna and Cassie drinking tea.

"Hi Robert, how's the car?"

"Brilliant, thank you, Mr. Parker."

"It's just Drew to friends Robert. Do you always go by Robert; never Bob or Bobby?"

"I don't mind Bob, but my mum and dad call me Bobby and I think it sounds a bit babyish. Cassie always calls me Robert and I like that."

"Robert it is then."

"The computer is fantastic, but my dad said he should pay you for it."

"It's a second-hand one we gave you for our protection. It cost us nothing. We confiscated it from a criminal who was using it to hack into the security system of one of my clients. All we did was wipe its memory, reinstall the operating system and software, then copy your data across. If you went out and bought it, it wouldn't cost you more than a hundred and fifty quid so tell your dad not to bother. We're not in the business of selling second-hand IT equipment."

"It's the family computer, so he and my mum use it too."

"So much the better," he said. "I'm going out now. I'm not sure how long I'll be. Perhaps we can go out to eat tonight if I'm back in time, otherwise order in."

"Are you taking the car, darling?" Anna asked.

"No I've ordered a cab. It should be here soon. Megan should be here sometime this afternoon."

Cassie immediately got excited. "Megan's coming? Is she bringing Rhian?"

"No, I don't think so."

He was in the cab when Lightfoot called back.

"I've taken a quick look at those two guys."

"Anything I should be concerned about?"

"On the face of things no but there might be a couple of things you might want me to take a closer look at."

"If you could go ahead and do that it would be great. I'm in a cab at the moment. Will you put your concerns in an email."

"No problem."

The cab dropped him at Dennis's home, a 1930s detached house with bow windows at the front, peeling paint on the window frames, and a garden in need of attention. There was no doorbell just a tarnished brass knocker attached to the letterbox.

A short, plump, grey-haired, old lady who appeared to be in her late sixties ears came to the door. "Yes?"

"Is Mr. Hargreaves available?"

"He's been dead for twenty-five years, so I doubt it."

"Dennis Hargreaves?"

"Oh you want Dennis. Why didn't you say so?" She turned and called up the stairs; "Dennis, one of your callers again. This one's American."

'This is like a remake of *The Ladykillers,* he thought.

"You'd better come in; you're letting the heat out."

It was the middle of June, and he wasn't sure if she was being funny. "Thank you Ma'am."

A middle-aged man came limping down the stairs smiling.

"Thank you mother. Why don't you put the kettle on and make sure you've got everything ready for book club?" He offered his hand to Drew. "So nice to meet you, Mr. Parker. Please come upstairs to my office."

His office in the three bedroomed house that didn't look like it had been decorated for at least thirty years, was in what would be called in real estate terms *bedroom two* and Drew didn't expect what he saw when he stepped through the door. His surprise must have registered on his face because Dennis smiled and said, "Yes I know, but when I left the civil service I decided to treat myself. This used to be my bedroom, the only one that mother will allow me to change. The house was once her parents."

With what appeared to be state of the art furniture and electronic equipment, the room looked as much like an office of the 2020s as it was possible to look in such a dusty old property.

"Do you do a lot of investigative work these days then Dennis?"

"Oh yes, almost all of my work is investigative, although I do some analytical, and research stuff as well."

"You must need to take a lot of security precautions then?"

"Definitely, I'm pretty hot on data security and everything I do is duplicated. Cloud-based back up of course and a disaster recovery system of my own design. The companies that provide that service are so expensive, and I don't need the sort of volume that they usually deal with."

"Sounds clever."

"Not that clever, but even though some people think I'm just a boring old forensic accountant, on the quiet I'm a bit of a computer geek. Anyway, Mr. Parker, please take a seat and tell me what it is you want me to do."

Over the next hour and a half, whilst describing recent events and all that happened two years earlier, Drew handed over copies of all the digital and hardcopy information about Manos Stamelis that had been gathered during the investigation after Cassie's kidnap.

"Good Lord, that's the most extraordinary tale. How confident are you in the accuracy of these records?"

"As far as they go, supremely confident. The man who did the work was at the top of his game, as I'm told by Digits are you."

"That's very pleasing to hear, I do hope I can live up to Mr. Glover's billing. You haven't drunk your tea, Mr. Parker."

47

"I'm not much of a tea drinker, but please thank your mother for me."

Hargreaves laughed. "Lots of people make that mistake; she's not my mother, she's my wife; she just prefers to be called that."

Drew took out his cell phone. "I'll need to call a cab to collect me."

"Where are you going?"

"To the BMW dealer in town."

"Why don't you share our cab, we can drop you off on the way? It's due in twenty minutes."

"That's very kind, thank you."

"That's a really nasty bruise on your face, and that dressing by your ear. What happened if you don't mind me asking?"

"Some guys drove me off the road near Knowle Hill last night."

"Good gracious, were you involved in that dreadful incident with the gunman?"

"Yeah, it's possible they were working for whoever the kidnappers are."

"Well, I'll have to make sure I do my very best to help put these people behind bars then. We can't have that sort of behaviour, can we?"

When it arrived, the cab was a C-Class Mercedes and Hargreaves ushered him into the front seat, giving him plenty of leg room.

"I'll get on with that work and be in touch as soon as possible, Mr. Parker," Hargreaves told Drew when got out of the car.

In the car dealership Drew surprised the salesman by announcing that he wanted to buy two cars and was happy to pay in full by bank transfer today if they could agree on the vehicles and terms. He gave the man the specifications he had in mind and waited while he trawled through online inventories of partner dealers. In the end Drew settled on an ex-demonstration dark grey X7 3 litre turbo diesel M Sport with only 4,600 miles on the clock that was at their Salisbury dealership. He then added a three-year-old blue Audi A3 with 8,200 miles that was available from stock.

The combined ticket price on the two cars was £107,650, Drew offered £95,000 on condition that the X7 was delivered to his home by Monday afternoon fitted with front and rear dash cams, and he could drive the Audi away that day. The man couldn't agree fast enough. It took longer to complete the paperwork than it had to choose the vehicles. When he drove out of the dealer's parking lot he left the salesman looking like he'd won the lottery.

Drew had a new issue to deal with by then. Whilst signing the papers he'd received a call from the police asking to come to his house to interview him about the incident the day before. He made arrangements to be there in an hour, giving him just enough time to make a short stop on the way."

SIX

16:00 hours, First Saturday - Pangbourne Grange

The remote control for the gate was still in the wrecked BMW so he had to press the button and ask to have them opened. Jason did the honours.

There were two cars already there; one was Robert's, and parked alongside it was Megan's Range Rover.

Everybody was in the living room when he went inside. "Hi everybody, hiya Megan."

"Hi, Drew, how goes it?"

"Pretty hectic last forty-eight hours to be honest, but the pieces are coming together. We'll have a chat later if that's okay. There's a cop due here in a minute to take a statement about yesterday. I just need to make a couple of calls first.

While his laptop booted up and went through its security protocols, he picked a number from the contact list on his cell phone that he'd never expected to call again.

"SAC Jackson speaking." The recipient answered. Barratt Jackson had been on the FBI team investigating Cassie's kidnapping two years earlier.

"Barratt, this is Drew Parker."

"Mr. Parker, I don't have your number in my phone any longer, so it never appeared. I'm sorry. How are you?"

"Okay I guess. You too, I hope. It's good to hear the about the promotion."

"Yeah well the investigation into your daughters kidnapping probably helped. The dust has only just settled from that by the way. But yeah I guess I'm okay too. What can I do for you?"

"I'm hoping you can help me out with a bit of information."

"As long as it's something I'm allowed to divulge, I'll do my best."

"In your investigations into that whole business two years ago, did you ever learn who Stamelis Russian handler was?"

"Sure, a guy called Dmitri Turgenev. Why do you need to know now?"

Drew gave him a brief rundown of recent events.

"That doesn't sound like anything that you need to be involving yourself in, if you'll forgive me for saying so."

"It isn't, but the Georgiou woman is emotionally blackmailing me."

"I wanted to go after her for her involvement in your daughter's kidnapping, but your wife was uncomfortable with it as I recall, and my bosses said it was all getting too complicated."

"Do you know what happened to Turgenev?"

"Last we heard, he'd 'disappeared', and we all know what that means."

"That's fantastic Barratt. Thanks for your help."

"Good luck with all that," the agent replied.

Whilst he'd been talking he'd been reading the email from Lightfoot about the two dead assailants.

They were Jay Hopkins 37 (the gunman) and Dale Wilson 60. Both had a string of convictions for violence, and both had served time. They came from Ilford in Northeast London, and both were members of a small neo-Nazi gang called Defend the Flag (DFT). As far as that went there weren't any surprises beyond the two areas of concern that Digits had highlighted:

First. During the days leading up to the kidnap both had made and received calls at similar times in the Finchley Road Area of London, less than a mile from the Georgiou home.

Second. The vehicles used in the attack had been identified by their Vehicle Identification Numbers and both had been reported stolen six months earlier from a hospital car park near Aylesbury in Buckinghamshire. Their false number plates had been stolen from similar vehicles in the Thame area of Oxfordshire.

Drew looked at the locations on a map and there was no apparent correlation with anything involving him or the Georgiou woman. Neither was there any indication where the vehicles had been from the time they'd been stolen to the time they'd been used to attack him. According to Digits, the police Automatic Number Plate Recognition system (ANPR) hadn't picked up the false plates on the M4 earlier. So, if Drew was the target, and it seemed certain he was, then they couldn't have followed him to the Bath Road, and must have known the motorway route was going to be compromised. What's more they appeared to have known when he was going to be there. If they knew he was coming from London, and the M4 became closed where it was, it was no great leap for them to assume he'd use the Bath Road.

He was still contemplating what he'd read when the gate bell rang announcing the arrival of the police. He went to open the gate and was surprised to see two cars drive through, and even more surprised to see two people get out of each car. He opened the door and waited for them to introduce themselves.

"Good afternoon, Mr. Parker?" the leading man asked.

"That's correct."

"Detective Sergeant Gasowski and Detective Constable Ballard from Reading Police," he said flashing his badge, and nodding to the woman beside him.

"And who're these other gentlemen?"

The older of the two other men stepped forward. "My name's Forester, I'm an Elite Agent with the National Crime Agency. This is my colleague, Field Agent Pelham."

"Please come in all of you. I'd been planning to use the study, but there aren't quite enough seats in there at the moment, so perhaps the dining room would be better. Come through."

Anna was at the living room door looking astonished as the entourage traipsed through.

"Take a seat all of you. I wasn't expecting a coach party Sergeant."

"If DC Ballard and I can complete our interview about the incident on the Bath Road first, then we'll get out of your hair and let the gentlemen from the NCA tell you why they're here."

"Sure. Go ahead; ask your questions."

"Can you describe the events as you recall them, Sir."

Drew explained the sequence of events in as much detail as he could remember up to being driven away in the ambulance, but he wasn't able to add much to what he'd told the cop in the hospital.

"And where were you coming from?"

"Wandsworth."

"Why were you there,, Sir?"

"I was meeting an associate."

"And who would that be?"

"Is there any reason that would be relevant?"

"Just getting background Sir. Did you know either of the men who attacked you?"

"As you haven't told me who they were, it's difficult to say."

"Their names were Jay Hopkins and Dale Wilson."

"I don't recall having dealings with anybody with those names."

"Have you had any confrontations with anybody who might wish you harm?"

"Sergeant, I've spent my life having confrontations with people; it's my job. Those who're still alive and not in prison no doubt all wish me harm. You do know what I do for a living don't you?"

Gasowski ignored the question. "What about recently? Any recent conflicts?"

"Most of my recent contracts have all been overseas."

"What about political clients."

"At least fifty percent of my clients are politicians, but recently none of them have been British."

"Do you have any political affiliations of your own?"

"None I'm prepared to share, and none that are likely to provoke attempted murder."

"So you haven't crossed swords with any far-right groups?"

"None because they were far-right, and none recently."

Ballard asked, "What about an organisation called *Defend The Flag*?"

Drew turned to her. "I don't recall ever hearing that name before, detective. Is that the group these guys belonged to?"

She ignored the question. "And you can't shed any light on yesterday's incident?"

"I'm afraid not unless it was a case of mistaken identity. However, have you thought about how they knew that whoever their target was would be on the Bath Road, at that time?" he asked. "I was only there because most of the M4 had been shut down. Neither the Land Rover nor the minibus had been anywhere near me when I diverted from the motorway, so they must have picked me up somewhere along that road. With the volume of traffic and little opportunity to overtake on the single carriageway, they were waiting for someone, that being the case then the incident on the motorway must have been planned."

"What was the cause of the motorway incident Sergeant," Forester asked, speaking for the first time.

"Somebody threw some dead sheep off a bridge, Sir."

"So it looks like the two men in the vehicles weren't working alone. There must have been at least two on the bridge, and probably one to interfere with the traffic on the Bath Road so that their vehicles could merge at the right place. This was a conspiracy."

The two cops showed themselves out leaving Drew to answer questions from the two NCA agents.

"I understand you've been employed by Ariana Georgiou to negotiate the release of her children," Forester said.

"Did Ms Georgiou tell you that?"

"No, but we're aware that you've been in touch with her."

"That's correct, I have."

"So what exactly is your business with her?"

"I'm not at liberty to say."

"Perhaps I should have mentioned earlier, Agent Pelham and I are with the NCA's Anti Kidnap and Extortion Branch."

"I kinda guessed that."

"In the UK, hostage negotiation would be our responsibility. Other people engaging in that could be considered as obstructing a police investigation."

"I'm also aware of that Agent Forester, although I'm not a hostage negotiator."

"You recovered your daughter from a kidnap gang two years ago."

"I didn't negotiate with the hostage takers."

"I gather you engaged in a gunfight with them though and three kidnappers died."

"I'm not sure where you're going with this Mr. Forester. If you're trying to draw some sort of parallel between what went on in the States two years ago with my daughter and what's happening with Ms Georgiou's children you're wasting your time. In the US I was legitimately armed, my wife was being held with a knife at her throat, so I shot the hostage taker. Then when my daughter was about to be shot by her attempted rapist I shot him. The third man died when he drove his motorcycle into a tree. I can't see what other actions I could have taken, nor see any similarity with the current situation. The kids aren't mine, I'm not armed, and Ms Georgiou isn't under any personal threat."

"You were involved with the disappearance of her father though."

"Is that what you think?"

"Ms Georgiou seems to think so."

"Manos Stamelis was an extremely dangerous man and caused my family a lot of pain and distress. I'm pleased to say that he's dead now and therefore unable to cause any more. When he died I was a thousand miles away."

"How do you know when he died?"

"After the trouble he caused my loved ones I made it my business to keep track of him."

"How did you do that?"

"He had a tracking implant in his right buttock."

"How did you know that?"

"I put it there."

"Where was he when he died?"

"He'd escaped from a migrant processing camp on the Greek Island of Leros. It's my guess his Russian handlers discovered that, and then had him killed."

"If you knew that, why didn't you inform Ms Georgiou?"

"Why would I?"

"It could be construed that you played a part in his death."

"Some people might choose to believe that."

"So why would Ms Georgiou involve you in the kidnap of her children?"

"I've asked myself that same question. If you find the answer please let me know."

"Ms Georgiou seems to think that you might know the whereabouts of some hidden wealth that belonged to her father."

"It's always been my assumption that when oligarchs invoke the displeasure of the Kremlin, their wealth is confiscated and finds its way back to the Russian coffers. My guess would be that's what happened on this occasion."

"So you didn't take the opportunity to help yourself to any of his money after he disappeared then?"

"I'm married to one of the world's wealthiest people, I've an annual income in seven figures and my personal wealth is over five million dollars all of which I can account for. I neither need nor have any desire for any money that has been tainted by that despicable bastard's activities."

After warning him of the perils of involving himself in police or NCA investigations the two agents left. Jason went to close the gates behind them while Drew joined the others in the living room.

"So what're we doing tonight, folks? Restaurant or order in?"

"It's too late to book a table so we'll have to order in," Anna told him.

"My vote is for curry from Shyla's place," Jason said. "By the way, whose is the little blue Audi in the drive?"

"It's ours, I bought it today."

Anna looked up. "That's a bit small for you isn't it, darling?"

"I didn't buy it for me, it's a family car, and for Cassie of course."

"You bought me a car?!"

"Like I say, it's a family car, but if you pass your driving test okay it'll probably be you that gets the most use out of it. Anyway, I like Jason's idea of curry, are we all okay with that?"

"They're not doing delivery at the moment, Daddy; their delivery guy had an accident. Robert and I could go and collect it if you want."

When they'd gone, Anna took Drew to one side. "Cassie asked if Robert could stay the night."

"What did you say?"

"I said yes. Do you think I did the right thing?"

"I think so. Are you expecting them to sleep together?"

"I suppose so, but she's not on the pill yet."

"Probably best to leave these on her bedside table then," he said handing her the pack of twelve condoms he'd bought on the way home.

SEVEN

06:30 hours, First Sunday – Pangbourne Grange

"Those bruises are worse than ever this morning, darling. Do you want me to rub something in them?"

"No, they'll be fine. Go back to sleep."

Drew began his exercise routine with five laps of the property, following it with forty-five minutes in the gym, before another forty minutes in the pool. It was the first time for a very long time he could remember that Cassie hadn't joined him for any part of his routine when they were both at home.

Anna was already in the kitchen with Jason when he joined them for breakfast. After wishing them a good morning he began to make his own. The talk was still mostly about the Bath Road attack, although Jason and Anna weren't aware of the conspiracy conclusion of the NCA agent, and although he agreed with it, Drew didn't enlighten them.

Just as he placed his plate on the table Cassie and Robert came into the room holding hands.

"Morning everybody," Cassie announced with a big smile. Robert stood beside her looking red-faced.

"Morning you two. Did you sleep well?" Jason asked.

"Yes thanks," Cassie replied.

Anna offered to make them a cooked breakfast, but they opted for cereals and toast.

"So what time does the cricket start Robert?" Drew asked.

"One o'clock."

"Where is it?"

"We're playing away today at Sonning just outside Reading."

"Just off the Bath Road, I've passed that. I can't promise to watch the whole match, but I'll try to see a little."

"You're going to watch Robert play cricket?" Cassie said.

"Why not? Robert was telling me about it in the pub the other day. I assume you're going."

"Well I hadn't thought about it, but I might now you've raised it. Is that alright Robert?"

"Yes, if you really want to. My dad might be there."

"It'd be great to meet him."

An hour later Drew was talking to one of the observation team watching the Georgiou home. "What's happening, Gordon?"

"Not a lot. She made a call to someone named Yaya. We couldn't hear what was said because there was too much background noise from the radio."

"Do you think she's found one of our bugs?"

"Either that or she suspects one."

"She went out at about ten fifteen last night. We followed her to an all-night convenience store on Finchley Road. She bought about ten items, didn't interact with anyone except the checkout guy and then went home. But she spent a long time choosing which particular packet of muesli, not just which brand but which packet."

Drew's next call was to someone he hadn't spoken to for two years.

"Mac, how're you doing?"

"Babycham, what's up?" The nickname came from his days in Delta. He didn't much like it but had come to accept it.

"Just wondering if you're busy at the moment."

"Not so much. I've been taking a break at my brother's home in Scotland, but golf was feeling a bit tame so I'm back in London now. Have you got something for me?"

"Yes, if you're up for it. It may be a onetime thing but has the potential to escalate."

"Tell me more?"

"Not on the phone. Do you like cricket?"

"Take it or leave it."

"I'll see you at Sonning Cricket Club at fifteen hundred."

"Shall I come ready to play?"

"Probably best. Kick off won't be until later though."

"I see you're all up with cricket terminology then."

"Whatever, the match is in Northeast London and play won't begin until twenty-three hundred. You'll need your bat, helmet, gloves, and knee pads."

His next call was to Lightfoot.

"Hi again. Thanks for the background on those two, that was real helpful. It appears there at least three others involved, I wondered if you could look at their communications and find out if any more of their friendly society were amongst them."

"No problem. Anything else?"

"Yes. I need to know if the DTF either own or have the use of property in the South Buckinghamshire, Oxfordshire area."

"I'll do my best, but that bit might not be straightforward."

Megan had been listening to most of the conversation from the door.

"You're throwing a lot of resources at this. I hope for your sake that Ms Georgiou has the wherewithal to pay for it."

The next call was to Angus Finlay. "Hi Angus, are you free for a meeting tomorrow morning?"

"Of course, what time and where?"

"Nine o'clock here, if that's okay."

"Is there anything I can do in the meantime?"

"Well there's something going on that I can't figure. I've just put someone on to doing an electronic investigation, but I wonder if an old school approach might bear more fruit."

He gave Angus a full account of the attack by the neo-Nazis.

"Have you had dealings with right-wing groups in the past?"

"The only direct contact was two years ago, when I prevented the assassination of a Democrat candidate by white supremacists in Kentucky, but it seems a bit of a stretch that they would wait all this time and cross the Atlantic to wreak revenge."

"My guess would be the same, but most of these extreme groups struggle for funding and will do anything to get their hands on cash. Remember back in the noughties how the IRA resorted to bank robbery as means of raising money. The Northern Bank heist in 2004 harvested £26 million and much of it was never recovered. What you've described sounds like a gun for hire crime. I can certainly look into that, although the NCA will already be doing it."

Nodding at everything that Finlay had said Drew replied, "If the NCA work anything like the FBI, I won't be placing too much faith in them sharing any of their findings with me. On the face of things as far as they're concerned they're probably treating this as just an unusual kidnapping, if I thought that that was the case I'd just tell them everything I know and let them get on with it. I'm sure as I can be that there's something much more personal going on."

"You're probably right. I'll start poking some sticks into a few rats' nests and see what stirs."

"Don't go putting yourself in danger though, Angus."

"I won't."

Megan joined him in the study. "Will my role just be babysitting your family?"

"Predominantly, but if you're up for it another pair of hands on my little outing tonight wouldn't hurt. Stamp's already involved." Stamp's real name was Terry Longhurst, Stamp was the man's service nickname after the famous actor.

"I know, he told me when I mentioned I was on my way here."

"Are you and him a permanent thing now?"

"Not really, but we spend a bit of time together and Rhian's grown quite fond of him. Neither of us are looking at settling down just yet," she said. "Tell me about tonight."

He described the op that he'd planned.

"You need to make this stick," she said.

"What do you mean?"

"These aren't the sort of people who're going to say, 'Okay you win' and forget about it. Most of them are thick as pig shit and won't know when to quit. If we don't put them out of action permanently or point them in completely the wrong direction they'll likely want to come back at you. I know they're amateurs, but they can still make life difficult for you. What's more they've clearly had someone speaking to them with access to sophisticated tracking equipment so who's to say they won't still have that."

"Good point; any suggestions?"

"How about we take one or two of the small fry and teach them the error of their ways, then use them to set one against the other. Then we can let the cops do the tidying up?"

"Great idea. Four of us should be able to handle it."

"Show me what intel you've got so far."

They spent the next two hours forming an op plan.

"Are you going to have something to eat before you go to the cricket?" Anna asked.

"Yeah. What are we having?"

"I thought we'd have the gazpacho I made yesterday because it's too early for a big meal. You might want to supplement it with something more substantial if you're not going to be here for dinner. I just overheard you making plans."

"That's great. Are you going to watch the game?"

"I could go, I suppose."

"If you do you'll need to cadge a ride home from Robert because I'm going to be going on somewhere."

Megan interrupted. "I'm not much of a cricket fan. Let me know where and when the RV is, and I'll catch you up."

Drew revised the location of the RV and informed all involved.

Ready to roll.

EIGHT

Anna and Drew parked up and walked to the cricket ground. Cassie saw them coming and walked over to meet them.

"Mummy, Daddy, you're just in time, Robert is batting number three."

"What does that mean?" Drew asked.

"That he will be next in when one of the others is out."

"Let's find a seat where we can watch the action."

Anna laughed.

"What's funny?"

"You'll see," Anna told him.

"They don't have seats unless you bring your own, Daddy. Come and meet Robert's mum and dad."

There were only about twenty onlookers, but Cassie led them towards a couple sitting on folding chairs of their own. The pair stood up when they saw the Parker-West family approaching.

"Mummy, Daddy, these are Robert's mum and dad. Mr. and Mrs. Taylor, these are my parents Anna and Drew."

The couple stepped forward to greet them and the father held out his hand. "Mrs. Parker-West, we're so pleased to meet you, and you, Mr. Parker-West."

Drew took his hand. "It's just Anna and Drew. Jack and Maureen isn't it."

The introductions were interrupted by a shout from the pitch. "Howzat?"

"That's the way to do it William!" a spectator shouted over a ripple of applause.

"It's Robert's turn to bat now, Daddy."

They watched the retiring batsman tuck his bat under his arm and walk off the pitch removing his gloves, Robert nodded to him as they passed each other on his way to his place at the crease.

"Out for a duck," Jack said. "The skipper won't be happy with that."

Drew searched the field for a duck but didn't comment.

"Please have my chair Anna," Jack offered.

"So what happens now?" Drew asked.

"There's two balls left in this over and Robert's receiving, but this bowler is really good."

Robert hit a four with his first ball, and chipped a single with his second which left him on take for the following over.

"Bobby was really nervous about you coming today," Maureen told them.

Anna smiled. "I hope we don't put him off."

The match continued with Robert putting twenty-seven on the scoreboard before being caught out with a bold stroke toward the boundary. There followed a minor collapse of four wickets for fifteen runs, then a recovery of twenty-one runs before being all out for sixty-one in the twentieth over.

"What happens now?" Drew asked.

"They do it all over again with the other team batting while Bobby's team fields," Jack explained.

"But they have tea first," Maureen added.

"Tea?"

"Normally with sandwiches and cake," Anna told him with a grin.

"No beer then?"

"So what did you think Mr. Parker?" Robert asked, joining them.

"Well I'm still looking for the duck, but apart from that it looks like fun."

Jack laughed. "So will we see you here again then, Drew?"

"Maybe, but I can't stay any longer today. I've a meeting with some colleagues in half an hour at the Duke of Wellington in Twyford."

"Nice pub. They do a decent craft ale in there."

"I don't drink I'm afraid though, Jack, but I'm sure you're right. Robert, would you mind giving them a small donation on my behalf to thank them for the education? I've got to go now. Well done by the way." He handed him two £50 notes.

He kissed Anna goodbye and Cassie walked him to the car.

"Thank you for coming, Daddy. Robert thinks you're amazing. I told him he was right."

"I've not done anything to deserve that, but thanks."

"Mummy told me that you were responsible for the box of condoms."

"Better safe than sorry eh?"

"We haven't used them yet."

"I didn't need to know that."

A five-minute drive got him to the pub where he found Megan, Mac, and Terry waiting in the beer garden with a jug of iced lemonade, four glasses and a selection of sandwiches.

Megan kicked the discussion off by outlining their plan.

"How up to date is the intel?" Terry asked.

"Overall, as recent as yesterday but we won't be certain of their precise individual locations until we're in theatre."

"Who're we taking first?"

"Harris if he's home. His cell phone made calls from the area just before and just after the crash, so it's reasonable to assume he was involved. We'll go after Godley next. His call patterns were the same, so he was there too.

"Finally we'll try to put Clive Droxford the gang leader out of the game. I'll probably tell him that he was grassed on by Godley. As far as we can see, Droxford wasn't directly involved last night, but we don't need him getting any ideas about revisiting this."

NINE

The front door of the small mid-terrace home just off the Ilford High Road, had presented no challenge to Megan's lock picking skills when she and Terry made their silent entry. They'd observed the house for over an hour and seen no sign of activity. Fully expecting the house to be unoccupied they did a quick sweep to confirm.

What they hadn't expected to find was the resident tied to his bed with a bullet hole in his head, and a note pinned to his chest that read, *TRY DEFEND THIS DTF – BETTER LEAVE WET WORK TO PROFESSIONALS. DPW*.

The body was still warm. It had probably been dead less than two hours.

"We need to get out of here and fucking quickly," Terry told her.

She nodded, took a photo, and grabbed the note before making a quick exfil, careful to make sure there was nobody in the street. As they climbed into Terry's car, Megan was already reporting what they'd found to Drew and Mac.

The other two team members had been waiting for Megan's report before making entry into a similar house two streets away.

Mac looked at Drew. "Stay there, Drew; you're far too distinctive to be caught on any CCTV in the area, I'll go in on my own, if it's the same again, I'll grab the note and exit through the rear.

Drew agreed, then watched and waited in the driving seat of Mac's car as his teammate casually walked along the street until he came to the house they'd been watching. Mac had no more difficulty making his entry than Megan had minutes earlier. No sooner was he inside than two police cars approached without sirens, one from each end of the street.

Drew gave Mac the heads up.

"Copy your message. Making exfil now. RV as agreed."

"Copy that."

As the two police cars stopped outside the house, Drew slowly reversed onto the block paved front garden of a house on his left and casually drove back towards the High Road where he parked behind Terry's 4x4.

Inside the grill house, Megan and Terry were already seated at one of the utility Formica topped tables. The only other diners were three teenage Asian boys seated on the far side of the restaurant.

The place sold both Indian and Chinese cuisine and the other two team members had already helped themselves to food from the buffet servery. Drew followed their example and took a seat at the table, but it was ten minutes before Mac joined them with a plate of his own.

"Sorry about the wait. There was an enormous fucking dog on my preferred exfil route, and I had to detour."

"Do you think you were spotted by a neighbour who called the cops, and it was just bad luck that they arrived when they did?" Terry wondered.

Drew shook his head. "I doubt it. They've probably got a sympathiser nearby who they pay to keep a lookout."

"Is it worth going back and having a word?"

"Not really. We'll listen to the police gossip and find out who put the call in, but it won't be a major player."

"What did you find in there, Mac?"

"Same as Meg and Terry. The guy was trussed up and killed with a head shot, probably over an hour before we got there. Same dumb message. I brought it away of course, but I'm not convinced that was the right move."

"How do you mean?" Drew asked.

"Well the grammar indicates that it wasn't written by an English speaker, so it was doubtful that it would fool the cops that you were the author, but it's an indicator that the real author intended to make you look like the culprit."

"Good point, but it may not have been put there just to mislead the police. Perhaps it's the rest of the gang they wanted to mislead."

"So what do we do about our planned courtesy call on Droxford tonight," Megan asked. "Do we abort?"

"Let's take a closer look at where he lives first," Drew decided. "Bluetooth me those photos."

After parking in a service road off the A12 they hiked across playing fields and were pleased to find that the large, detached property backed onto the grounds of King Georges Hospital, which gave them plenty of opportunities to evade the police should the need arise.

"He's probably got CCTV." Megan said.

"We ought to be able to deal with that if we're not disturbed."

"Why not let me go in first and see the lie of the land."

"Okay, you're the smallest so if window entry is possible then you're best placed to do it, but Terry you go with her."

Watched by Drew and Mac, Megan and Terry easily climbed the rear fence into the garden, both masked up as they all had been for their earlier infiltrations. The two observers listened to the brief military instructions and reports from Megan as she affected her entry into the house without activating an alarm, or at least not one that could be heard.

Then they heard her say, "Dog," and she went quiet for a minute or so.

"What's happening Stamp?"

"It's okay, she's got it."

Several minutes passed.

"All clear ground floor," Megan reported.

"Stamp going in."

Another two minutes passed. "All clear. Target secured."

Drew and Mac quickly scaled the fence and entered the house via the French door into the conservatory, passing the unconscious dog which had been tasered and then sedated. They quickly mounted the stairs where they found Clive Droxford naked and secured with cable ties and gagged with duct tape. Lying next to him was a boy no older than nineteen, equally naked, and similarly restrained.

After looking at the two for a few moments without speaking, he took several photos with his phone.

"Makepeace, would you take the boy into the next room, find out who he is and let him get dressed," Drew said using her SAS handle for the first time.

She cut the cable tie on his ankles, and led the terrified kid into the next room, grabbing some of what appeared to be his clothes on the way.

"Clive? It is Clive isn't it?" Drew said.

The man nodded.

"Do you know who I am?"

The terrified man vigorously shook his head.

Drew whipped off his ski-mask. "Now do you know who I am?"

This time a nod.

"Good because, in a moment I'm going to show you some photos of what happens to people who get mixed up in my affairs, and I'm hoping it'll encourage you to avoid doing it in the future. Do you understand?" he nodded.

"This is your little friend Godley. See that bullet hole in his head, the end for him was quick; I doubt he suffered. And this is your pal Harris. If you look carefully you can see that he's got a similar neat little hole. Can you see where I'm going with this?"

Droxford nodded; his eyes were wide as he attempted to say something behind the tape.

"Hush now, Clive; you'll get your turn to speak. I expect you're thinking that I'm going to make a nice little hole like that in your head as well, but that's not how I do business. I don't shoot unarmed people unless they're a direct threat to me, my family, or my friends. You see, I didn't shoot your pals, so do you want to take a guess who did?"

Clive shook his head.

"Never mind, I'll tell you. It was the people who paid you to kill me. I don't know if they were killed because they failed in their task, or because they wanted to shut them up. But now I've got your attention, you are going to tell me in great detail who it was that put the contract on me. I won't kill you if you don't. That would be too easyhat I'll do is send copies of the snaps I took of you with your little boyfriend to every member of your quaint boys' club. I gather they're not fond of members of the gay community, so imagine what they'll say when they discover that their leader is a pink pirate and has been disguising his preferences all the time. So are you going to tell me everything you know about the assholes that want me dead?"

Clive nodded as tears dripped down his face and Drew ripped the tape from the man's mouth.

"Before we start, is that your laptop over there?"

"Y-yes."

"Tell me the password."

"It's DFT43V3R all capitals," he dictated as Terry typed them in and then nodded to confirm they worked.

"Now tell me slowly and accurately who sent you to kill me."

"I don't know their names, but I think they were Russian. They approached me in the pub and offered me ten grand to kill you. They gave me five up front, with another five to follow if we got the job done."

"Describe them to me."

"The one doing all the talking was about seventy, he didn't look well he limped, the other one about forty-five or fifty."

"Tell me about the vehicles your pals were using to come after me."

"We were told to collect them from a place in Oxfordshire. It was called Thame or something. Jay and Dale went with Albie to collect them. They were outside Screwfix with the keys on top of the back wheel."

"Those vehicles must have been in storage for months. Why give them to you lot to use in that crazy attack that your dumb pals attempted?"

"They weren't supposed to use them like that. They were told to wave you down on the Pangbourne Road and the second one was supposed to shoot you as they drove past, and we were supposed to take the cars back to where they got them after. Then Dale said he wasn't sure he could hit you from a moving car. So they got together and dreamed up that stupid idea of the dead sheep and driving you off the road."

"Have the Russians been in contact with you since?"

"No."

"How did you know where I was going to be and when?"

"They had a tracker on your car, and they sent me a text to tell me."

"On your own phone?"

"No on that one over there." He nodded towards what was obviously a burner on the bedside table."

"What happened to the five grand?"

"It's in my safe."

"Where's that?"

"In the front bedroom, under the bed."

Terry went to look and returned with a smile on his face. "It's just a metal tool chest with a padlock that's screwed to the floor."

"Where's the key?"

"The other members will kill me if you take that money."

"You should have thought about that before taking a contract to kill me. Key?"

"I won't tell you."

Drew pressed a taser onto his scrotum and pressed the trigger. Droxford screamed and went limp.

"If you don't want me to do it again, you need to tell me where the key is."

"Taped to the bottom of the top drawer over there."

There was nearly fifteen thousand pounds in the toolbox, they found a small holdall and put all the cash into it except a five-pound note.

"You bastard."

"Very astute observation, but nonetheless I need to be compensated for all the pain, distress, damage, and expense you've caused. We're leaving now and we'll ask your young friend to release you after we've gone. Then you can decide what you want to do, but just so you know, if you decide to come after me again, that no killing thing won't apply."

Three minutes later they were scaling the rear fence. In another ten they were in their cars.

At 02:25 they arrived back at the Duke of Wellington pub, where after a quick debrief, they dispersed in their own cars,.

TEN

"Don't you ever rest?" Anna asked.

"This isn't a time for resting. There might be two kids out there in danger, although I'm beginning to have my doubts about that."

"What do you mean?"

"I've nothing tangible at the moment, but something tells me that the Georgiou woman isn't playing straight with me, and if that's the case then maybe her daughters won't be in as much danger as she makes out."

Cassie met him on the landing as usual.

"Morning, sweetheart. Are you looking forward to your driving lesson?"

"Morning, Daddy. Yes I am, but I'm a bit nervous. How long are the lessons; you didn't say?"

"I booked three hours a day, 5 days a week for two weeks. They may not be the same time every day. You'll have to sort that out with the instructor. Her name is Davina, but she likes to be called Dav."

They did five laps, half an hour in the gym and the same in the pool.

"Jack and Maureen are nice, aren't they?" she said, as they dried off after coming out of the pool.

"Yes, once they got over treating us like royalty."

"Robert says they thought you and Mummy were really nice too."

"I'm sorry I couldn't stay longer. Who won the cricket match?"

"The other side won by three runs when they got a four with the last ball. Robert was bowling and he was angry with himself, but the others all said he played really well."

"I'm not sure I'd be able to go very often."

"Robert wouldn't expect you to. He was pleased you took an interest. He thinks you messed with his car so it wouldn't start that morning."

"I'll take the fifth," Drew replied. Cassie smiled.

Angus Finlay arrived punctually at nine o'clock at the same time as the driving instructor. Drew watched Cassie sit in the passenger seat before Dav drove them away.

"Morning Drew," Angus said, his Scottish accent as obvious as ever.

71

"Angus; hi. Come through."

Anna and Jason smiled at the tall ex-cop as he passed. He was a large man, although not as big as Drew.

When they were in the study, Angus closed the door behind him. "Before we go any further, I take it you're aware of the three deaths in Ilford last night."

"I was aware of two, Paul Godley and Brian Harris. Who was the third?"

"His name was Albert Abbott. All three were members of a small fascist group called *Defend the Flag*. Can you assure me you had nothing to do with their deaths?"

"If you're asking, did I kill or arrange their killing, absolutely not. Myself and one or two colleagues visited Godley and Harris last night with the object of discouraging them from further attempts to kill me. However, when we arrived, we found them both dead. Here are some photos of how we found them."

Drew showed Angus the photos on his laptop.

"As far as I know, there weren't any notices on those two bodies when the police arrived."

"No there weren't. We removed them. We didn't want the police wasting either their time or ours eliminating me from their enquiries. Was there one on Abbott's body?"

"Yes, there was. I haven't seen a picture, but I'm given to understand it was much the same as those."

"Tell me is there any mention of Clive Droxford?"

"Not yet. Why do you ask?"

"Because we visited him as well and took a number of embarrassing photos like this." He scrolled to a picture of naked Droxford with his bed mate. "I don't think they'll be well received by his fellow fascists if they found their way into the public domain."

"I see what you mean. But I shouldn't be too concerned by the notice. No decent copper would pay too much attention to that. It's far too obviously designed to misdirect. Not only that, it must have been prepared in advance which sort of damages any credibility."

Drew described the information that Droxford had given them about the Russians.

"Thame you say. Not far from where the vehicles were taken. That's interesting. I don't understand why two vehicles stolen from the same place at the same time should disappear for six months and then suddenly both make a reappearance at the same crime scene. So I've been looking at other crimes where it's possible that they might have been used before with different plates, because the numbers used on both vehicles were from other vehicles, same model, same colour but not reported stolen."

"Why do you say that Thame was interesting?"

"Because a Land Rover Defender of that colour was involved in a kidnap in Princes Risborough, which isn't far, and another in a farmhouse burglary a month before that."

"What about the minibus?"

"A white minibus and possibly a Land Rover defender was thought to be involved in a prisoner escape from Grendon last month."

"Who was the escapee?"

Angus smiled. "I was hoping you'd ask that. His name is Tobias Althorp."

"That name sounds familiar."

"It should do, he was an accounts executive for your wife's company until he was sent to prison last year for embezzling £1.75 million."

"Has he been recaptured?"

"No."

"Have the police made the connection?"

"Not yet, as far as I know."

"Have you found any direct connection to Ms Georgiou?"

"Not yet, but I'll keep looking."

"What about the kidnap?"

"His company paid up and he was released after a few days."

"It's a bit suspicious about the Land Rover, though if it does turn out to be connected. Who was the hostage?"

"Oliver Babcock; worked for a hedge fund."

"I'd love to know where they were keeping those two vehicles."

"I'll keep working on it."

"Something else is bothering me. Why an out-of-date SUV and a minibus? If you were stealing vehicles to order, what sort of crime calls for transport like that?"

"Buggered if I know," the Scotsman said, shaking his head.

"If they needed those cars returned to where they were collected from, it suggests they were planning on using them again. If that's the case they'll need to replace them. Is it possible to keep an eye out for a similar combination theft."

"It's probably technically possible, but in practical terms there's not a chance in Hell that the powers-that-be would throw money at it. There are too many variables involved and too many different police forces. The only reason I picked it up was because I knew what vehicles I was looking for. If they just replace them with similar vehicles, and that's a big if, they could choose any number of mixes."

"I guess you're right. Can you think of anything we're missing on the attack side of things?"

"I imagine you've got other people working on the kidnapped girls."

"That's right, but it's mostly electronic detective work at the moment because we've got no physical clues and no witnesses."

"I might as well leave you to get on with what you're working on. Meanwhile I'll continue to dig a bit deeper into these vehicles and where they were stored."

"Before you go, give me the address of the guy that was kidnapped. Where did you say it was?"

"Princes Risborough."

"That's it."

"The house is called Green Trees, it's in Upper Icknield Way. I'll text you the postcode. I guess you're going to pay him a visit."

"That's right; what's his name again?"

"Oliver Babcock."

Angus left and Drew decided to look a bit closer at Babcock. His LinkedIn profile listed his most recent post as Financial Controller at Alhambra Capital Management, a UK based company that was listed as a Multi Strategy, Global Macro, and Military Hardware Investment Fund. He appeared to be currently inactive. A hedge fund executive, with a connection to investment in arms manufacture. Drew was intrigued.

Anna was working in the library when he asked if she wanted coffee.

"Jason is just making some, come in and join me for a few minutes."

Drew sat in one of the armchairs in the window alcove and she turned to him with a smile. "How are you, darling? After the accident I mean."

"I'm okay, the bruises will be gone in a week or so. There's no permanent damage but I guess I won't be too pretty to look at for a while."

"How's the investigation going?"

"Making progress, but there's definitely more to this than meets the eye. I haven't found any concrete evidence of a connection between the kidnapping and the attack on me, but I'm certain there is one. Have you ever heard of Oliver Babcock?"

"I don't think so."

"What about Alhambra Capital Management?"

"Oh yes, I've definitely heard of them. They've got a ten percent holding in NorArm Silico. Please don't tell me they're mixed up in it."

"It's too soon to say, but Babcock was their financial controller until a few months ago, when he was kidnapped, then released a few days later after the company paid a ransom. It doesn't look like he's worked since."

"I remember Jared Carrington talking about that. Carrington holds their seat on our board."

"What about Tobias Althorp?"

"That little shit! He's in prison isn't he? How can he be involved?"

Drew explained about the escape before telling her he was going to pay Babcock a visit after lunch."

Anna knew better than to question him too closely about his work, so in spite of her worries that this latest operation would involve their family and her company, she resisted the temptation to ask more. She changed the subject. "I wonder how Cassie is getting on."

"She'll be back soon, so you can ask her."

"Are you taking the new Audi?"

"No, the new BMW should be here soon, I'll take that."

"You didn't say you'd replaced the X7."

"I couldn't stand driving around in that tiny A3 for long, it would cripple me."

Cassie arrived home as they were talking.

"How did it go, darling?"

"It was fun in the end, but I was really nervous at first."

"Where did you go?"

"We went to a school somewhere and after she'd confirmed that I had a learner's licence and that I understood all the controls, we spent an hour practicing manoeuvres driving around the playground. She laid out loads of traffic cones and had me steer in and out of them. Then she drove me to a residential estate in Reading and I just went where she told me. That was a bit scary, but I think I did okay."

Anna smiled. "Well done, darling, I'm proud of you."

"Daddy's lessons helped a lot."

Jason came to the doorway. "Lunch is ready. It's just sandwiches today; I've been a bit busy."

"What've you been up to then?"

"I've been doing preliminary telephone interviews to replace Shyla."

Drew's ears pricked up. "You know that they'll need to be deep vetted, don't you."

"Of course, Anna authorised first stage vetting by Megan's friend. There were only four potentials. They all looked good on paper, but two ruled themselves out because they had too many other commitments. The other two are coming for interviews tomorrow afternoon."

"Do they know they'll be deep vetted, and what that means."

"I did explain that to all of them, but none of them know where the post is yet. One said that if it was for our MP she wasn't interested. I'll call them after lunch and give the short-listed ones the news."

Halfway through lunch the new car arrived. Drew signed all the papers and took possession of the key fobs. He still needed to arrange collection of his personal belongings that were in the old car, including the remote controls for the gates and garage so he called the police station, who informed him that his wrecked car was at the car breaker's yard near Wokingham, but his personal belongings had been retained by their CSI team. With another call he arranged to collect them on his way to Risborough.

When she handed over the small box of belongings, the woman at the CSI desk confirmed what Droxford had told them. There had indeed been a tracker on his car.

ELEVEN

16:00 hours, First Monday – Princes Risborough, Buckinghamshire

As Drew approached Oliver Babcock's home he noted that there were parking restrictions on the road and there were two cars already on the short driveway, so he drove past and turned into a side road. The first thing he saw as he turned was a maroon Land Rover Defender. His inbuilt alert system went immediately to Defcon one.

In broad daylight, and with no obvious way to make a stealthy approach, he walked back to the driveway entrance to the property and strode toward the front door of the thatched Tudor period cottage as if making a routine visit. As he drew close to the house he spotted movement through one of the front windows. A man wearing a ski mask was rummaging through a filing cabinet, and a handgun rested on a nearby desk.

Drew lifted his phone from his pocket, dialled 999 and reported an armed home invasion in progress.

Before leaving Pangbourne, Drew had established that the Babcock home had only been sold a few months earlier and the floor plans had been still available on the agent's website. With some idea of the building's layout he remembered a side entrance.

In a few long strides he was at the side door. Silently he turned the handle and was relieved to find it unlocked. When he pushed the door, the soft creak of the hinges was barely audible. A single pace put him in a position to see the masked man bending over the bottom drawer of the cabinet pulling out folders and files before discarding them on the floor.

There were voices from elsewhere on the ground floor, which were persistent enough to disguise his movement across the carpeted floor until he was almost behind the intruder. The man was so distracted by his task that when he finally sensed Drew's presence he had no chance to utter a sound before the big fist hit him in the side of his head. The intruder collapsed, but Drew caught him, pressed a finger to one of his carotid arteries, and lowered him unconscious, almost silently, to the floor.

He picked up the gun and made his way toward the voices. A man with a strong Russian accent was speaking. "If you not give me answers I need, I kill your wife. If you still not say I kill your son."

A muffled voice replied. "I don't know, I really don't. I'm begging you. You have to believe me."

"Althorp, you shoot her now."

"But what if he really doesn't know?"

"I say shoot her, or I shoot you."

The sound of the shot inside the low-ceilinged house was deafening, and almost drowned a woman's muffled scream.

"You fucking English coward, I tell you shoot her.

Drew burst into the room as a second shot rang out and a masked man holding a gun fell to the floor clutching his stomach.

Assessing the situation with the benefit of his extensive military experience, he saw a badly beaten man tied to a chair, a woman and young boy trussed and gagged on a sofa, and a third masked man with a gun turning towards him.

Drew threw himself to the floor firing three shots as he fell. The masked man cried out, dropped his weapon, and fled through the double doors into the garden. Hauling himself to his feet, Drew kicked the wounded man's gun out of his reach and moved to give chase but the man on the floor tripped him as he writhed in pain.

By the time he got to the garden the escaping man was nowhere in sight, so he ran back inside only to find that the first man had recovered and fled as well.

The sound of approaching police sirens in the distance discouraged him from giving chase so he called 999 again and told them that the danger was over. Two perpetrators had fled the scene, one with an injury; a third was seriously wounded and still on the scene while the three residents required medical attention.

Drew untied the woman who immediately went to her husband, while he released the boy.

"Who are you? What are you doing here?" the woman asked.

"My name's Drew Parker; I was on my way to see your husband and I discovered your little house party. I hope you didn't mind me gate-crashing."

"Thank you; thank you so much."

There was no time for more discussion before a police car arrived. He laid the gun he'd been holding on the floor near the front door, opened it and walked outside. The police patrol car was parked across the driveway and two unarmed officers sheltered behind it.

He held his hands out to the side and called out to them. "There's been shooting. There's one severely wounded intruder inside, maybe dying, one very badly beaten occupant, and his wife and child who're both suffering severe post traumatic shock. I'm unarmed. There are three handguns inside, one just inside the door behind me, one near the garden room door and the other under the sofa in the living room. Two intruders escaped the scene, probably in a maroon Land Rover."

"Lay on the floor face down with your hands out to the side," A cop shouted.

Drew calmly complied and allowed the cop to handcuff him.

An Armed Response Unit arrived a short time later, and after announcing the place was clear and extracting the woman and boy, paramedics were allowed into the scene, but not in time to save the wounded intruder.

It was nine-thirty before Drew was told he was no longer being treated as a suspect and allowed to leave. Earlier, he'd been driven to High Wycombe Police Station, questioned for an hour, then again for another twenty minutes before being told that they would probably need to speak to him again.

The senior detective, an Inspector Jefferies, had tried hard to find some way to incriminate him or get him to incriminate himself, but the statements of Mrs. Babcock, her nine-year-old son, and the injured Babcock all verified everything Drew had said. After he'd given a brief outline of the possible connections with the Bath Road incident, and the kidnapping of the Georgiou girls, and explained the potential for involvement of the National Crime Agency the senior cop backed off.

Drew asked for a ride back to the crime scene to collect his car, but Jefferies sarcastically replied that they didn't provide taxi services. Then added, "This isn't the Wild West here, Mr. Parker. This is the United Kingdom. We don't settle our differences with a shootout in the street, so if you've made your home here you need to get used to that idea."

Drew smiled and shook his head. He'd dealt with cops like Jefferies many times before, their heads so far up their own asses they couldn't see anything but their own ideas. He used his phone to find a cab company.

When the cab dropped him near his car he spotted a police car pulling into Babcock's driveway. Leaving his car where it was, he walked to their house and got there just as Mrs. Babcock was helping her husband from the car.

The driver of the police car challenged him. "I'm sorry Sir, but you can't be here" but Mrs. Babcock intervened.

"No; please don't send Mr. Parker away. He saved our lives. I want to thank him."

"I won't stay long. I just wanted to make myself known to you and ask if it would be okay to return in a day or two to speak to you properly."

"Of course. We want to know what brought you here," the woman said.

"I wanted to ask about the people who've been harassing you. I believe they have malicious intents toward my own family."

Babcock himself hadn't spoken until that point, when he did his words were barely intelligible. "They're madmen. I had no idea what they were talking about."

"Would you be happy to speak to me tomorrow evening, or the day after perhaps?"

"I don't know, I'll have to think about it."

"I'll give you my card. If you decide you might like to help, just give me a call."

At close to midnight he drove through the gates of Pangbourne Grange.

When he walked into the house from the garage, Anna, Cassie, and Jason were waiting for him.

"Why are you all still awake?"

"Why do you think," Anna asked? "We've spent half the evening, being questioned by the police after you were involved in yet another shooting incident with yet another bunch of criminals, and guess what, your phone was turned off."

"I guess the cops must have put it on silent when they took it off me. Sorry, I didn't spot your missed calls."

"What happened, Daddy?"

"I went to speak to a kidnap survivor and when I got there the kidnappers had returned and were threatening to kill his wife and son, so I intervened."

"The police told us that you'd shot someone, and they died."

"You know what they say; 'Never let the truth spoil a good story.' There were three of them, I took a gun off one without killing him.

80

One of the other assholes shot the third one who died from his wound, and I shot at the one still standing. I think I winged him, but he was well enough to get away along with the one I'd taken the gun off. That's when the cops arrived. They never told me that they sent someone here."

"They wanted to search your office," Jason announced. "I told them that unless they had a warrant they weren't going anywhere near it."

"Well done, Jason."

"How is Babcock?"

"More than a little beat up, and a great deal traumatised. I haven't had chance to speak to him properly. I doubt he'd be back at work any time soon, even if he did have a job."

"After the police left I called Jared Carrington. He told me that after the kidnap, Babcock resigned with a big payoff."

"Ah; indeed".

TWELVE

08:30 hours, First Tuesday – Pangbourne Grange.

The gate bell rang to alert them to a police car awaiting admittance. When the car discharged its occupants, Drew was surprised to see Sergeant Gasowski from Reading Police, and DI Jefferies from Wycombe.

"Good morning, officers," Drew greeted them. "Please come in."

He took them through to his study, offering them tea or coffee, but they declined.

"How can I help you this morning?"

Jefferies began with, "I want to know what you were doing at the Babcock property yesterday."

"I thought I explained in my statement, I was hoping that Mr. Babcock would have information that might be relevant to Friday's attack on me."

"I don't see the connection. What would make you think that?"

"A similar vehicle was used when he was kidnapped."

"How would you know that?"

"I have my sources as I'm sure you do. Was I wrong?"

"I don't know at present. Even so it's a bit of a stretch to come to that conclusion."

"I think after what happened yesterday, we can assume I might be onto something, don't you?"

"What would the connection be?"

"Both vehicles in the attack on me were stolen from Stoke Mandeville Hospital car park at the same time six months ago, and both were using false number plates stolen somewhere else at roughly the same time. They must have been stored out of sight in the intervening period and I was curious why. Me and my associates looked for instances of unsolved crimes that involved vehicles with similar descriptions, and Mr. Babcock's kidnap was one. When we looked closer at Mr. Babcock we discovered that at the time of his abduction, he was financial controller for one of the largest investors in my wife's company."

"A coincidence surely."

"Maybe but the man who died at the scene was prison escapee Tobias Althorp, a disgraced former senior accounts executive in my wife's company. A white minibus and maroon Land Rover Defender were involved in his escape."

"How do you know these things?"

"If I'm right, does it matter? And if it helps you to know, there was a maroon-coloured Land Rover Defender at the scene yesterday."

"You're talking in riddles now. The Land Rover involved in the incident on the Bath Road was a write off and the driver was killed."

"You must know that the two dead drivers weren't working alone, and it would be my guess they were being paid to do it. I've never had any involvement with either of them or the group they belonged to."

"What's that got to do with your wife's company?"

"Do you want me to do all your job for you? Past attacks on me and my family are well documented. At least one of the intruders yesterday was probably Russian, and the previous attacks had all been instigated in Russia. I don't know the precise connection between all these things, but they sure as Hell aren't just a coincidence, and I'm just as sure that I'm going to find out."

"Investigation of crime in this country, is the responsibility of the police."

"Yeah? How's that working out?"

"We won't tolerate vigilante action, Mr. Parker."

"Is there a law in the UK that stops me from investigating who's trying to kill me?"

"No, as long as you don't interfere with witnesses, destroy evidence, or obstruct the police."

"That's okay then. I've been as helpful as I can be so far, and I haven't been obstructive. I called the police to the crime in progress yesterday, and if you'd been able to get there in time I wouldn't have needed to be anything other than a witness."

"Is there a connection between all of this and the abduction of Ariana Georgiou's daughters?"

"Without a doubt. Although as yet I have no idea what it is."

"I'm guessing you've made no progress in finding her children either," Jefferies said with a smug smile.

"No, but then as far as I know, neither have the police."

"So you believe that the attack on you, Oliver Babcock's abduction, the attack on the Babcock home yesterday, and the kidnap of Ms Georgiou's children are all connected and it's all to do with your wife and the Russians; is that right?"

83

"More or less, yes."

"That is the most ridiculous conspiracy theory I've heard for years. I think you should stick to being a bodyguard, Mr. Parker and leave criminal investigation to the police."

"Well Inspector Jefferies, if you've got nothing better to do with your time than to come here and make patronising and offensive remarks then I suggest you go away and do some of that investigating that you claim to be so good at. As for me, I'm too busy for this."

"We haven't finished asking questions yet."

"That's a shame, because I've finished answering them, and in case you were wondering; I recorded that interview, so if I ever feel the need to make a complaint. I'll find it easy to recall your precise words. Thank you and goodbye."

"What an asshole," Drew remarked, as the gate closed behind them.

Jason laughed. "I was going to ask if you all wanted coffee, and I overheard the last few moments of that. It's a miracle he solves any crimes at all."

"He made it clear he just doesn't like Yanks. Has Cassie already left for her driving lesson?"

"Yes. She said if you go out before she gets back, to tell you she loves you."

"I've no plans to go out at the moment, but that may change."

"Will you be here when I interview the new cook?"

"I'm not qualified to interview cooks, but I'll arrange the vetting when you've decided.

"There's only one candidate now. When I explained what was involved in deep vetting the other one told me that she didn't want people delving into her personal business."

"Won't Anna be here?"

"She's not sure. She's meeting with the security guy at Silico to talk about what happened to Mr. Babcock."

Drew spent the next hour or more trying to find some way to connect Babcock with Russia or Ariana without success. Then he received a call from Digits. "Hi Glover, how goes it?"

"If my enquiries are right, then you've certainly got involved in something pretty complicated. I've had to use quite a lot of sources to piece it all together, and it's going to cost a bit."

"I'm not concerned about the cost. Just tell me what you've found out."

"This is the story so far, much of which you'll already know, but to keep the narrative straight in my head, here goes. Correct me if I get something wrong. As we know Manos Stamelis's Russian handler was a guy called Dmitri Turgenev, who was very, very close to Putin throughout his climb up the political greasy pole. That Turgenev was able to hand control of such an enormous chunk of Russian assets to Stamelis speaks volumes about how much clout he must have had.

"However, there are no friends in politics, especially in Putin's Russia. The next bit is partially conjecture on my part. The assets handed to Stamelis were in the form of huge sums of money to turn into profit initially via the shipbuilding industry. It was almost unheard of for a foreigner to be entrusted with sums of that size, but he produced exceptional returns.

"Through the shipbuilding connection Stamelis grew close to Lemonis who developed a relationship with his daughter Ariana. Then at some point, after moving his assets into the US hi-tech industry following the death of your wife's first husband, and at Stamelis suggestion, Lemonis established a friendship with Anna, culminating in their marriage. The bright idea of trying to gain control of Silico stemmed from that if it hadn't been the plan all along.

"When the first attempt failed, it caused the loss of much of the investment that the Russians had ploughed into the scheme. However, either Stamelis or Turgenev persuaded Putin to allow them one last attempt to salvage something from the rubble. That's how the plan that involved Cassie's kidnapping two years ago came about. The total failure of that resulted in every asset controlled by Stamelis either being lost, or access to it denied by the Russian government. That was when Putin said enough was enough and pulled the plug on Turgenev. The once most favoured colleague was stripped of all he owned and exiled to Omsk in Siberia to manage a ticket office in a railway station. That for any other Russian of sixty-seven in poor health would have been the end of that, except..."

"Except what?"

"One night in March last year Turgenev disappeared, and when neither he nor his body turned up a search was authorised. Not because anybody gave a rat's ass for his wellbeing, but because they needed to make sure he hadn't escaped a single second of what his prolonged death sentence was supposed to be. It seems that no sign of him has been seen since, and much to Putin's chagrin it's suspected that he's escaped, which of course is frowned upon."

"So where is he?"

"I haven't finished my tale yet. Turgenev had a second cousin called Killip, who lived in Kingisepp, close to where they'd both been brought up. It was soon discovered that Killip disappeared a few days after Dmitri. Naturally, it was deduced that Killip had assisted in Dmitri's escape, and indeed Killip's body was washed up on the Estonian coast a few weeks later. He'd been shot. The mystery was how Dmitri got from Omsk to Kingisepp. Neither of them owned a car and it's at least a three-day drive. So it's clear that there must have been a third person involved. At present, that's as far as the Russian investigations have got."

"Does that mean you've unearthed something more?"

"I think so, yes. I can't explain how the Ruskies haven't picked up on it yet, but another man disappeared a few weeks earlier, who I believe could be connected. His name is Miron Sokolov who worked as an accountant at one of Turgenev's businesses. In the aftermath of Turgenev's disgrace, Sokolov lost his job as well. Sokolov has an aunt in Tallinn called Iliya Tarasova and would have been ideally placed to engineer their escape over the Estonian border."

"So Turgenev and this guy Sokolov are now in the EU."

"That's my estimation, yes."

"What about ID though?"

"Once again this is speculation on my part. Either Turgenev or Sokolov had some money salted away and they'll have used that to finance their run for it."

"Good false IDs cost a lot of money."

"It's my theory that's why Sokolov needed Turgenev. He wouldn't have been able to skim enough off the top to do it on his own, not in the job he'd held. Turgenev would have been needed for that alone."

Drew sighed in frustration. "I get that these two might be the Ruskies responsible for the kidnapping, but where do I come into it? Why try to kill me? Is it revenge on Turgenev's part, or are they just scared I might stop them doing whatever it is they're trying?"

"God knows. Maybe they're pissed off that the Georgiou woman has got you involved, but apart from that, we can't be sure the Stamelis treasure trove that they're after even exists."

"Or what the fuck maroon Land Rovers have to do with it," Drew added with exasperation.

"Say what?"

Drew explained the issue with the vehicles.

"That sounds to me that they're setting you up for a red herring somewhere later on down the line."

"I guess you're right, but I don't see how I can avoid following the lead."

"I'll leave you to ponder that. In the meantime, I'm going to try to hack into the Estonian passport office and look for passports issued after Turgenev's disappearance that might be our two Russian friends."

Drew smiled at his contact's extraordinary abilities. "Good luck with that."

He next took the opportunity to call Hargreaves. "Dennis, I know I haven't really given you a lot of time, but I thought I'd call to see how it's going."

"It's all jogging along absolutely fine, helped enormously by the first-class job my predecessor did. As far as I can tell he missed absolutely nothing, although there's one anomaly that intrigues me. I doubt it would have troubled you at the time because you were searching for assets, but it's annoying me, and I've been searching for explanations."

"Tell me about it?"

"In July three years ago he appears to have received an income of $110 million in the form of a loan. It's odd because he was already in funds to the tune of more than $800 million at the time and there doesn't appear to have been any acquisitions that might account for it. Furthermore he repaid the sum plus interest two months later."

"Could he have just been trying to appear as if he had more collateral than he did?"

"I considered that but, most people examining the wherewithal of someone involving those sorts of sums, would want to see a lot more than a balance sheet, and so would the lender if it were a loan. Therefore if that were the case, then those looking for evidence of collateral were doing an exceedingly poor job."

"Who were the lenders?"

"The Nevada Foothills Capital Management Trust."

"What do you think it means?"

"My educated guess would be is that is exactly as you suggest an attempt to make himself appear wealthier than he was. However for him to do this and get away with it he'd have needed the collusion of one or more than one person very high up in the investment fund to get away with it."

"Such as?"

"The portfolio manager, the chief financial controller, the chief executive, or the chairman; most likely the first two."

"Thank you Dennis, that's been very helpful."

"Do you want me to keep looking?"

"Are you likely to find anything?"

"Without a close look at the Nevada Foothills books it's doubtful."

"Then just leave it for the time being. Send me an invoice, and make sure it covers everything you've done. You may well have given me a key to unlock this whole thing."

Cassie returned from her driving lesson really upbeat about it. "I drove around the housing estate for over two hours and Dav didn't have to correct me once. She said she might let me go on the main road tomorrow."

"That's real quick, sweetheart, well done."

"What time is the new cook coming."

"I think Jason said he'd be here in about half an hour."

Cassie turned in surprise. "It's a man?"

"That's alright, isn't it?"

"Of course it is. I suppose that makes me as guilty of gender stereotyping as anybody else."

"We haven't accepted him yet, and he'll have to be deep vetted."

"Of course," she said.

THIRTEEN

14:00 hours, First Tuesday - Hampstead home of Ariana Georgiou

Drew rang the doorbell and waited.

Her abrupt response at seeing him was, "You didn't say you were coming."

"Is it a problem?"

"I could have been out."

"You weren't."

"I could have had visitors."

"You haven't."

"How did you know? Are you spying on me?"

"If you mean keeping a watchful eye over a client in danger, then yes."

"Danger, what do you mean?"

"Are you being deliberately obtuse or are you just dim? Your daughters have been abducted and held for a ransom of something that you claim you've no knowledge of or which may not even exist. Does it not occur to you that if the kidnappers are that desperate they might come for you next."

"Is that usual, for kidnappers to do something like that?"

"There's nothing usual about any of this. Taking the children of wealthy people hostage is a common enough practice in some countries perhaps, but not in this one. From then on it only gets more bizarre. They haven't demanded money even though you're quite capable of giving it. They've only demanded the location of or access to money that they can't be certain still exists even if it did in the first place. If all that weren't extraordinary enough, even though there are a number of better qualified alternatives, the target of the extortion hires a sworn adversary to find her children, and then leaves him to get on with the job for days without making even a single enquiry about progress."

"I told you why I hired you, and I've been assuming that you've been doing your best. The police are having no more success than you are."

"What did you have for breakfast?"

"What are you talking about?"

"Just tell me?"

89

"Toast."

"Don't you like muesli?"

"Have you gone mad?"

"At least three times since you engaged me to find your daughters, you've left the house attempting to evade the people watching you, visited an all-night grocery store, to buy muesli or at least examine the store's stock of Swiss style breakfast cereal. What're you hiding?"

"They don't have the brand I like."

"Don't bullshit me, Ariana. How can I find your kids if you won't tell me the truth?"

"I can't tell you; they'll hurt Elektra."

"How do you know that?"

"When I gave you the copy of the ransom note there was part of it missing."

"I already knew that, but now you need to show me the whole thing."

"What if they're listening?"

"The only people listening are my people, take my word for it."

"You put bugs in my house?!"

"Yes."

"Why?"

"Because I don't trust you."

"You've got to remove them. It's an invasion of my privacy. I don't like it."

"Tough. If they go, then so do I. Same applies to the missing part of the note."

"You're a cruel man."

"I'm not the one who colluded in the kidnap, rape, and murder of children. Show me."

Ariana walked to a bureau and took the original note from a drawer. "If this leads to Elektra being hurt, I'll send someone to kill you."

He took the piece of paper from her. "If it does, I'll deserve it." Then he read the note in its entirety

Your daughters being looked after nothing bad happen to them if you do what we say.

Russian government take all your fathers properties when he disappear, but we know that he had big holdings in property and money that they not

take. We want know where all fathers other money is. When we know we will know how to deal with it.

When you ready to give information make new Twitter account @ManosIsHere with photo of father as profile picture and make name El Stam, with the password Revenge15sw33t. Then we be in touch with how to deliver the information to us. When information confirmed we return daughters.

We are patient people and not expect an answer in one day, but we not wait forever. If we don't have information we need by 31 July, you not see daughters again.

Do svidaniya.

CUT THIS PART OF MESSAGE OFF AND PHOTOCOPY BEFORE SHOW POLICE.

If we need contact with you again, we leave message inside a 650G pack of Dorset Cereals Simple Muesli marked with gold star sticker in all-night convenience store near Finchley Road railway station. If you need reply put message inside the box and put back in store. If you tell police about this part of message, we hurt oldest daughter and send pictures.

"So that was another lie you told me."

"What do you mean?"

"Explain how you copied it without the police seeing?"

"I opened the envelope while the uniformed cops searched the house, then I used the printer in the study before the detectives arrived. How did you know that I hid part of the note?"

"When you copied it, the copy showed a very fine line where the original was smaller than the paper the copy was printed on. Whether the police have spotted it I don't know, but I doubt it, or they would have asked about it. So far they haven't followed you to the store."

"What're you going to do about it?"

"For the time being, nothing. Keep up your nightly visits to the store, if they leave you a message then buy a copy of a TV listings magazine. If you're replying then buy something from the kosher or ethnic shelves."

"How will you know?"

"We'll know."

After her first visit to the store Drew had asked Digits to hack into the store's CCTV which was fortunately a good up to date system with cloud storage. So far nobody else had messed with the muesli display other than the store staff.

"Before you go taking your own safety for granted, you should know about an incident which I believe is connected to this business. Several months ago a man was kidnapped and threatened until he gave them information. He says he told them everything he knew. This week the kidnappers returned, severely beat him, and threatened to shoot his wife and son in front of his eyes unless he told them more. The family were lucky to survive after a chance intervention. There were three of them, one was killed, but the other two escaped. They were Russian."

"How do you know it was connected?"

"I'm not prepared to go into detail; you'll have to take my word for it. Have you ever heard of Nevada Foothills Capital Management Trust?"

"No."

Drew couldn't be certain, but he thought he'd seen a momentary reaction. "How about Alhambra Capital Management?"

"No, I don't think so." There was no tell this time, but he was convinced she was lying.

"I'm going to leave you now, but you need to remember, if I find out you've been lying to me again, I'll be gone."

"Haven't you found out anything?"

"I've actually learned quite a lot, but nothing I'm yet prepared to share with you."

Before returning home he visited Digits, and they talked through their various discoveries.

"She sounds like a slippery character to me. Do you want me to keep an electronic eye on her."

"I've been monopolising your time a bit lately. I don't want you to ignore your other clients."

"I've nothing urgent happening with them at the moment, and your stuff is much more interesting, so nothing to worry about on that score. At the moment the Estonian Passport database is giving me a headache, but I'll get there in the end. It's language that's holding me up at the moment. Same goes with their driving licences."

Drew left Digits and on the way home he thought about his visit to Ariana, wondering if he'd shaken her enough for her to reveal what was really happening.

"Robert's got a job!" Cassie triumphantly told him as he came into the kitchen. The kitchen was the hub of the Parker-West household during the daytime, and where everybody congregated until they were ushered out by whoever was cooking the evening meal.

"That's great news. Is it okay if I ask where?"

"A small company in Upper Basildon, not far from here."

"What's he going to be doing?"

"His job title will be Junior Graphic & Website Designer, but he'll mostly be doing general office duties. He showed them his portfolio and they said they'd help support him through his college course with a view to him doing design work if it goes okay."

"When did he apply for that?"

"Months ago. He hadn't heard anything, and he thought he'd been unsuccessful, but the girl they first gave the job to didn't work out, so they looked out his application and called him yesterday. He went for an interview this morning. He starts on Monday."

"I think it's wonderful news, darling," Anna said.

"It doesn't pay very much."

"I don't expect it does."

"We've saved you some dinner if you're hungry."

They chatted for a time while Drew ate his meal. Afterwards he said, "Have you got a minute, darling, there's something I need to run by you."

They went through to the library.

"I didn't want to talk about this in front of Jason and Cassie in case you think it's something to be concerned about. Have you ever heard of Nevada Foothills Capital Management Trust?"

"Yes I have. Please don't tell me they've cropped up in your investigations as well."

"In a rather oblique way, yes. It may mean nothing, but three years ago they gave Stamelis a short-term loan of $110million. It was paid back in full very shortly after, but it's an anomaly in his financial background that Dennis Hargreaves picked up."

"Nevada Foothills was already a big shareholder in Silico at that time and still are now. If they were loaning out that sort of money, we should have been told."

"Do they have a seat on your board?"

"Yes they bloody do. Steve Boardman holds it, the man you called a smarmy bastard."

"Is it going to be a problem?"

"I doubt it, not if it happened three years ago, but we'll need to know why we weren't informed at the time, and I'm not sure if it's something we should report to the regulator. I'll speak to the controller tomorrow,"

"If it's at all possible, it would be good if you could hold off making an official complaint for the time being."

"At the moment, I don't have any evidence other than what you've told me, and that might be considered to be illegally obtained, so I won't be initiating a formal inquiry."

"Ok, then."

FOURTEEN

08:00 hours, Second Wednesday – Pangbourne Grange

"What've you got planned today, darling," Anna asked.

"I'm going to be looking at a small business park in Thame where these assholes might have been storing their vehicles."

Megan's ears pricked up. "Has Lightfoot found an actual location?"

"Not yet, but I have a theory. We know where the minibus and Land Rover were picked up from and where they were to be returned to. It seems reasonable that they won't have been stored too far away. Thame isn't a big town, so it's unlikely that there are that many suitable places."

"A bit of a long shot."

"True, but with nothing else to work on for the minute, I thought it worth a try. Fancy a run out?"

"Absolutely. How about we take my car just in case they've got wind of your new one."

During the drive to Thame, Drew brought Megan up to date with every aspect of the investigation.

"I'm no investigator, but I once had to get involved in something on my own behalf which turned out quite complex, but this is weird," Megan told him. "There are so many aspects to this that at first glance don't appear connected, and yet the fact it's possible that they must be is becoming indisputable."

"I don't think we'll know for sure how they're connected until we're certain who's driving this. For example, I'm certain that Dmitri Turgenev and/or Miron Sokolov Initiated the chain of events, but I'm not sure that they're entirely still in control, even if they think they are."

"What do you mean?"

"Why the second go at Babcock? They must have thought they'd got everything they needed out of him the first time, or why else release him. It seems to me that they're getting desperate. If they'd wanted Georgiou to find the money on her own they would have told her not to involve anybody else. Then there's the dead letter thing with the muesli. That suggests that they expect someone else to be involved. And why try to kill me? I think there's a third party."

When they reached the business park in Thame, Megan parked outside Screwfix while Drew went inside, bought a two-foot wrecking bar, and asked if they recalled a maroon Land Rover and a White minibus being parked outside, maybe overnight. One server remembered the vehicles but hadn't seen who left them and none of them were able to help with where they might have been stored nearby.

It wasn't long before they discovered that there were no units in that business park or nearby that weren't actively occupied, so they drove around the neighbourhood hoping to chance on something, but it was a bigger town than they'd thought. After an hour Megan declared she needed a drink, so she stopped at a parade of shops and waited while Drew went into a newsagent that sold coffee.

Just inside the door he bumped into an elderly man hurrying to leave. Drew grasped his arm to stop him falling, apologised, and asked if he was okay. The man snatched his arm away and grumpily rushed off without speaking.

The shop was busy and even though there were two people serving, there was still a queue. At the counter, he ordered the drinks and while the girl was making them, he asked, "I'm told there's a guy around here that sells Land Rovers. You wouldn't know where I could find him would you?"

"I don't know if he sells them, but the man you bumped into as you came through the door; I've seen him in more than one, and they're always maroon. I only noticed because they're the same as my dad's."

"Where does he hang out, do you know?"

"He's got a yard behind the church; I think he rents it from a farmer. I think he must be Polish or something. When he comes in here, I can't understand a word he says most of the time." She gave Drew directions, he paid for the coffee and rejoined Megan in the car.

"Bingo. I think I just missed one of them, Turgenev would be my guess from his age."

"Do you mean that old guy you nearly sent flying?"

"That's him, did you see where he went?"

"He got into a little hatchback and drove off round the corner like his butt was on fire. My engine was turned off, so I never caught it on dashcam."

"I think I've got some idea where he's gone. The shop girl told me how to get there."

They put their cups in the cup holders and Megan followed his directions, but he must have memorised them incorrectly, because they couldn't find it.

"She said it was behind a church," Drew remarked.

They drove around searching for a church, or something resembling one. In the end they had to stop someone to ask where the church was, but as Megan reversed into a side road to turn around, a fire appliance went speeding past, followed shortly after by a second and a police car. A thick plume of smoke above the buildings was an indicator of where they were headed.

Megan followed the speeding vehicles, but as they headed into a narrow single-track road, a maroon Land Rover Defender and a small hatchback emerged. A second police car sounding its siren behind them forced them to move over, but by the time they'd manoeuvred to allow the cop car to pass, the two fleeing vehicles were long gone.

"Shit!" Drew shouted, as he thumped the dashboard.

"Let's go have a look at what's on fire," Megan said, in an effort to placate him.

She parked where she wouldn't obstruct anyone, and they followed the emergency vehicles on foot. The lane led past the church to a farmyard where the firefighters had deployed hoses to attack a blazing barn from three sides and appeared to be making good progress.

Megan approached a firefighter operating the pump on one appliance. "What's in there, do you know?"

"Two or three cars and a minibus, so I'm told."

"Any people inside?"

"None reported."

"Too soon to talk about cause I suppose."

"I shouldn't say, but if it ends up as anything other than arson I'd be surprised."

"Who owns it?"

"Couldn't say, but the farmer died about a year ago I think. It's been empty ever since."

"What about the house?"

"That too."

"Thanks for that mate." She walked back to where Drew was standing. "Do you think they've been keeping the girls in that rundown farmhouse?"

"No, I don't think they're keeping them anywhere. If they're being held somewhere, it wouldn't have been here or by them. I'm no longer convinced they were ever kidnapped in the first place."

"So you think that Georgiou is involved in some kind of scam?"

"Whether she's directly involved, or taking advantage of the situation, I don't know, but something about this whole thing stinks."

"I'll have dashcam footage of their cars as they passed us. Difficult to know what we'll gain from it though, the number plates will be false, and they've probably been changed already but we might catch a picture of the drivers' faces."

"Send the file off to Lightfoot and see if he can do anything with it and ask him to try and find out who owns that farm."

They were soon on their way back to Pangbourne, having little else to show for their morning.

Anna was pleased to see the pair return but led Drew through to the study. "I called our controller about that loan. He said there's nothing we can do about it now, but we should have been told about it at the time. He'll be revisiting their books to ensure that nothing like it has happened since."

"Don't mention it to Boardman yet, unless you have to."

"The least amount of time I spend speaking to him the better. I doubt you've had time to vet the new cook yet have you?"

"I asked Lightfoot to do it, I'll see if he's got back to me." He booted up his laptop. "Have you all had lunch?"

"Yes, do you want me to get you something?"

"That would be great if you've got time."

"What do you fancy?"

"What I'd really like would be an old-fashioned American hamburger, but I'll settle for a couple of your British sandwiches."

Anna laughed and left him at his work. When she returned she brought a plate with two UK sized beefburgers in buns. "Best we could do, darling, will they be okay?"

He laughed. "They'll be fantastic, sweetheart. Your new cook passed vetting without problems. When's he going to start?"

"He's here already. He was the one who produced those burgers. I told him you wanted to meet him before he started, so he came in. Do you want me to bring him in?"

"No, I'll come through."

He walked into the kitchen where a tall young black man stood to meet him.

"Hi, you must be Eli. Guess you're going to be our new part-time cook. I'm Drew."

Eli took Drew's offered hand and shook it looking puzzled and scared in equal measure, looking to Anna and Jason for reassurance.

"It turned out that Eli wasn't looking for a part-time post, but we were so impressed with the demonstration meal he did yesterday, I offered him the job full-time, subject to your approval of course."

"Well Eli, you certainly know how to rustle up a couple of hamburgers in a hurry, and if Anna and Jason are impressed with your cooking, I'm pretty sure I won't have any complaints. Welcome to the household, it's nice to meet you."

"Thank you, Sir."

"You only need to call me Sir when you've done something wrong, Sit down and tell me about yourself. I don't mean all that stuff you write on your résumé; I know all about that."

"I don't know what to say."

"I know you're Elijah Freeman, you're twenty years old, and you took a Level One Professional Culinary Arts course at Reading College. Your course tutors all remarked that you were an exceptional student, but you never went on to do Levels Two and Three. I was curious why you didn't follow it up."

"Er well..."

"Don't worry, this isn't a second interview, and if you'd rather not say, that's okay. There are a few things about my past that I haven't told everybody in this house except Anna."

"My Mum and Dad ran a pub in Newbury and the plan was that I'd take over running the restaurant when he retired, but dad was killed by some guys that didn't like the idea of a black guy running a pub. My mum couldn't run it without him, and the brewery cancelled the lease. They wouldn't consider me as a landlord. So the idea of pub management sort of lost its appeal. I love cooking and I think I'm pretty good at it, but it's not a very secure job. Since then, I've lost two sous chef jobs after restaurants went bust, and I thought working for a family might be a bit more stable."

"Well we hope so too. How much have my family told you about me?"

"They said you run a bodyguard business."

"I guess that's true but there's a lot more to it than that, and some of it might be a bit surprising. I imagine that Anna and Jason have told you about the need for tight security and discretion by everybody who works here, but I'll explain it a bit more to put it into perspective. My work, and Anna's business both demand absolute commitment to confidentiality about our lives and those of everyone in the household, and by that I mean it could mean the difference between life and death.

"Anna and Cassie have both been the victims of kidnap attempts. In fact six years ago Anna's eldest daughter was kidnapped and murdered, and then two years ago Cassie was actually abducted. There has been an attempt on my life last week, it wasn't the first and probably won't be the last. I provide protection for some very high-profile individuals, politicians, movie stars, and very wealthy people. Anna is one of the world's wealthiest women, so she attracts a great deal of unwanted attention from time to time. You've been offered the post, because we're happy that we can trust you, but I'm telling you all this in case you want to reconsider accepting it."

"No, Sir. I do want the job; it's a privilege to be given the opportunity."

"It's still just Drew, and it's not a privilege; it's a job that you earned, so it's great to have you on the team. Have you met everyone else?"

"I think so."

"Eli met everyone yesterday, except you. It turns out he went to the same school as Robert."

"Yes, I spotted that. Did you know each other?"

"We weren't friends, but we knew who each other was."

"So are you staying for dinner?" Drew offered.

"You want me to cook again?"

"No, I mean as a guest. That's okay Anna, isn't it?"

"Of course, it's a lovely idea, a good opportunity for us all to get to know each other. My cooking won't be up to your standard though."

"Thank you, that's kind. I'd better let my mum know."

He began typing a text to his mother.

"Where's Cassie?" Drew asked.

"She's out with Robert. She's treating him to a celebratory meal at that Italian restaurant we were going to try."

"So Eli, tonight it's just Anna, me, Jason, Megan, and you. Have you met Megan?"

"Yes, I met her yesterday."

"Megan's a guest here for a week or two to provide a little extra security, while a little nastiness is going on. Just a precaution."

"Have you got a girlfriend, Eli?" Anna asked.

"Her name's Rachel. She's a sort of second cousin. We've known each other since we were kids."

"That's sweet. Does she live nearby?"

"In Reading."

"You'll have to bring her to meet us one day."

"So how did you hear about this job?" Drew asked.

"I read the ad in the local paper; I had no idea it was for such a rich family."

"We're just a family. The fact that we've got more money than most others is irrelevant. Don't get dazzled by banknotes. The very fact that I'm a member of the family should give that away. I was just a bad kid, from a trailer park in Delaware that got luckier than I deserved when I met this wonderful woman beside me. And by that, I mean it had nothing to do with her money."

"The ad just said, 'Working family require cook, short hours, competitive pay. Apply with CV to the email address below'." Eli said.

"We only had six applicants," Jason said. "Two were completely unsuitable, two more ruled themselves out for one reason or another and one didn't want to be vetted. So if you hadn't worked out, I'd have had to start again."

"So what did you imagine it was going to be like then, Eli?" Anna asked.

"I kind of expected it would be a stockbroker with a couple of kids, and wife who couldn't be bothered to cook. Then when my satnav brought me to your gates, I thought I'd typed the postcode in wrong, and nearly turned around and went home."

"What finally got you the job was when I asked if you could make a meal for us at short notice from whatever ingredients were available, I was talking hypothetically," Jason told him, "but you just got up and looked in the cupboards and in a couple of minutes you gave me a choice of four things. Proof enough you're capable to me."

FIFTEEN

06:50 hours, Second Wednesday – Pangbourne Grange

"Did you have a good time last night?" Drew asked when Cassie stopped at the oak tree.

"It was really nice. Robert had never eaten in an Italian restaurant before. His parents rarely go out, and he doesn't have many friends."

"So the food was good was it?"

"Yes, really good. You and Mummy should try it."

"It'll have to wait until this crap with the Georgiou woman is finished."

"Robert stayed over last night."

"I saw his car."

"Is that okay?"

"Sure; I trust your judgement."

"We..."

"It's all I need to know."

"Robert told me again that he thinks you're amazing."

"He hardly knows me yet."

"I told him about the business with Theo, and about Manos. Is that okay?"

"As long as he knows that he can't speak about those things to anybody else."

"We were talking about animals because he's interested in wildlife photography. I showed him the pictures of the bears in Kentucky, and the conversation went on from there. He asked about how you lost your fingers."

"Yeah well that was mostly false pride and not listening to your mom."

"He said that someone ought to write a book or make a film about you."

"People shouldn't make films about dumb military grunts like me. They should make them about the women who stop us falling. People like my grandma, my sister Lina, your mom, or you."

"Me? What did I do?"

"You and your mom were the final things that turned me from a dumb violent thug for hire into an almost human being. You made me look at myself and make an effort to be a proper person."

"That's crap, Daddy, you're not dumb. You're the smartest person I know, and you're only what you are now because you were like it all along. You just didn't have the opportunity to show it. I remember when you told me about why you left Delta Force. It was the good person inside you that made you do that."

Drew changed the subject. "Shall we do half an hour in the gym before we swim?"

They were halfway through their in the pool routine when Robert joined them. "Is it okay if I swim too?" he asked.

"No problem Robert. No point in having a pool this size if it doesn't get used.

Later, Drew was reviewing the footage from Megan's dashcam when his phone buzzed. It was Digits.

"Glover, how's it going?"

"Well, I think I'm pretty sure that I know the new identities that Turgenev and Sokolov are using, and I've got their Passport photos, issued in April this year. I've sent you an email with all the details. Turgenev is now Martin Leppik, and Sokolov is Andrus Sepp. Both are now in the UK using their Estonian passports. It's their second visit and they've been here since the fourth of May. They landed at Stansted from Tallinn, stayed the night in an airport hotel, and then disappeared."

"Shit, so you've no idea where they are now then?"

"Hold your horses. Now this is the bit where you gasp in admiration and tell me what a genius I am."

"Go on."

"I did a search for new UK passports in the intervening period, narrowed it down to men of approximately the same age, then did facial recognition on the photos, and bingo. Our Russian pals were issued UK passports the week before they arrived in the UK the second time. They're now Marian and Filip Bronski, brothers born to a Polish RAF pilot, and British mother. The boys had never held a passport before because they both have Down's syndrome and live in a care home in Bromsgrove."

"Jesus that's clever, but they must have had UK help to get that far."

"Yes and it goes further. They've got UK bank accounts."

"Can we track them with those?"

"Yes, although they're not very active. Deposits have been in cash; significant sums, all less than £5000 at a time, and all in random places."

"What about withdrawals and purchases?"

"Both make very few cash withdrawals, I guess they don't need to; and they make very few purchases probably for the same reason. The main purchases have been three vehicles, a maroon 1991 Land Rover Defender 110. Cost £5,500, Sepp paid a deposit of £550 and the rest in cash. He then bought a white 2003 Ford Transit minibus. Cost £2,600, he paid a deposit of £260 and the rest in cash. Then Leppik bought a 2012 grey Ford Fiesta. Cost £3,100, he paid in full by card."

"When did they buy them?"

"The Land Rover and minibus were both bought in the first week of May, but the Fiesta was last week."

"What address have they been using to make all these transactions?"

"Here's where it gets interesting, the address they've been using is a two-bedroom flat in Harrow. It would be my guess that, it's an accommodation address, and they're having their mail redirected to a private mailbox elsewhere."

"Who owns the place in Harrow?"

"I'm having problems pinning that down at the moment. .t's at the bottom of a long line of companies."

Drew described his and Megan's trip to Thame the day before. "Is there any possibility that the place in Harrow and the farm near Thame could be owned by the same people?"

"It's worth looking into. I'll get back to you."

"Leave it, I'll get Lightfoot to do it, he's already looking into the farm."

Drew printed out the photos that Digits had sent him, then compared them with stills from Megan's dashcam. The driver of the Fiesta was unmistakably Turgenev (AKA Martin Leppik, AKA Marian Bronski), but even though the picture wasn't good, the driver of the Land Rover was almost certainly not Sokolov. There's at least one other person working closely alongside them.

When he joined Jason, Cassie, and Robert in the kitchen he put the two photographs on the table while he poured himself a coffee.

"Do you want a cup Marilyn?" he asked the head domestic, who was passing through on the way to the coach house.

"Do you know what, Mr. Parker, I think a cup of caffeine right now would be a life saver, thank you."

Drew smiled and handed her the cup he'd poured for himself.

Marilyn grabbed some creamer from the fridge. "We're not all as tough as you Americans you know. Some of us need to calm it down a bit occasionally."

"If all the extra visitors are causing you too much work, just get Jason to authorise more hours for some of your staff."

"I've already offered that Drew, but she keeps telling me it's okay."

Marilyn sat at the table and pointed to the photos. "Who're those men?"

"They're persons of interest in something that's happening at the moment."

"Two men approached me in the village yesterday afternoon. He was one of them." She pointed at Turgenev.

"What did they want?"

"They said they worked for Hello magazine and were doing a story about you and your wife and wondered if I'd like to contribute. Offered me five hundred pounds. I told them to fuck off. Sorry for swearing."

"Don't worry about it and well done. Did they have an accent?"

"That one didn't speak; just sort of hung around in the background. The other one sounded Scottish but pretended to be posh."

Drew told her to hold on for a minute, before rushing out to the study. When he returned he showed a printed still of the Land Rover driver. "Is that him?"

"Yes, that's him; slimy bastard."

"Marilyn, you are a star. Make sure you give her a bonus, Jason."

"Why didn't you say something about it before?" Cassie asked.

"I'd have mentioned it before I went home, but we're always getting approached by gossip columnists, celebrity magazines and paparazzi, so we don't think it's such a big deal anymore."

"It's always a big deal, Marilyn," Drew explained, "because that's how people like that get information to harm people like us."

Drew returned to the study to ask Digits to run an Internet facial recognition search for the Land Rover driver. He knew that it could take a long time. It wasn't like a Google image match. As he ended the call, he smiled grimly. The one good thing about all this was that Ariana Georgiou would get a massive bill at the end, probably well into seven figures. The people who were working for him didn't come cheap. Much of what they did was on the very edges of the law, if not totally illegal; they couldn't be expected to work for peanuts.

It was late afternoon before Anna emerged from her study for anything other than a cup of tea and a snack to eat. Eli had already arrived and had started preparing the evening meal.

"Hello, Eli, I didn't realise you'd already started."

"Jason called and told me that you've been working hard all day and asked if I could start straightaway."

"That's fantastic. Well done Jason. I'm not much of a cook. I used to quite enjoy using my limited repertoire, but lately the whole business of being Chairman of the board, is getting to be much more burdensome that it used to be, and time is precious."

"It won't be anything very fancy tonight; I haven't had time to get a handle on what you have in stock, but I'll do a quick inventory before I go home and make a list for Jason. I'll also prepare something for tomorrow."

"That's the difference between a professional and a bumbling amateur like me. Does anybody know where my husband and daughter are?"

"They're behind the stables fighting each other. It was Cassie's idea; I don't think Robert was quite so keen."

"I hope they're gentle with him. Drew's idea of self-defence classes looks a lot more like assault training to me."

SIXTEEN

03:15 hours, Second Thursday – Pangbourne Grange

Drew and Anna woke to a loud bang somewhere outside the house.

"Stay there but put some clothes on!" Drew instructed, before quickly pulling on some training pants, a top and a pair of sneakers. Megan joined him as he ran downstairs after giving Cassie and Robert the same instruction.

After opening the front door by pressing his hand against the palm reader, the two professionals burst into the open air, with Megan holding an automatic pistol. Robert's car and the new Audi were on fire, and too far gone to make any amateur attempt at firefighting worthwhile.

Jason came running outside to join them.

"Call the fire department," Drew ordered,

"I have already. What happened?" the housekeeper asked, jumping as another bursting tire exploded.

"This doesn't look like an accident."

"I'd better open the gates for the fire engines," Jason said, hurrying back inside the house. Seconds later he was back. "The gate controls aren't working. I'll open them manually."

"No, you stay here, I'll do it. Get everybody out of the house and here in front with Megan where we can see them." He jogged to the gates, disengaged the electric controls, and opened them.

The fire appliances were there in fifteen minutes, by which time there was nothing worth saving left of either car. The officer in charge confirmed what he already knew; it was arson. Someone had poured a flammable liquid (probably petrol) over both cars and lit it.

The fire officer told him, "It would have been burning sometime before the bursting tyre woke you, so the chances of salvaging anything from either car will be pretty remote."

The police had been informed but car crime where nobody had been hurt wasn't at the top of their priorities, so he wasn't expecting a quick response. Drew wouldn't necessarily welcome any more police intrusion into his life so he wouldn't chase them about it just yet.

After he and Megan had made a thorough inspection of the house for evidence of intrusion, he hurried everybody back inside.

"I don't understand, Drew," Anna asked? "Why didn't the alarm let us know that someone was in the grounds,"

"That's something I don't understand either."

"It looked as if it was working okay when I set it at bedtime," Jason confirmed. "They only serviced it yesterday."

"Wait a second; yesterday? It's not due for at least another two months. Did you check his credentials?"

"He had the right ID card."

"How closely did you check it?"

"Oh God, do you think I might have allowed someone in to do us harm. I'm sorry, I'm so sorry."

"Don't worry about it for the moment. We'll review our security arrangements in the morning. I need to see who, if anybody, tampered with the alarm. The engineer may have inadvertently deactivated it somehow, but I doubt he avoided being caught on camera."

Nobody wanted to go back to bed, so they congregated in the living room.

Jason was inconsolable. "What if one of you'd been hurt, it would have been my fault."

Anna comforted him, but Cassie told him off. "If anybody had been hurt it would have been the person that did it not you. So stop blaming yourself. We're not all security experts, and we can all make mistakes. We don't even know if you did make a mistake yet."

Drew's first action was to call the alarm company who agreed to send one of their 24-hour call-out team. Next he checked the camera recordings. Needless to say, the recordings made by the integrated alarm system stopped seconds after the guy interfered with the control box and without catching a useable picture of his face.

What the guy hadn't accounted for was the secondary camera system, which had been in place before Drew had even known Anna and Cassie. When the most recent system was installed he asked for the original to be maintained. The alarm engineer's face was full frontal and instantly recognisable by anyone who knew him. He printed out a screenshot and waited for the genuine engineer to arrive.

When Drew joined them in the living room, they were all drinking one sort of alcohol or other. Megan was holding a beer, Robert and Cassie were drinking wine, and Anna was about to top up her cognac.

"What's this, a party?" Drew said with a smile.

"I think we earned a drink, after nearly being burned to death in our beds. What's the damage Drew? Is it bad?"

"None on the house as far as I can see, but the two cars are write offs. Apart from that the drive will need a bit of a rake over."

"Robert's worried about how he's going to get to his new job on Monday," Cassie said with her arm through his.

"You'll have another car before then Robert, don't worry."

"How?"

"The person causing all this grief is going to pay for it, just as they will for the repairs to the other one."

"They mightn't agree."

"They won't have a choice."

The front doorbell rang. Megan and Drew went to answer it. It was the alarm engineer. After checking his credentials, Drew let him in.

They watched as he opened the control box, and within seconds using a small screwdriver he removed a tiny, plastic cube with wires attached.

"That's the problem. Someone has installed this. It's a device to turn the system off. It's activated by mobile phone, the same technology they use to detonate IEDs."

"Can you tell which mobile phone?"

"Somebody might be able to, but I can't. I expect it'll be a burner so probably not worth the trouble."

"I'll hang onto it anyway."

"Do you recognise this guy?" Drew showed him the picture of the phoney engineer.

"That's Wes Fletcher. He's one of our Surrey team. Are you saying it was him that fitted that device?"

"I'm not saying anything, but thanks. Can you give the system a full test before you go?"

"No problem."

It was almost five a.m. before the engineer left with thanks ringing in his ears and a fifty-pound note in his pocket. Cassie and Robert had gone back to bed, as had Jason, relieved to find he had no way of knowing that the original engineer wasn't genuine.

Anna looked ashen face when Drew stepped back in the room.

"What's up, sweetheart, it's all over now."

She handed him her cell phone with an open text message.

YOU OR ONE OF YOUR FAMILY WILL BE IN THE CAR NEXT TIME BITCH. DON'T MEDDLE IN THINGS THAT

DON'T CONCERN YOU, AND DON'T EVEN THINK ABOUT CALLING THE COPS.

"Don't delete it, sweetheart I'll have it traced."

"What do they mean?"

Drew speculated, "It must have something to do with the enquiries you've made about Alhambra or Nevada Foothills."

"I don't think it can have anything to do with Nevada. We haven't initiated anything to do with them yet. All that's happened so far is that I've asked a question."

"What've you done about Alhambra."

"Only asked Jared Carrington to find out more about Oliver Babcock, why he was kidnapped, and if he gave them something else to be released other than the money that the company forked out."

"What did Carrington say?"

"He said he'd look into it, but he hasn't got back to me yet."

"Go back to bed and see if you can get some rest."

"Only if you come with me. I need a cuddle."

He conceded because he'd do anything she asked, despite knowing that he wouldn't sleep. There was a raging fire of hatred building inside him and he desperately needed to find out who was behind this direct threat to his family.

He lay with her spooned against her back, until he felt her relax and begin to breathe regularly, then as the morning light began creeping around the curtains he got out of bed and dressed.

As he silently closed their bedroom door he heard Robert say, "I love you." Then Cassie's reply, "Hush, go back to sleep."

In the kitchen Jason was already making coffee and Megan was with him.

"You couldn't sleep either then?" Jason asked.

"Things to do today, and things I need to think through."

"I'm so sorry Drew, I should have been more careful."

"Jason, everybody makes mistakes. In this case it was understandable, because I hadn't made it clear that the engineers shouldn't be admitted without a prior appointment and checking with the company. If it had been me that let him in, it would have been unforgivable, but it wasn't, so don't beat yourself up about it. We both know you won't let it happen again."

"But that lovely new car, and Robert's..."

"Cars can be replaced."

"The laptop you gave him was in it."

"So can laptops."

"Would you like me to cook you breakfast?" Jason asked.

"Let me do it," Cassie said from the door. "Robert's going to have a cooked breakfast as well today."

As she kissed her father's cheek, Megan, and Jason both said good morning,.

"Robert is really worried about you buying him another car."

"Would he prefer to buy one for himself?"

"He can't afford to."

"So he'd prefer not to have a car."

"No, he needs a car for work."

"So what's he going to do?"

"Borrow the money."

"Who from?"

"His mum and dad."

"When I checked him out it was obvious that his parents didn't have a lot of breathing space in their budget, so how's that going to work?"

"A bank?"

"He's eighteen; until now he's never had a full-time job, and as you say, the one he's about to start doesn't pay very well."

"What's he going to do?"

"How about I buy the car and he pays me back when he's earning enough to do it."

"You're a genius, Daddy. Thank you." She kissed him again and placed the plate in front of him.

"Is your car okay, Megan? I should have asked earlier."

"A little heat bloom on one side, but I think it'll polish out if I can get around to it."

Two minutes later Robert appeared, and Drew said, "Cassie tells me that you're worried about me buying you another car."

"Yes..."

Drew interrupted him and they repeated the same conversation he'd had with Cassie.

"But that might take years," the teenager said. "I could claim on my insurance."

"If you do that, I doubt they'll pay enough to buy another car and you wouldn't be able to afford next year's policy. Robert, without wishing to make a big deal out of it, let me put this in perspective. The woman who's at least in part responsible for this whole mess has known assets of around two hundred and fifty million dollars and she's never done a single day's work in her life. She was gifted that money by her father. He didn't earn it either. It was stolen from the Russian people. I've had to employ a lot of very talented people including Megan here to try to get to the bottom of what's going on, and I'm sure not going to be doing it out of my own pocket. So when I bill this woman it'll be top dollar, and a few thousand for a couple of cars will barely register."

Robert was clearly shocked. "Really!"

"When I was your age I was a soldier, and I've been putting myself in harm's way in one way or another ever since. It's how I earn a living, but I've been trained, and it's my choice. That's why I don't get too mad when it happens to me, such as the attempt on my life on Friday, but that van driver on the Bath Road, my family, none of you had a choice; you got dragged into this for no reason. In my world, people who do that have to pay the price for their actions one way or another. So today I'm going to get you and Cassie new cars, and if you want to treat it as a loan then so be it, but I won't give a shit if I never see a red cent of it again. Same goes for the laptop by the way."

"Thank you."

"Let's eat before it gets cold."

At half past eight he called Digits and related the night's events. "Would you be able to do anything with this little device they installed in our alarm controls?"

"I'd love to try. How soon can you get it to me?"

"Sometime this morning I hope, I've a couple of things to do first."

He spoke to the girl he'd got to upgrade Robert's computer the first time, and asked her to replace the laptop, but with a new one suitable for graphic design work, and to include appropriate software. He also asked her to provide an additional one for his parents with similar specification as the one that was burned in the car.

In a call to the car dealer he'd dealt with before, he told him that he wanted two more cars of a similar quality and standard as the A3. At least one had to be delivered to his home by Saturday and he wanted the two burnt out cars to be removed by Friday at the latest.

The dealer agreed to get back to him with recommendations before the end of the day.

As he tapped at his keyboard composing an email to the dealer with Robert's details for the registration of one of the cars, Anna came up behind him and put her arms around his neck. "You abandoned me."

"Sorry, sweetheart, I had things to do."

"What are you intending to do about last night?"

"I'm going to revisit Oliver Babcock. He's a lying asshole."

"How do you know?"

"Because what he's said so far doesn't make sense."

"How do you mean?"

"Because nobody kidnapping for extortion would release their hostage without being sure they'd got what they wanted, and in this case it wouldn't have been money."

"Why not?"

"Who ever heard of a financial controller being a kidnap risk?"

She was about to reply when his phone rang from an unknown number, and she listened to his half of the conversation.

"Hello...How can I help you?...You surprise me (he said sarcastically) ...Where are you?...Okay, I've got to go into London first, but I'll be with you as soon as I can." He ended the call and turned to her. "Well I wasn't expecting that."

"Who was it?"

"Babcock's wife, Elizabeth."

"What did she want?"

"She said her husband hasn't been telling the truth, not to the police and not to her."

"So why call you?"

"She's frightened, too frightened to talk to the cops, and thinks that I might be able to help."

"It isn't a trap is it?"

"I doubt it. She sounded major league pissed off with hubby. They're in a police safe house in Maidenhead at the moment."

"Why are you going into London?"

"I'm going to give that device from the control box to Digits to have a look at."

"Why don't you courier it? I've got a reliable company that I use."

"Great idea. Then I could get straight off to Maidenhead. Maybe catch them on the hop."

Before he left he called Lightfoot and asked if he could find an address for Wes Fletcher and anything else about him that might be useful.

SEVENTEEN

09:50 hours, Second Thursday - Police safe house, Maidenhead, Berkshire

He was outside the small Maidenhead address, just in time to catch Detective Inspector Jefferies leaving.

"Good morning Inspector."

"What the Hell are you doing here?" the irascible cop demanded.

"I've been invited. You?"

"I'm investigating a crime."

"Me too."

"As I told you before, that's our job."

"And as I asked before, how's that going?"

"This is a police safe house. Revealing its whereabouts would be a criminal offence under a number of pieces of legislation, so you need to take very great care, Mr. Parker."

"I've no intention nor need to reveal its whereabouts Inspector. I'm sure you're busy, as am I, so don't let me keep you from your important work."

The cop strode to his car and looked back at Drew with a contemptuous expression before he drove away.

"Come inside, Mr. Parker," Elizabeth Babcock said, having witnessed the whole exchange from the open door.

"Why is he speaking to you like that?"

"Professional jealousy I expect. Some cops aren't fond of guys like me. I shouldn't worry about it. How's your husband Mrs. Babcock?"

"No better than he ought to be. He's brought all this upon himself."

"How about your son?"

"I think he'll be okay. We've sent him to stay with my sister in Ireland."

"Do you want to tell me what's wrong, or shall we leave it to your husband?"

"I don't think I know the whole story, but I want to be there while you drag it out of him, the stupid bastard. He didn't want me to call you, but he knows that there might not be anybody else who can help. I've read about you, Mr. Parker, and I doubt you'll listen to his lies."

"Okay, where is he?"

"In the lounge, and he'll have overheard all we've just said."

She opened the door into the small living room where Oliver Babcock sat in an armchair. His head was bandaged, nose broken, he had stitches on his eyebrow, his face so swollen that one eye was closed. One arm was in a sling, the other hand bandaged and strapped to a medical splint.

Before he spoke a word, Drew took a bug detector from his pocket and quickly moved it around the room. After finding nothing he began.

"Mr. Babcock, your wife thinks you've been less than accurate with your account of what's been going on and I believe her. Are you going to tell me the truth. I won't beat it out of you, that's not my style, but what I can do is hand over what I do know about you to the cops, and that's enough to send you to prison. I should warn you though that prison wouldn't be a safe place for you. You've been mixing with some very dangerous people. What's it gonna be?"

The injured man remained silent, but his shoulders shook, and tears rolled down his face.

"Oliver, stop snivelling. This is your mess and Mr. Parker might be your only chance to salvage something from it. I don't want any more gun-wielding criminals bursting into my home threatening me and our son with torture and death."

"I don't know where to start."

Drew didn't know what Babcock's diction was like before the beating, but most voice recognition software would struggle to understand anything he now said through his distorted face and his two missing teeth.

"Start with why the first kidnappers let you go without getting what they wanted, so they had to come back for a second try." Babcock didn't answer. "The men who were here the other day, weren't the same people, were they?"

"The first kidnap was a fraud, Mr. Parker," Elizabeth told him. "He spent the days he was supposed to be missing in a luxury hotel in London drinking champagne and eating like a king, while my son and I worried ourselves sick for days, over a kidnap that never took place."

"Are you going to make your wife tell me everything, or are you going to dig deep into that thing you used to call a conscience for a spark of integrity and tell me yourself?"

Babcock remained silent, unable to look either of them in the eye.

Exasperated by her husband's cowardice, Elizabeth continued. "Oliver was lured to a hotel room by a young girl, who may or may not have been underage and he was filmed having sex with her. Apparently my husband enjoyed the experience so much, when she called him to arrange a second date, he agreed, but only to be met by Jared Carrington, Alhambra's Portfolio Manager, and another man. He was shown the film of his disgusting tryst and told about a risk-free opportunity for them to make a huge amount of money.

"I don't know the fine detail, but as far as I can ascertain the fund is holding massive capital on behalf of an anonymous investor who'd disappeared and was assumed to be dead. The intermediary agent, the other man in the room, assured them that the deceased man had left no family heirs, and nobody was looking for him. Carrington and the agent had come up with a plan to transfer ownership of the investment to a new account holder, then divide the spoils between them, but to do so undetected they needed Oliver's help.

"Carrington and the agent then told Oliver, that now he knew of their plan he had only two choices, to either collude with them to make it happen or they would release the movie of him with the girl who they say was thirteen. Oliver maintains that she looked over sixteen because, and I quote, 'She had tits'.

"Oliver, however, seemed happy to go along with the plot, having nursed the idea for some years that he'd been inadequately remunerated for his work. So he went to the office approved the transactions that Carrington had initiated, then returned to the Chelsea hotel. A ransom note demanding £5million was manufactured and sent to Alhambra's Chairman and copied to me. The company's insurance fund paid whoever sent the note - my guess it was the agent, Oliver was released then rewarded with £20 million worth of equity from the dead man's account, and a £2 million compensation package from the fund's insurance. That's how he paid for this house. He hasn't worked since."

"So who was the intermediary, Oliver?"

"Hith name was Perthey Melton," He struggled to say.

A cold shiver went down Drew's spine. "Did you say Percy Belton?"

"Yeth, it woth the name on all the paperth."

Drew took out his phone and scrolled through the images until he came to one of his wedding with himself and Anna in the centre and the man giving her away by her side. He zoomed in on the man's face.

"Is that the man?"

Babcock struggled to indicate the man behind the real Percy who was the imposter.

"Do you know who he is?" Elizabeth asked.

"Yes."

"Whose wedding was that?"

"Mine," he replied But before giving her the chance to ask anything else, he asked, "So who were the men who beat you to a pulp the other day?"

"He doesn't know, or if he does he's not saying. I've asked him over and over again."

"Does the name Manos Stamelis mean anything to you?"

"Those men, the bastards who beat Oliver up kept asking about him. They wanted to know where his money is. Who is he?"

"He's the man whose money your husband stole. He's dead, but it's not true that he doesn't have an heir; he's got a daughter. And her children have been kidnapped to make her reveal where that money is. She alleges she doesn't know either."

Drew continued. "Mr. Babcock, when these violent armed thugs beat you up in front of your son and threatened to kill your wife, why didn't you tell them where the money is, and why didn't you tell the police why they came?"

"He won't tell you, Mr. Parker, he's too ashamed. He didn't tell the gangsters, because he didn't want to give the money back, and he didn't tell the police for the same reason. He was prepared to let them shoot me, and maybe even our son, rather than give up the money he stole."

"I didn't think they would do it," Babcock struggled to articulate.

"Well Mr. Babcock you really are a worthless piece of shit. You must be really proud of yourself."

"What are you going to do?" Babcock managed to ask.

"I'm going to carry on trying to find the two missing children and working to put the assholes that you colluded with behind bars, alongside the two Russians who did this to you. Not because they did this to you, but because last night they put my family at risk.

"But that's not what you were asking though, was it? What you really meant by your question was what am I going to do about you, isn't that right? The answer is nothing yet. Although if you want my advice, you should pick up the phone as soon as I leave here, call the police, and tell them everything your wife has just told me. Because when I bring down all these people, you can be sure that the cops are going to be knocking on your door, and after that you won't be in a safe house you'll be in a remand prison. But you're too much of a coward to do that aren't you?"

Drew turned to the woman. "Goodbye Elizabeth, and good luck."

After slipping into the driving seat of his car he thought for a moment and selected a number from the contact list on his phone.

"Drew, what can I do for you?"

"Percy, are you alone?"

"No, but I can be if necessary."

He asked whoever was with him to leave the room.

"I am now."

"Where are you?"

"I'm at the factory. They asked me to come in for an ad hoc shareholder meeting. It starts in about half an hour."

"Who's the meeting with?"

"Jared Carrington - he's a Silico board member - and one or two others, including Giles."

"Is Giles a shareholder?"

"A minor one but yes."

Giles Braithwaite was Percy's personal assistant, the man standing behind him in the photo.

"Percy, I need you to listen to me very carefully. I've reason to believe that you're in very great and imminent danger. Stop what you are doing, and leave the building. Don't go home, don't use your own car. Get one of your most trusted security officers to drive you to the Grange as soon as possible, and don't tell anyone where you're going; anyone at all. Leave your phone on the desk."

"What's going on Drew?"

"It's too complicated to explain over the phone, but until we've spoken, don't trust anybody except Anna, Cassie, or me. At the moment they don't know what's happening either. I'll be home in about fifty minutes."

"Shall I bring Giles?"

"Absolutely not, and don't tell him you're leaving either.

"But..."

"This is serious Percy. Please just do as I ask. If I'm wrong you can ball me out later."

Percy agreed and ended the call.

EIGHTEEN

13:30 hours, Second Thursday – Pangbourne Grange

Drew's drive home seemed to take forever. If anything were to happen to Percy, Anna and Cassie would be heartbroken.

He pressed the remote as he approached the Grange, and the ornate wrought iron gates began to open, and he swung through them, barely managing to avoid putting scratches down the side of his new car.

Inside the house he found Jason and Megan in the kitchen and Anna in the library. He guessed that Cassie was in her bedroom with Robert.

"Is Percy here yet?" he asked his wife.

"No. Are we expecting him?"

He explained what he'd learned from Babcock. She was horrified.

"I'll call him." She picked her phone from the desk.

"I told him to leave his phone at the factory so he couldn't be tracked."

"I bet he didn't leave his other phone there," she said, dialling his second number and putting it on speaker.

"Percy, where are you?"

"I'm on the hard shoulder of the M4 westbound carriageway just after the entry slip road from the A329. Some lunatics drove us off the road, and we hit a crash barrier."

"Are you alright?"

"I'm fine, but I think my driver's got a broken arm."

Drew interrupted. "What about the other car?"

"A police car was on the motorway as we joined it. They saw it happen and gave chase, so I've no idea who he was, or where he is. There's an ambulance and another two police cars here now."

"I'll come and get you. Don't tell the police anything about what I told you earlier if you can avoid it."

"Okay, but don't collect me, the police have already told me they'll drive me."

"Take care though, I'm certain it wasn't a random thing."

It was nearly an hour before the police car delivered Percy to their door, and the driver was one of those that had attended the Bath Road incident. Meaning that someone in police HQ would almost certainly make the connection, if not now then sometime soon. He felt he was so close to making a breakthrough though, he didn't want any interference from well-intentioned cops.

"Percy, darling, are you okay?" Anna said, rushing to help him from the car.

Cassie had come downstairs and waited to one side to express her own concerns for the elderly man's welfare.

"Uncle Percy, we've been so worried. Are you sure you're not hurt?"

"Seat belts and airbags took the brunt of it I've just got a few bumps but thankfully the bullets never came anywhere near us thank God."

"Bullets! They tried to shoot you!?"

Once they'd got Percy settled in the family room with a large single malt, he asked, "Are you going to tell me what the fuck is going on Drew?" It was a measure of how shaken up he was. He rarely cursed, especially in front of Anna, and never in front of his goddaughter. "I'm so sorry; I shouldn't have said that."

Cassie giggled. "You're forgiven, I've used that word a lot in the last couple of years. There are so many people around that evoke that response."

Drew explained what had been happening over the previous week, much of which was news to Percy. "But what's any of this got to do with me?"

As Drew explained what he'd learned from Babcock, Percy took a turn for the worse. He dropped his glass, turned white and began to hyperventilate. At first they thought he was having a heart attack and Cassie suggested calling for an ambulance.

Drew told her to wait. "I think it's a panic attack. Percy, do you have any pain? Raise your hand if the answer's no. Okay just try to breathe slowly, count to five between each breath if you can."

After five minutes his breathing began to slow and after fifteen it was normal, and his skin tone had returned to its usual pink.

"You frightened the life out of me there Percy. Cassie's been in tears," Anna told him.

It took a moment or two for Percy to respond. When he did, it was to Drew. "How sure are you?"

"Until you told me about the attack on the M4, only about 80 percent, but now closer to 95. Tell me about this ad hoc meeting. How common are those?"

"It was the first one I've heard of; especially unusual because it was actually at the Silico plant."

"I've never heard of one either," Anna confirmed. "Who called it?"

"Carrington."

"Who were the invitees?"

"Myself, Giles, two other board members and two shareholders I've never met before."

"When did you receive the invitation?"

"About nine-thirty this morning I think it was."

"Just this morning," Drew reacted.

"Yes, they said that's why they were holding it at the plant."

"Was the invitation just for you, or you and Giles?"

"No Giles invitation came separately."

"Did you think it was odd?"

"Yes, very. Giles' holding in the company is miniscule, and other than AGMs he wouldn't expect an invitation to any meeting. Surely you don't think he's mixed up in this, do you?"

"How long has he been your PA?"

"About six years I think. I'd have to look it up; I can't be sure. No wait a minute, it was just after Theo died." He paused. "Oh God, do you think he could have been manoeuvred into place by Manos."

"It's possible, but if so I wouldn't blame yourself. That bastard has been running rings around a lot of people for years, including the Kremlin."

"But what does it mean now? Stamelis is dead, isn't he?"

"Yes, I'm absolutely certain of that. I think that what's happening now is a two-handed grab for whatever he managed to stash away that even the Kremlin didn't know about. On the one side are the people who've been milking it for their own benefit ever since he died; they're trying to make it their own. And bizarrely at the same time and for the same reason, Turgenev and Sokolov have learnt or guessed about it and they're doing the same thing."

"So how does Ariana come into this?"

"At present I'm not sure. She may be making a play of her own, or she could be being used by one side or the other. Either way I'm not convinced she's an innocent party; nor do I believe her kids have been abducted. She's playing a dangerous game though, because if whichever side it is that's using her, finds out that she's been playing both ends against the middle, the girls are likely to become pawns."

"What do I do now?"

"Percy, I think you should stay with us for a day or two, while we try to figure out if Giles is involved and if so what his next move is. If he is, it's my guess that he'll realise he's been rumbled and run for the hills."

"I've no clothes. Surely I can nip home and get a few things."

"If you give me the key and a list of what you want I'll go after we've eaten."

Cassie came back to the room. "Uncle Percy, I'd like you to meet my boyfriend, Robert."

The gate bell rang announcing Eli's arrival.

Drew let him in, then left the others to get to know each other.

He booted up his laptop and checked his emails. The first one he read was from Digits who'd identified the driver of the Land Rover in Thame as Brian Sturges, a former specialist Explosive Ordnance Disposal expert in the Royal Logistic Corps. He'd been Court Martialled and dishonourably dismissed the service after sexually assaulting a female corporal. He had a background of crazy behaviour, with a long list of disciplinary offences including some involving extreme violence, and a reputation for his mercurial temper. No known current address, but his parental home was in Reigate, Sussex. Drew wondered how the Hell the guy had ever been allowed anywhere near explosives.

The timing gadget had been programmed to be activated by an unregistered SIM card purchased in Thame and only used twice; once to call a second burner, and once to activate the timer from a location somewhere close to Pangbourne Grange. However the second burner had been used in various locations including Thame to call yet another burner in the vicinity of Finchley Road.

Digits ended by promising to carry on picking at the loose threads on that electronic trail.

The last-minute additional person for dinner didn't faze Eli, and the meal turned out to be another confirmation that Jason had made the right choice.

They'd barely finished eating when the bell alerted them to an anticipated visit from the police. Jason pressed the button to open the gates, and Drew went to the door to greet them. He wasn't exactly shocked to see Sergeant Gasowski and Constable Ballard from Reading Police get out of the car.

"Good evening detectives; please come in."

"Good evening, Mr. Parker. We understand that Percival Belton was with you this afternoon. Is he still here?"

"Yes he is. Go through into the living room. I'll tell him you're here."

"It's okay Drew, I overheard. Will you join us, that's alright officers, isn't it?"

Gasowski didn't look best pleased but agreed.

They all took seats and Gasowski began by asking Percy if he was okay.

"Before we start, would you mind clarifying how you know, Mr. Parker."

"Certainly. I'm a shareholder in Mrs. West's company NorArm Silico and a lifetime friend of the family. I was on my way here when the attack occurred."

"Why do you categorise it as an attack? Do you have any reason to believe the incident was deliberate?"

"The gunfire was a bit of a giveaway, don't you think?" Percy said, with uncharacteristic sarcasm.

"Gunfire?"

"Surely you know that shots were fired."

"Given the speed and the way things happened you could have been mistaken. You must have been quite scared at the time."

"I was a bit shaken up at the time Sergeant and I may be old, but I'm not senile. I heard the shots and I saw the gun. Are you telling me that nobody in the police car saw it?"

"We haven't been able to interview the driver yet. Unfortunately his car was involved in a collision of its own, and the driver sustained a head injury. He was alone in the vehicle."

"Oh dear, is he alright?"

"I hear he's expected to be okay, one of my colleagues from Newbury is going to be speaking to him once the doctors have given the go ahead. He's in the Great Western Hospital in Swindon."

"Swindon? Where did the accident happen?"

"Lambourn, just off junction 15."

"Has nobody other than me mentioned the gun?"

"Not so far."

"Didn't he report it by radio?"

"I've heard nothing to say he did."

"Excuse me Sergeant," Drew interrupted. "Maybe your colleague in Swindon ought to be made aware about the allegation of firearms involvement before he speaks to your injured officer. Perhaps he could confirm what Percy has just said, because I'm guessing that you haven't yet arrested anybody."

"No, not yet. Ballard, can you call the Inspector and let him know."

Ballard stepped out of the room.

"So if as you say this was an armed attack, are you alleging it was against you or your driver?"

"My guess it would have been against me."

"Why?"

"Because they may have believed that I was about to uncover some illegal trading in Silico shares."

"Who'd be aware that you were about to do that though?"

"The only people outside myself, Mr. Parker and Mrs. West would be those responsible for the illegal trading."

"Can you be more specific?"

"I'm sorry Sergeant, I don't wish to be offensive, but this may be a little bit above your pay grade. If Mr. and Mrs. Parker-West are correct, today's attack may be part of an international conspiracy that is currently being investigated by the National Crime Agency."

"Are you suggesting it is connected to the shooting incidents in Buckinghamshire and on the Bath Road involving Mr. Parker here?"

"That's correct, and other recent serious crimes including the abduction of two small children."

"You are going to have to give me more than that, Mr. Belton."

"It involves a plan to hijack the holdings in a hedge fund belonging to a man who died intestate, a hedge fund that has substantial shares in Mrs. West's company, which as you probably know is a major defence contractor for the UK and NATO. Destabilising the company could have international security implications. So I hope you'll forgive me for not wishing to go into too much detail."

"It does sound a bit far-fetched; you have to agree."

"Sergeant Gasowski, excuse me for butting in again," Drew interrupted. "But you were here the other day with Inspector Jefferies also from Thames Valley Police and I seem to recall him making similar offensive remarks. If you can't treat a victim of crime with respect, I suggest you go away and come back when you've learned some manners."

"I apologise, Mr. Belton. What I meant to say was that it's an extraordinary sequence of incidents and you are probably right, there's much more to this than I originally thought. I'll consult with my inspector who'll likely want to revisit this with you at some time in the near future. In the meantime can you confirm how best to contact you?"

"I'll be staying here for a few days. I left my mobile phone at the Silico plant, but there's someone here 24/7 if you call on the landline. Drew will give you the number."

Ballard came back in the room and told them that the injured policemen had confirmed that he'd seen a firearm, but not until the end of the chase. It was what caused him to crash. The driver of the other car had escaped, and his car had been found on fire near Wantage, about ten miles away.

Five minutes after the cops left, Drew was in his car, anxious to get on. When he'd offered to collect things from Percy's home he'd had a second motive, and that was to search the room that Giles used whenever he stayed over.

The big, two storey, detached house was in a cul-de-sac of similar sized but individually designed properties, likely all worth well over a million pounds. Even though it was beginning to get dark, Drew had no trouble locating Percy's home. He'd been there several times before. After parking on the block paved driveway, he walked to the front entrance, but as he went to present the key to the lock he noticed that the door was already partially open. It didn't appear to have been forced, so somebody must have used a key or picked the lock.

It was likely that anybody still inside the building would have heard his car pull up, but on the off chance that the brand-new vehicle had been quiet enough to be missed, he stealthily moved inside. Careful to avoid his sneakers squeaking on the highly polished natural wood hallway floor, he made a quick survey of the ground floor. Finding no-one, nor any evidence that anyone had been there, he carefully climbed the stairs.

He remembered that as well as the family bathroom, there were five bedrooms and a linen cupboard off the landing. At the top of the stairs he paused and listened. The door to the room used by Giles was directly ahead of him, and there was a door to a smaller room to his immediate left. A streetlamp had come alight since he'd entered the house and that gave enough light through the landing window behind him to see that the doors to all the rooms were partially open.

Remaining absolutely still and silent is a very difficult skill to master. Frightened or stressed people find it almost impossible to breathe quietly, and when people move they can't help but make some kind of noise, like the shuffle of feet or the rustle of clothing. However, it was a skill that all special forces operators like Drew were schooled in because it could mean the difference between life and death.

At first there was nothing, and he began to believe he was alone, but then he heard it, the momentary brush of a foot or door across carpet. Somebody else was in the house, but the sound was so brief and indistinct he hadn't been able to precisely pinpoint its source. It was likely that the intruder was Giles, as he was the one with a key. If so, then he'd be in the room he normally used but Drew couldn't dismiss the possibility he'd be in another, so not wanting to start a violent confrontation unnecessarily, he stayed where he was, and flipped a switch on the wall to illuminate the landing.

"I know you're there, Giles. You need to come out now."

The door to Giles' room began to slowly open and he appeared from behind it, a terrified expression across his face. It was at that moment Drew's head exploded in pain.

As he fell to the floor a voice with a slight accent said, "We need to get out of here, now!"

"I haven't got it. It's not there," Giles replied."

"I don't give a fuck. We've got to get away from here. This is all getting out of hand and I'm not going to jail. Move, before he wakes up if you don't come now, I'll go without you."

"What if you've killed him."

"All the more reason to go."

The assailant stepped over his legs and ran down the stairs. Giles hurried to follow, and he tried to move past the barely conscious Drew only to find a hand reaching out to grab his ankle. The intruder tripped, pitched forward down the stairs, and after a momentary cry, lay still.

Drew pushed himself into a sitting position, put his hand to his head and it came away covered in blood. "Fuck," he cursed.

Still dazed from the blow, and clutching the banister, he staggered down to the half landing where Giles' motionless body lay face down with a pool of blood spreading on the carpet near his head. Kneeling, Drew felt for a pulse. At first he felt nothing, but when he moved his fingers it was there, steady, and strong. He sat back on the stairs, and pulled his cell phone from his pocket to call for an ambulance and the police.

After trying to stand and having to reach for the wall to steady himself, he recognised the symptoms of concussion and sat back to wait, but not before calling Megan to tell her what had occurred.

Paramedics were the first to arrive, and quickly established that the unconscious casualty was alive before one left him to stem the bleeding from the gash on Drew's head.

A second ambulance arrived at the same time as a police car.

Drew couldn't be entirely sure of the sequence of events that followed, but the comatose Giles was transferred to a stretcher and taken away in one ambulance leaving the remaining two female paramedics to treat him.

He remembered a policeman trying to question him about who he was, and what had happened. In the end, one of the green clad paramedics stood toe to toe with the cop, and blasted him. "This man is suffering from concussion. Any answers he gives you could mean anything or nothing. If you don't stop now I'll make a formal complaint."

The cop backed off and the two medics helped Drew stand, and walked him to the ambulance just as Megan arrived with Anna, Percy, and Cassie.

"I'm sorry about this, sweetheart," he told his wife. "I'm okay really, but they want to check me out."

Meanwhile Percy was trying to explain to one of the cops that it was his house.

Eventually the ambulance left for the Royal Berkshire hospital, with a cop car and Megan in close pursuit.

The hospital accident and emergency department was busy, and it was more than an hour before he was seen by a doctor, during which time the cops refused to allow Anna to see him.

By the time the doctors had stitched the flap of skin on the back of his head and given him the okay for discharge, he'd had time to sort through what had happened. Nonetheless, the cops were no longer interested in an impromptu interview. Instead they arrested him and put him in cuffs. They gave him only enough time to tell Anna to make sure that Percy was okay and that he'd call when he was ready to be collected.

"You ain't going anywhere mate. You're going to be charged with assault causing grievous bodily harm," the cop announced.

At the station, he was checked in by the custody sergeant then locked in a cell. Other than infrequent welfare checks from officers looking through the vision panel and a mug of tea passed through the serving hatch, he heard nothing until the morning. They'd taken his clothes and given him a grey track suit to put on, but it was far too small. After a brief discussion, an officer fetched one of the disposable jump suits that they kept for crime scene examination, but that wouldn't fit either, so he spent the night in his underwear.

NINETEEN

09:00 hours, Second Friday – Reading Police Station

A rule that had been drilled into Drew in the army; food and sleep should be taken when they were available because you could never be sure when you'd next get either. He hadn't been offered anything to eat, but he'd used the time to catch up on sleep.

He was finally offered a jumpsuit that he could get into and a pair of flip flops that didn't fit. Apart from a headache he was rested and alert by the time they came to escort him to an interview room.

He waited for another ten minutes before the door opened again and Jefferies and Gasowski entered. The presence of the Inspector from the High Wycombe station surprised him, but he didn't remark on it.

"Good morning, Mr. Parker." Drew remained silent. "Not speaking today? You've had plenty to say when we've previously met."

"I was told that I don't have to say anything. I choose not to."

The two police officers then spent another ten minutes trying to coax a response from him, but he remained silent. In the end they gave up and stood to leave the room.

"Before you go officers. I don't want to tell you your job, but I was reading that little book they gave me when they locked me up. It said something about you being obliged to tell me about my right to free legal advice after I'm arrested and before being questioned at a police station. Perhaps you could arrange something like that before you call again."

"Arrange a duty solicitor for him will you Gasowski?" the frustrated Inspector asked.

"It also mentioned something about using my own solicitor. If it helps, mine is Patricia Spenser at Ruskin and Firth."

Jefferies stormed out, Gasowski shook his head and followed.

A uniformed officer then took him back to the cell where he lay down and closed his eyes, expecting a long wait. Ten minutes later though, the officer returned to tell him his solicitor was there and took him back to the interview room but when he entered, it wasn't to find the forty-year-old Patricia waiting for him. Instead it was a much younger woman in a wheelchair.

"Good morning, Mr. Parker. I'm Alison Scrivens. Pleased to meet you. Pat sent me because I'm one of the firm's criminal defence specialists, whereas, as you know, she tends to work more in family and commercial law; the areas that pay well."

They shook hands. "Nice to meet you Alison."

"Just call me Alli. They tell me that they're considering charging you with grievous bodily harm of someone called Giles Braithwaite, and that you're not helping yourself by refusing to answer questions."

"Don't they have to have evidence before they do that?"

"They tell me that you were found by the side of a critically injured man covered in his blood."

"I was certainly by the side of a critically injured man covered in blood, although I doubt that much of it was his. I was bleeding like a stuck pig." He turned and pointed to the dressing on the back of his head.

"What're those other stitches?"

"There's quite a bit of history leading up to last night's events."

"Tell me."

It took forty minutes to describe to Alli most of what had happened since that first phone call from Ariana nine days earlier. She listened and made copious notes in a thick hard-back notebook. At the end she said, "Right, well that was one of the most interesting tales I've heard in a long while. For the time being though 95% of it is irrelevant."

"How so?"

"Because, until they say otherwise, you've only been arrested for an alleged offence that occurred last night. I suggest we draw up a statement and refuse to answer any more questions until they've got some actual evidence to put to you. If they have I might suggest you do a no comment interview which is pretty much what you've done until now. If they haven't, I'll challenge the legitimacy for continued arrest, and we can all get on with our day."

"Sounds great. How did you get here so quickly?"

"Your wife called Pat hours ago, so I was already on the way here and I was in the car park when the police called."

When they'd written the statement, Alli asked him to knock on the door to tell the cop outside that they were ready.

It was another ten minutes before Jefferies returned with Gasowski.

"Are you ready to answer questions now then, Mr. Parker?"

"Did you have a nice breakfast Inspector? Only you still have half of it on your chin," Alli told him.

Jefferies wiped crumbs from his face. "We all have to eat, Ms Scrivens."

"Not my client though it seems. He's been here since midnight and been given only a cup of lukewarm tea and this beaker of water."

"I apologise for that. Let me arrange to have something brought through now."

"Don't bother, I doubt he'll be here much longer."

"We'll see about that," the belligerent inspector said.

"My client won't be answering any questions. He's prepared a statement to explain his presence at the Reading home of Mr. Belton last night, and the events that unfolded."

They read the statement and then Jefferies looked up. "I'm afraid that isn't enough, so let's move on."

"Mr. Parker has given you a full account of what happened in his statement, and you can see that any suggestion that he attacked Giles Braithwaite is ludicrous, so there's no need for you to hold him any longer.

"I'm afraid we can't take Mr. Parker's word for that."

"Of course not, so if you have any contradictory evidence we'll be pleased to hear it."

"There was blood everywhere, on the landing, down the stairs, on the stair carpet and all over the walls," Gasowski offered.

"All reasonably explained in my client's statement."

"We've yet to interview the victim, Ms Scrivens,."

"You've yet to establish that he is the victim, and not a perpetrator. My client was in the house by invitation; the injured man wasn't. My client didn't hit himself over the back of the head, and if that's what you're intimating, it would be a first in my experience."

"The injured man had a key so he could quite easily have been there legitimately to collect belongings."

"My understanding from the house owner is that Mr. Braithwaite had no belongings at the house as far as he was aware. Have you spoken to Mr. Belton?"

"Not yet."

"Then I'd suggest you've no reason to hold my client."

"There are other matters I want to speak to your client about."

"And has my client been arrested for them?"

"Not yet."

"Then presumably these matters have nothing to do with last night's episode, is that right?"

"It's possible they do."

"But you've no evidence of the connection to put to Mr. Parker?"

"Not at the moment."

"Then make an appointment, provide information about why you wish to speak to him, and we'll be pleased to oblige. My client has had a long, tiring, and uncomfortable night, so unless you have further substantive criminal matters for which you believe him responsible and wish to put to him, you should unarrest him and allow him to leave."

Jefferies glared at her and sat silently for a moment. "Very well. Do that will you, Gasowski."

"Until the results from the forensic team are back, I'm afraid my inspector will only authorise release under investigation on police bail."

"You'd better get on with it then, Sergeant," Alli told him.

The sergeant led them through to the custody suite, and after being told the bail conditions - a curfew of 8pm to 8am, not to contact Percy, and surrendering his passport the following day - Drew was released.

Alli explained that the conditions were bullshit, and she thought the preliminary forensic report would be available in less than twenty-four hours and should be enough to clear him even before he'd had time to hand over his passport.

Anna was waiting in the foyer of the station with Cassie where Drew thanked Alli.

"Piece of cake. I don't know whose idea it was to arrest you. If they'd waited for the results of the blood tests, they would most likely have told their own tale. It's my guess that Jefferies was jumping on the bandwagon in the hope he could squeeze something out of you about other things while you were in custody, although why he was doing the interview and not a more junior officer from his own station I don't know."

"I didn't even get to speak."

"Did you want to?"

"Not especially."

"That's okay then." They shook hands and Cassie held the door as she wheeled herself outside.

He turned to his family. "I'm sorry about all that, sweetheart."

"We've been worried sick. Nobody would give us any idea what was going on. They wouldn't even tell Percy."

"I asked Megan to tell you."

"I know, darling, but you were concussed, and she told me that half of what you said was gibberish."

"What're you doing here, Cassie? Shouldn't you be having a driving lesson?"

"I was too worried about you, so I cancelled it."

"Are you going to cook me one of your jumbo *Full Monty* breakfasts then?"

She started to cry. "I don't understand why people keep trying to hurt us, Daddy?"

"It won't be forever, darling, once we've put this to bed, Stamelis' ghost will have been well and truly exorcised. Let's go home."

"Where's Percy?" he asked when they were in the car.

"He refused to come back with us last night. He said he wanted to oversee what the police were doing."

"What about your clothes, Daddy? You look like one of those CSI people in that suit."

"They kept my clothes for the forensic people to test."

"Let me ring Percy quickly."

Dialling their friend's landline he had to wait a while before he picked up. "Percy, how are you?"

"Very tired. More to the point, what about you?"

"I'm fine, a bit of a bump on the head, otherwise okay. Listen I want you to do me a favour; don't go to collect your car. I want it checked for IEDs before anyone moves it."

"A bomb?!"

"I'm just being hyper cautious at the moment, because there's an explosives expert mixed up in this. I'll get Anna to have someone check it over before we tell the cops."

"Dear God, who are these people?"

"At least one of them is formerly FSB. Just take extra care. If you're worried you can come and stay with us again."

"I don't know anyone who can check for bombs," Anna said, after he'd ended the call.

"No, but I do. I'll make a call when we get back."

"Why don't you just tell the police everything and leave them to sort it out, Daddy?"

"Because, last time we did that they left things hanging in the air. This needs to end, permanently. The Russians are still trying to get a wedge into Silico for whatever reason, and Ariana Georgiou; they all need to be left in a position where they can no longer be a threat to this family."

When they got there, the gates to Pangbourne Grange were open and a car they didn't recognise was there, along with a truck lifting the second of the two burnt out cars onto its bed.

Jason came out to meet them. "Those two men who were here the other day with the police are back, he said. "I asked them to wait in the family room, but a minute ago one of them started looking around your study."

Once they were inside they found both men in the study.

"Agent Forester, Agent Pelham, what can I do for you?"

Forester looked up. "We thought it was time we had another little chat."

"And while you were about it you thought you'd interfere with my personal belongings did you?"

"Just interested how an operation like yours works, Mr. Parker, that's all."

"I imagine it's much like any other small recruitment agency. But now you've satisfied your curiosity, why don't we have that little chat you spoke of. Take a seat."

"You've had a busy week, Mr. Parker," Pelham remarked.

"Yes, I have."

"Three shooting incidents, two car crashes, and an aggravated burglary, not to mention two arson attacks."

"That would just be two shooting incidents, one car crash, and one arson attack Agent Pelham. If you're referring to the attack on Mr. Belton, I wasn't present."

"Of course that's true, but you were at the scene of an arson in Thame, weren't you?"

"Yes I was at the scene of a fire there. Nothing to do with me though. Just curious how a firefighting operation like that works. Fascinating profession firefighting don't you think?"

"Why were you in Thame in the first place though?" Forester asked. "Given the urgent nature of your involvement in the Georgiou affair I'd have thought you'd be concentrating your efforts on that."

"Just following a line of enquiry. It didn't lead anywhere."

"Have you made any progress in discovering the whereabouts of the two Georgiou children at all?"

"I've strong theories about who's responsible, with little concrete evidence to substantiate them, but as to where the girls are, I've no idea. How about you?"

"We're not at liberty to share the progress of our investigations, Mr. Parker."

"I'll take that as meaning you're no further on than I am then."

"Would you like to share your theories?"

"Not until they're more than just that. Theories I mean."

"What about the catalogue of unfortunate events and criminal activities you've been leaving in your wake? Would any of your theories be that some of them may be connected to the abductions?"

"All of them, directly or indirectly."

"Then why not share?"

"Because they're just that, theories, and I've already been described by one police officer as ridiculous when I voiced some of them."

"That would be Detective Inspector Jefferies and your thoughts about the maroon Land Rovers."

"That's right."

"We've looked into that, and we believe that there may be something in it, although we haven't figured out what yet."

"Neither have we, other than that they may be trying to set up some sort of red herring for the end game. What makes you think I may be right?"

"The list of vehicles damaged in the barn fire in Thame are consistent with that hypothesis," Forester confirmed. "Are you saying that you've now ruled it out?"

"No, in fact we're more certain than ever that the vehicles and those premises were connected to my theory."

"Why?"

"As we approached the fire scene two other vehicles made a hasty escape, the driver of one was someone who's a person of interest in my investigation."

"Who's that?"

"His real name is Dmitri Turgenev a former member of the Russian FSB, but now using one of two other identities. Martin Leppik an Estonian, or Marian Bronski a UK citizen."

"How on earth have you been able to conclude that?"

"I'm not prepared to reveal my sources, but I'm a hundred percent confident of its accuracy. The fleeing vehicles were captured on the dashcam of the car I was travelling in, and the drivers have been subsequently identified; one was Turgenev."

"What about the second driver?"

"His name is Brian Sturgess, formerly a Private in the Royal Logistic Corps, and specialist Explosive Ordnance Disposal expert. He was Court Martialled and dishonourably discharged on a sexual assault charge."

"Most of this information can only have been gathered illegally." Pelham remarked.

"If you say so, Agent Pelham, but given the serious nature of what we're talking about, is that really going to be your focus?"

"If this Turgenev is former FSB as you say, are you suggesting some sort of national security issue?"

"I doubt it very much. No doubt you won't find it difficult to verify that Putin had him stripped of his wealth and exiled to Siberia. This is his attempt to recover wealth that Manos Stamelis allegedly concealed from the Russian government."

"Is he acting alone?"

"We're working on the assumption that his escape was assisted by a Miron Sokolov who's now using one of two other identities. Andrus Sepp an Estonian, or Filip Bronski brother of Marian. They're both now in the UK. All those things are verifiable."

"What else are you keeping from us, Mr. Parker?"

"Nothing that I'm completely confident of. There's one thing that needs to be done as a matter of urgency though, and you're much better placed to do it than I am."

"What's that?"

"Mr. Belton was on his way from the Silico plant where he'd been invited at short notice for an impromptu meeting of shareholders when he was shot at by an unidentified gunman. A meeting of that nature has never happened in the past, and my wife, the chair of the board had no knowledge of it. Percy left the plant before the meeting started because I warned him that I thought that his life was in danger. I advised him to leave his car at the plant."

"Where are you going with this, Mr. Parker?"

"Given that we've identified one of Turgenev's accomplices as an explosives expert, I suggest you have someone check his car for IEDs as soon as possible."

"For God's sake, Parker! Why haven't you said so before!?"

"I only came to that conclusion on my way home from the police station where I've been held in custody for nine or ten hours concussed from a head injury. I was going to get one of my former military contacts to do it but seeing as you're here."

"Pelham, get on to that right away." The junior man left the room.

"Why did you think that Mr. Belton was at risk?"

"His name, or should I say someone using his name came up elsewhere in my enquiries."

"In what context?"

"I'm not sure yet that is relevant, so I'd rather not say."

"How can you say that, after Belton was attacked?"

"I believe the target was the person who's been using Percy's name."

"Are you suggesting that whoever it was that instigated the meeting is responsible for the attack and therefore complicit in the conspiracy, and mixed up with the missing girls?"

"Responsible for the attack, possibly. Although they may have been tricked into arranging the meeting. Involved with the kidnapping, almost certainly not. As to one of them being mixed up in any hidden wealth of Stamelis, absolutely."

"Why are you being so coy about what you do or don't know about all of this, Mr. Parker?"

"Mr. Forester, that bastard Stamelis has been attempting to destroy my family's life for six or seven years now, and every time the various law enforcement agencies have failed to put an end to it. He's dead now and yet he's still haunting us, and I'm not going to allow anybody to imagine that coming back at us again would be a good idea. If there's any hidden wealth I need to put it completely out of reach, and make sure they everybody knows it. Before you ask, I don't want it."

"Aren't you willing to tell us anything more?"

"Only that there's more than one element to this. There are the Russians who want the money, if there is any, but by now I'm pretty sure there must be. Then there's the people who've had control of it since Stamelis died, and there may be more than one of them; and lastly there's whoever is holding the children, that's if they have indeed been abducted."

"You believe they haven't been abducted?!"

"I'm not convinced."

"Why not?"

"Because Ariana Georgiou is almost as untrustworthy and slimy as her father, and if she's got wind of a big wedge of money that her father had control of she'll have convinced herself that it's rightfully hers. That's precisely what she's done with a multi-million-dollar property on Tinos that her father acquired a few months before he disappeared. She's adopted it as her own, and is taking an income from it. If she could find a way to commandeer this wealth by exploiting a situation created by Turgenev or colluding with him, she wouldn't hesitate."

"How would you prevent her gaining control of it?"

"I'm hardly likely to tell you am I, even if I had decided?"

As soon as the two NCA agents left, Drew called Percy to warn him that people would be checking his car for IEDs before the end of the day. It seemed the most immediately vital thing to attend to.

TWENTY

Drew joined Anna and Cassie in the family room and flopped into a chair.

"You look exhausted, darling," his wife told him.

"I am. It's a normal response to concussion."

"That was the second time in a week, Daddy. We don't want you to get brain damage like rugby and American football players."

"You've been working hard and putting yourself at risk without a break for over a week, from early in the morning until late at night, sometimes through the night as well. I know you're a strong tough man, but you're not invulnerable."

"I'm not planning anything else today, I'll be fine in the morning. Is Robert coming over to collect his new car. It should be here this afternoon."

"His dad is bringing him over after the shop closes."

"We overheard some of the things you told those men, Daddy. What do you think has happened to the little girls, do you really believe they haven't been kidnapped?"

"I suppose it's possible that they have, but I remember how she behaved two years ago after I briefly allowed her to believe that I'd taken them. She was frantic, pleading with me to tell her where they were, and threatening to kill her father if he didn't comply with the instructions I was giving him. When she called me last week there was no trace of that sort of concern; nor has there been on any occasion since. She hasn't even bothered to harass me for information on progress. I don't believe she thinks the girls are in danger at all, but if she's playing games here, she may well be putting them at risk."

"Oh God I can't bear the thought that we're involved in this. The torture I felt when Izzy was taken, and then when Cassie was missing was unbearable. I wouldn't wish that on my worst enemy."

"Ariana Georgiou is your worst enemy. Don't forget all those phone calls she made to you. But the reason I told Forester about my theory was to get him to concentrate on that aspect of this business. He can lean on her much more effectively than I can."

The car dealer arrived midway through the afternoon. He'd come in his own car but leading a small transporter with two Audi A3s on the back, one gray and one blue. Drew had approved the choice of vehicles and agreed prices in an exchange of emails the previous day.

After the vehicles were unloaded, the transporter was dismissed by the dealer who then went into a fawning explanation of what a privilege it was to do business with such an eminent person. Drew's tolerance threshold for obsequious bullshit always hovered just above zero, and his response was curt. "Let's just sign the papers and get on with our day can we?"

Cassie waited until the gates closed behind the dealer's car. "Which one's Robert's Daddy?"

"The grey one. Is that okay?"

"I don't mind, I just want to put something inside it for a surprise before he gets here."

"What's that then?"

"It's sort of private."

"Sure, I shouldn't have asked. Here's the key fob."

Robert's parents arrived at five-thirty with their son in the back seat. Anna invited them all to stay for dinner, Jack and Maureen said they wouldn't, but Robert was going to be staying over and he'd brought a small overnight bag with him.

"You have such a lovely house," Maureen told Anna.

"We're very lucky. It was a wedding gift from my father on my first marriage."

"I hadn't realised you'd been married before,"

"Twice, Henry and I were at uni at the same time. Then we started Silico together. Sadly, he was killed in a motoring accident when Cassie was about six. I did marry again, not altogether successfully, but he died in awkward circumstances when Cassie was eleven. Drew and I married two years later."

"Your dad must have been very wealthy to be able to give you a house like this. Sorry, is it rude to say that?"

"Not at all. Daddy was extremely rich, and I suppose it makes me a bit of a spoilt brat I'm afraid. Would you like to look around?" She led her away, and Cassie took Robert to look over his new car.

"Do you mind if we have a word, Drew?" Jack asked.

"Sure, what's up?"

"Look, it's not that we don't appreciate it, but all this with the new car and computers, it makes me uncomfortable. We could have claimed on the insurance for those."

"I completely understand where you're coming from, but look at it like this. In the first instance, I paid for the repairs to Robert's old car because I authorised them without Robert's permission. However, I won't be paying for its replacement, I'll be reimbursed for that by the person who's responsible. The same goes for the cost of replacing Cassie's car, and the laptop in Robert's. The only thing that will come out of my pocket is the cost of your laptop that we originally replaced, and the second cheap laptop that's just a small gift from me to you and Maureen.

"I don't want to go into detail but the people responsible for the damage to Robert's car have also been responsible for quite a lot of things. The police are involved now so hopefully we can put it all behind us soon.

"Robert is starting a new job on Monday which he hopes will lead to a career in graphic design, and I'm told that you need a high spec piece of kit for that, so the person paying is going to have to live with the extra cost of that. I doubt they'll notice."

"But it's so much money."

"I was born in a trailer park outside Dover in Delaware, I've no idea who my father was, but my mom was a no good drunk and drug addict paying for her habits on her back. She'd go out on the street and leave me and my seven-year-old older sister Lina alone without food. Sometimes she'd bring guys back to the house she'd met an hour before, have sex with them for money, or let them sexually interfere with us. She'd even walk out on us for three days at a time, so we had to beg strangers for food. So I know what it's like to not have a lot of money.

"I know life ain't quite as bad as that for you and your family, but Cassie is a real privileged kid. She knows that, and tries to have a balanced view of life. Your Robert seems a real nice kid, and it seems like a little bit of a leg up wouldn't do him any harm. He certainly doesn't need to lumber himself with a huge debt to start out in life. He's Cassie's first boyfriend, and if it doesn't work out, I wouldn't want the difference in their circumstances to be the reason.

"I was just a soldier when I met her mom, but we still managed to make it work. By the time we got together I'd been able to acquire something of a nest egg. If I hadn't, it might not have been so easy. Robert should look on this as a little bit of good fortune. If he decides to pay me back at some time in the future, that's up to him, but I won't expect it, whether or not their relationship works out."

"Why the computer for us though?"

"When Robert starts college, he's likely going to need to monopolise the computer, so I thought, why not? Look Jack, I'm married to one of the richest women in the country if not the world, but not a penny of this comes from her. What I do for a living pays ridiculous money, so I'm pretty comfortable myself these days. I've never been in a position to be a bit generous before, so if I've offended you I'm sorry."

"This is all just a bit overwhelming I suppose."

"Don't let it be. Me and Anna are just the same as you and Maureen, we've just been luckier with money than you have. These days, Anna gives the majority of her income away; I haven't got to that stage yet."

Jack was about to reply when Drew's phone rang.

"Alli, how's it going?"

"Fine thanks. Thought I'd let you know that you're off the hook. Forensics came back. Too early for DNA, but the blood groups and patterns support your version of events. Braithwaite is awake, his injuries are all consistent with him having hit his head on the newel post as he fell, and he's refusing to answer questions. Your bail has been lifted."

"Thanks Alli, I think a bottle of wine is about to be winging your way. Do you have a preference?"

"That would be lovely, thank you. I'm a prosecco girl myself."

He ended the call with a smile, Alli was a smart cookie and no mistake.

"Sorry about that, Jack."

"It's alright. How are you after last night? Cassie told Robert about it, and there was a bit on the local TV news. It didn't mention you, but we put two and two together."

"I was a bit woozy for an hour or two but I'm okay now. The hospital told me to avoid alcohol and not to drive for twenty-four hours. I don't drink and it's already twenty-four hours, so I might nip out and collect my car later."

"Can we give you a lift?"

"That's kind, but I don't want to go until after dinner. Maybe Robert will run me over."

Soon after Robert's parents had left, the family had their meal. Then Robert and Cassie drove Drew to Percy's house before going to a pub to meet one of his friends from cricket.

Drew hadn't told Percy he was coming and so wasn't sure if he'd be home. He rang the bell and there was a short pause until their family friend opened the door.

"Drew, what're you doing here?"

"I came to collect my car. You weren't planning on keeping it, were you?"

"They told me you weren't allowed to speak to me."

"I wasn't, but I've been cleared, so normal relations can be resumed."

"Come in. How are you?"

"Your pal's friend did her best to scalp me but didn't quite succeed. I don't know what she hit me with, but it certainly hurt."

"I think it must have been that little statuette of the sheepdog. I didn't realise it was a woman that hit you?"

"That's right."

"The police didn't tell me that."

"That's because when I made my statement, I hadn't quite got everything straight in my head," Drew said, running his hand over the dressing. "Has Giles got any lady friends you know about?"

"I shouldn't think so. He's bi-sexual but predominantly has gay relationships."

"Another thing that's come to mind during the day today is something that Giles said after the woman hit me. He said, 'I haven't got it, it's not there.' Have you any idea what that means? Did he store stuff here?"

"No, no, nothing like that. He keeps an overnight bag in his car for when he needs to stay away. He hasn't slept here for months."

"Do you think he could have been hiding things from you or planning to take something of yours."

"I can't imagine what. I don't keep any important information here, and I've never had access to sensitive military material."

"No valuable artefacts, things like that?"

"I'm quite well off but I don't indulge in art investments."

"Weird. How bad is the damage?"

Mostly superficial. I've got a team of crime scene cleaners coming tomorrow but if they can't clean the carpet, I'll just replace it and claim on the insurance."

"What're you going to do about Braithwaite?"

"Well, he can't work for me any longer of course. But now I'm not a full-time part of the team at Silico, I probably won't replace him."

Drew decided there was nothing more he could learn and left Percy to it.

Later as he climbed into bed beside Anna, she said, "Cassie asked me to buy another box of condoms this morning."

"It's good they're taking care."

"I asked Jason to get them for me. He didn't ask why."

Drew laughed.

TWENTY-ONE

06:45 hours, Second Saturday – Pangbourne Grange

Drew was just finishing his first lap when Cassie joined him on his run. She didn't speak; neither did he. Three laps later she stopped by the tree. After several moments of silence he asked if she'd had a good evening with Robert's friend.

"Yes, it was fun. It was his friend Piers from cricket, the one who brought him to the play at school. He had his girlfriend with him."

"What was she like?"

"She goes to Padbury College with him. They've both still got a year left. She thought I went to the same school as Robert. Then, after Piers mentioned that I used to go to Downley, she wanted to talk about what our parents did, where we lived and that sort of thing."

"And what do her parents do?"

"Her dad does something in insurance, and her mum is an event planner. It turned out they live on the same road as Uncle Percy. I told her that Percy was my godfather. She said about what happened, the police, ambulances, and the gossip of the neighbours. I told her I knew about it, but I didn't mention that you were involved.

"Anyway, Robert keeps telling me he loves me, Daddy. I don't know what to say."

"I'm not really the right guy to give romantic advice, sweetheart. How do you feel about it?"

"I like him, quite a lot, and I like it when we do things but I'm not ready to talk about love and that sort of thing yet."

"Have you told him that?"

"Yes."

"Sounds like you've got it under control. As long as he's not making you feel pressured."

"No, it's fine, I suppose. I just don't want to hurt him."

"What was the girl's name – Piers' girlfriend?"

"Tamara."

"Would you be upset, if I asked you to do me a favor?"

"Of course I wouldn't, what do you want?"

"I was going to suggest you inviting Piers and Tamara round for a pool party this afternoon."

"That's a great idea, I haven't had a pool party since Izzy died, can I ask another couple of friends from school?"

"I guess that would be okay."

"I'll have to go and buy a few things, inflatables and stuff."

"Get Robert to take you. Pay with your card, I'll put the money back in your account."

"You don't need to. There's loads in there. Do you mind me asking why you suggested it? It's not the sort of thing you usually enjoy?"

"I want to ask Tamara about what happened. There were a lot of neighbours rubber necking when they put me in the ambulance, she might know more. I just don't want to make a big deal out of it."

"I understand. Shall I get Jason to ask Eli if he can come in today to do the food? He wouldn't normally work on a Saturday."

"Ask your mom if she thinks it's a good idea. Remember she doesn't know I've suggested it yet."

Drew and Megan spent most of the morning in the study with the door closed oblivious to the chaos developing outside. The preparations for what he'd imagined would be half a dozen kids sitting around the pool listening to music and drinking alcohol-free cocktails in between water games had evolved into something a bit more elaborate.

Halfway through the morning, Drew had a call from Forester to inform him that they hadn't found an IED in Percy's car, but they'd discovered a cell phone operated device that could deactivate the lane and cruise controls and turn off the power steering of his VW Tiguan. Operated in conjunction with someone driving aggressively in another car, it would have been possible to manufacture a serious collision. In normal circumstances it would likely have been missed by someone not looking for it. Drew had always suspected that something like that was responsible for the death of Anna's first husband.

He'd had the call on speaker, and when it ended he turned to Megan. "Perhaps now they'll take my so-called conspiracy theories a bit more seriously."

"Only if the NCA share that information with the cops."

They'd spent the time going over everything they'd learned, looking for a chink of light, something that they might have missed. Between them, they used their contacts, hacked, and conducted illegal searches of records and databanks without result. In the end they decided there was nothing more they could do until something else happened.

When they decided to take a coffee break, they found the kitchen a hive of activity, with the big table barely visible under the spread and the worktops faring little better.

"This is a bit more elaborate than I imagined, how many are coming?"

"Cassie tells me there are ten guests. Thank God that Eli agreed to come in to help," Jason explained.

"Did we already have all this stuff in the house?"

"Eli made up a list and Robert ran into town and did a quick supermarket sweep."

"Where are Anna and Cassie?"

"Last I heard they were by the pool blowing up inflatable toys."

He shook his head and turned to go and find them, only to hear Megan laughing. "What did you expect when you suggested a party to a teenager?"

In the pool room Cassie was using a foot pump to blow up an inflatable flamingo while Anna was struggling to push back the big bifold doors that opened onto the patio. He'd never once seen them open before.

"Here, give me a hand with this will you, darling?"

"Jason said that there are going to be ten guests. Is that right?"

"Maybe twelve now. Cassie invited Rhian and her girlfriend as well. It's a two-hour drive, so we're not sure if she'll make it."

"We're nearly ready, Daddy. What do you think?"

"It looks great," he said, his faux display of enthusiasm convincing nobody. "What time are you expecting them?"

"I told them two o'clock. Was that alright?" Cassie said? "Will you be okay doing the barbecue because Eli's got to leave by five?"

"I guess." Other than cooking small wild animals over a rudimentary fire while on ops or exercises, he'd never barbecued anything in his life.

He wandered back to the kitchen. "I'm told I'm in charge of the barbecue Eli. Have you got any tips?"

"Mostly it's just a case of not cooking things too close to the coals and turning them regularly so they don't burn. The only things you need to be careful with are the chicken legs, but I'll part cook them before I go if you want."

"Eli is a genius, darling. We could never have done all this without him," Anna said as she followed him into the kitchen.

"I guess she's right, Eli. Thanks for coming in at such short notice."

"The offer of double pay helped persuade me, Drew."

He smiled. "Bet it did. Worth it though."

The first guest arrived forty minutes later. Cassie pressed the bell. "It's Andrea from school!" she said excitedly.

The girl and her boyfriend were no sooner out of their car than another arrived with four more guests inside. Half an hour later Drew was finding it difficult to keep up with the introductions, and he pulled Cassie aside. "Did you actually invite all these people?"

"Yes, except the couple that brought Sophie and Julian."

"Point them out to me when you get the chance."

By two-forty, the driveway was like a parking lot, and everyone expected had arrived except for Rhian and her plus one.

"Take these drinks to the patio will you, darling?" Anna asked. She pointed at two giant jugs of something he didn't recognise.

Someone had found a long folding table to put beside the other tables that were already there and it already carried dozens of plastic wine glasses and tumblers on it.

This is great," he said to Cassie. "Where did you get all this disposable tableware from. Did we already have it?"

"No; Mummy called Tamara's mum, and she told us about a place that she uses, and they agreed to deliver."

He looked around. He'd never seen so much naked flesh in one place in his life. Nothing was exposed that shouldn't have been, but some of the scraps of cloth worn by both sexes left little to the imagination.

After Cassie pointed out Tamara and the two uninvited guests, Bradley and Charlene, Drew attempted to stay out of the way, only responding to requests for more food and drinks.

At four-thirty he lit the barbecue and left it to warm up. That was when he noticed that the party was beginning to warm up quicker than he'd have expected. As a non-drinker it didn't take long to detect the presence of alcohol when he taste tested a jug of punch of watermelon lemonade. He tried the other jug and wasn't surprised to find the same thing.

He banged the barbecue tongs on the LPG bottle until they all stopped talking. "Good afternoon everybody, I hope you're all having a great time. I'll be starting to barbecue the meat menu soon, but before you get to eat, I need the driver of each vehicle to drop the keys to their car into this tumbler. The invitation didn't include an overnight stay, but as someone or some people have decided to introduce alcohol into the drinks, and none of you have any idea how much you've consumed, I'm forced to assume that none of you are fit to drive. I expect you're wondering how you're going to get home. The options include calling a cab, calling your parents, or you're welcome to stay the night. If you choose the third option I don't guarantee privacy or comfort though, and if anyone is sick on the carpet, they get to clean it up themselves. In the meantime continue to have a good time, and if you want to chance it, feel free to finish this batch of drinks. But if any more booze finds its way into the beverages, I won't be quite so forgiving."

There was silence for a moment or two before someone said, "I say Mr. Parker is a cool dude." It was Bradley raising his glass. "We need to say cheers to him." A few weak cheers followed.

Drew ignored him and turned back to the barbecue.

An hour later and Drew had succeeded in cooking a lot of meat without cremating anything too badly, and the party had become more raucous than ever. Girls were giggling and boys were throwing them in the water. He left the patio to collect a second batch of burgers, but as he returned, his curiosity was roused when he spotted Bradley laughing as he left the drinks table empty-handed.

Drew continued to watch as the boy sat down then put something into the pocket of a pair of pants on the floor beside him and grinned to himself.

After the initial welcomes, Anna and Megan had avoided the proceedings and left the teenagers to themselves, leaving Drew as the only adult around the pool. He rested the uncooked burgers he'd just brought from the kitchen beside the barbecue then casually walked through the discarded paper plates, plastic glasses, and pieces of clothing until he came up behind Bradley and his girlfriend. They hadn't noticed him until he nudged their pile of clothes with his foot and heard the unmistakable clink of glass.

The boy turned and looked up at the big man standing behind him. "Hi, Mr. Parker. That was really cool how you arranged for all us kids to have an all-night party without getting in the shit with our parents."

"Do you think so?"

"Yeah; we all get to sleep over and spend the night with our girls and mum and dad can't complain."

"So you're imagining this is some sort of teen orgy under our roof all sanctioned by me?"

"Well..."

"Are these your clothes?"

"Er yeah."

Drew picked up a shirt revealing empty bottles of vodka and white rum, and an almost empty bottle of something else. "What's all this then Brad?"

"It just a little lubricant, helps people loosen up."

"Is that right? Did the invitation say, *bring a bottle*? I can't remember. Oh but then you weren't invited so you wouldn't know. Let's ask." In a louder voice he called, "Say everybody, can you help us out here, cos I can't remember. Did the invitations say to bring a bottle, Brad here doesn't know?" Nobody spoke. "Seems they don't recall it saying that Brad. But as you're such a generous guy you decided to bring some anyway. That's real magnanimous of you.

"Look here folks, Brad's not only brought bottles of vodka and rum, but guess what; he's also brought a bottle of 25-year-old single malt, worth about five hundred quid as I recall. I know that because it's the same as the unopened bottle we had in our living room. My, your folks must give you a real good allowance. I don't usually drink, but people tell me that this brand is real good stuff. It's a shame you drank most of it already, or I might have been tempted to find out for myself. Brad here says this stuff helps people loosen up, but as a non-drinker I wouldn't know."

Drew bent down and picked up the pants he'd seen Brad hide something in. "I'm wondering what else you brought to help people loosen up. Let's look in here." He fished in the pockets and came up with a car key, a cell phone, and then a small anonymous looking glass container about the size of an aftershave bottle. It was half full.

"What's this then Brad?"

"It's a vitamin supplement; like Berocca, only liquid. It's harmless."

"So drink it."

"I've already had today's dose."

"But if it's harmless it won't matter will it?"

"Y-you're not supposed to exceed the dose."

"So how does that work if you don't know if or how much you're taking; might it not be dangerous then? What about you Charlene, do you use this stuff?"

152

"No, I don't know what it is."

"Your boyfriend says it's harmless after all, and he takes it."

"I don't want to take anything without knowing what it is."

"You're a sensible girl. Bradley doesn't want to exceed the dose I wonder if that's because it isn't a vitamin supplement like he said. Is that true Brad?"

"Y-yes."

"So what is it then Bradley?"

"It's roofie, but it's really weak; doesn't have hardly any effect."

"And with your first-class degree in toxicology, you know that do you?"

Charlene looked at Brad in horror. "Have you used it on me?"

"A bit, the other night. We had a real good time; don't you remember? It didn't do you any harm, did it babe?"

"Have you just added it to those two jugs on the table?" Drew demanded to know.

"Hardly any, it won't do-"

"Shut up and get dressed, you're leaving. What about you Charlene, are you going with him?"

"Can I stay? I don't want to go anywhere with him, bastard."

"Sure, if that's what you want."

Bradley finished dressing. "Give me my car keys then."

"No."

"You can't keep them."

"Watch me."

"I'll call the police."

"You really want to call the cops after confessing to administering a date rape drug without consent in front of your ten victims, here's your phone, help yourself."

"It's my dad's car."

"I'd suggest calling him then. You can wait for him outside the gate."

Drew showed him to the door, watched him walk down the drive, and then closed the gate behind him.

"What's going on, darling?" Anna asked.

"I'll tell you in a minute. Is there anything else needs barbecuing?"

"Just a few sausages if anybody wants them."

"Sorry about that folks," he told the rest of the partygoers around the pool, silencing the hubbub. The drama's over now. Let's try not to let it spoil the rest of the day."

"How did you know about the drugs, Mr. Parker," one of the girls asked.

"No disrespect to you great young people but you were all starting to enjoy yourselves a bit too enthusiastically, so I tasted the drinks, that's when I tasted the alcohol. If it had been just a little bit of booze I might have given him a pass, but it was the best part of two and a half bottles of spirit, one of which he stole from me. Then I spotted him with the Rohypnol. There was no way he was getting a pass for that."

"Why didn't you call the police?"

"If I had, everybody here would have been questioned and the cops would have a record of that, and if Bradley were to be prosecuted and found guilty he'd have a criminal record for the rest of his life, maybe even a prison sentence." Drew didn't want some kind of black mark against his or Anna's name either, but he didn't mention that.

He took the two contaminated jugs and left them to try and regain the party spirit.

He asked Jason to prepare two more jugs of drink just as the gate bell rang and Megan went to admit her adoptive cousin Rhian."

"What was that all about in there?" Anna asked.

Drew gave her a brief rundown.

"For God's sake, the first time she asks a few friends around like normal girls and look what happens."

"I don't think the day will be a total loss. I've just given them licence to stay over if they want to and if their parents are okay with it."

"Great, who's going to clear up after them?"

"They are."

Rhian came through the door. "Drew baby, how are you? And you Anna, you're looking sexy as usual."

"Rhian, lovely to see you again. Did you come alone?"

"No, of course not. Tina come inside," she called. "Sorry she's a bit shy."

A tall thin girl with long straight black hair tentatively appeared in the doorway.

"Everybody, this is my very lovely friend Tina. Tina these are, Anna, the lady of the house, Jason the other lady of the house, and Drew the only man I'd consider going straight for."

Megan smiled. "I should have warned you beforehand, Rhian has come out of her shell a bit since you last saw her."

"Where's that cute daughter of yours?"

"She's by the pool with a lot of other friends," Anna replied. "Go through. I hope it won't be too much for Tina."

TWENTY-TWO

After Bradley had left, the party gathered pace again, thanks in no small part to the introduction of Rhian. The adults had all retired to the family room and were trying to ignore the loud music from the pool room when the gate bell rang. Drew went to answer. It was Bradley's father. He opened the gate and went to meet him. The man and his son met him halfway.

"Brad, I thought I told you that you weren't welcome here. Go and wait for your father by the gate."

"Who the Hell do you think you are, Parker?"

"I know who I am, but I don't think you know who your son is."

"What does that mean?"

"When your son is off my property I'll tell you."

"We've only come to collect the car; I don't understand why you wouldn't let him take it before. It's not blocked in."

"You can take the car, but your son isn't going to be driving it on my property, and if I see him driving it on the road I'll report him to the police."

"For what?"

"Drink and drug driving."

"You can't prove that."

"Maybe not but I can prove he's administered a date rape drug to at least ten people, because I have a video recording of him confessing to it."

"Brad what's he talking about?"

The kid looked at the ground without replying.

After Drew had given the father a brief summary he was furious.

"Get back to your mother's car, you stupid little shit." The boy slunk away. "I'll get my wife to collect the car in the morning."

"Thank you Mr..."

"Wyatt, Brian Wyatt."

When he went back inside, Tamara was in the kitchen refilling one of the jugs.

"That was a good thing you did earlier, Mr. Parker. With Brad I mean."

"Do you know him?"

"No, but what you said about him not getting a criminal record, that's true. He told me earlier that he wanted to be a banker like his father. If he had a record he wouldn't be allowed, would he?"

"You're right, I don't think he would. It's Tamara isn't it?"

"That's right."

"Cassie tells me that you know our friend Percy Belton."

"He lives across the street from us."

"Did she tell you that I was inside Percy's house when it all happened last night?"

"Really!"

"Percy had been hurt in a traffic accident a few hours earlier and was staying here with us, so I'd gone to collect him a few clothes. It turned out that there were two people already in the house who weren't supposed to be there. One of them hit me over the head with something very heavy. That's what this dressing on my head is covering."

"I didn't know about any of that. The police asked us loads of questions; if we'd seen anything or anybody; that sort of stuff, but they didn't tell us what really happened. They took a copy of our CCTV recordings though."

"I was wondering if you might have seen something, earlier in the day, or maybe over the day or two before. There were two of them in the house; one was a woman."

"There was a woman in the street the day before. I took our dog for a walk and when I came out of the house she was looking at our neighbour's house. When I came back she was still looking at houses including Mr. Belton's. When she saw me, she asked me if I knew if there were any houses in the road up for sale."

"What happened then?"

"Nothing, I just told her I didn't know and went home."

"I know that most houses in the street have security cameras, does yours cover the street as well?"

"Yes, my dad says it's a great system. He replaced the one that came with the house."

"Do you think your mom and dad would allow me to have a copy of their CCTV recording from the day before the break in? It may be nothing, but I'd like to check."

"I don't think they'd mind, not if you tell them what you told me. They know I'm here and they know who you are. I'll call them and tell them you asked."

"Are you staying over?"

"Oh yeah, it's going to be fun."

"Are you going to the cricket with Piers tomorrow?"

She laughed. "You must be joking, it's the most boring game on the planet isn't it? Anyway it's in Crowthorne and I need to be home, we've got visitors tomorrow afternoon."

"How about I drop you home in the morning?"

"That'd be great, it'd save my mum collecting me. Thanks, Mr. Parker," she said, before returning to the party.

He went back to join the others in the living room where he found them all laughing,

"What's so funny?"

In between chuckles, Megan explained. "Jason just said, if that lot are going to be staying over, then it's a good job he bought Cassie the giant pack of condoms."

Drew laughed as well.

When they'd regained their composure, Anna asked, "How many are in a giant pack Jason?"

"Hundred and forty-four." That started them all off again. "I didn't want to keep going back. It's embarrassing. They know me in there; they'll think I'm some sort of sex maniac."

Cassie appeared at the door. "What're you lot all laughing at?"

"Nothing, darling, just something that Jason said. Is everything still going okay?"

"They want to know where they're going to be sleeping."

The adults looked at each other and started laughing again.

Eventually, Anna told her. "You're all supposed to be adults, or very nearly adults so I'm not going to be policing where you all sleep or who you sleep with. So just remind them that I don't want to find evidence of it all over the house tomorrow. And Drew says he expects you all to pitch in and help clear up in the morning. You know where the linen is, and you know where the spare rooms are. Try not to keep the rest of us awake with a live soundtrack from Fifty Shades of Gray."

"Mummy!" she said, mildly shocked. She disappeared for a couple seconds before briefly popping her head around the doorframe again. "I didn't know you'd watched that, Mummy."

"Of course I have, and read the books," she called after her daughter.

"Mummy, there must be a whole other side of you I never knew about."

When the youngsters had all decided that the prospect of the night with their partner held more allure than drinking lukewarm soft drinks and nibbling at barbecue remnants, they dispersed to their chosen sleeping quarters. The couple that occupied the room next to Anna and Drew, enthusiastically took advantage of a whole night without parental supervision. They were obviously either unaware or unconcerned that the interconnecting door was providing little sound insulation to their activities; and twice they were woken by people knocking on Cassie's door to ask for another condom.

TWENTY-THREE

08:00 hours, Second Sunday – Pangbourne House

Thankfully, the plastic glasses that Tamara's mother had recommended were all coloured and easily spotted, so after diving for three on the bottom and clearing the water of inflatable toys, Drew was eventually able to begin his laps. Alone in the pool he was nearing the end of his morning routine when he was joined by Cassie, with Robert and two other couples including Piers and Tamara.

"Morning, Daddy," she said as she caught him up.

"Morning, sweetheart. Did you have a good time yesterday?"

"It was fun, thank you."

"No problem, but I did have an alternative motive."

"I know, but that didn't matter. Tamara said you're going to drive her home today."

"That's right."

"Can I come with you; I want to see if Uncle Percy is okay?"

"Aren't you going to cricket with Robert?"

"I don't think I want to go every week."

Drew finished his laps and climbed out of the water.

The remaining overnighters surfaced from different places in the house including the spare bedroom in the coach house. Different varieties of breakfast were taken in shifts as couples undertook various duties returning order to the house.

Half of the guests had left by the time Bradley and his mother arrived to collect the car. He stayed in the driving seat of his mother's car and waited while she introduced herself to Drew.

"Mr. Parker, I'm Sarah Wyatt. I want to apologise for our son's unforgiveable behaviour yesterday, and to thank you for not reporting him to the police. A police record could have been catastrophic for his future."

"He's just a kid. We all make mistakes when we're kids. I made quite a few of my own and if I hadn't been given a break by a few people, my life would have turned out quite different."

"I tried to get him to apologise but he's too much of a coward. So we've banned him from driving, cut his allowance and grounded him for three months. Although I doubt that last bit will stick. Thank you again."

"No problem."

They were on their way to drop Tamara off when she asked, "Cassie, why do you call your parents Mummy and Daddy, but everybody else's mum and dad?"

"Mummy has been there all my life and she's always been called that, but Drew didn't come along until I was eleven and at first he was just Drew. When he married Mummy, and kept risking himself to save our lives, I wanted to show him that I thought of him as my real dad, not just the man who was married to my mum."

"Save your lives?"

Drew interrupted. "Can we change the subject?"

After parking on Percy's drive, Drew and Tamara crossed the road to her house while Cassie went to her godfather's door.

Tamara's front door was opened as they approached by an attractive, thirty-something, woman

"Mr. Parker is it, or Mr. West, I'm never sure what to do when there's a hyphen? Lovely to meet you, come in," she said.

"It's just Drew, and I'm real sorry but I forgot to ask Tamara your family name in advance."

"It's Pritchard, Amelia Pritchard. Tammy told me the tale about the goings on at your house yesterday. Her father and I thought that you handled the situation very well, I'm not sure we'd have been quite so restrained."

"Just didn't want anybody getting in a car loaded without realising it or what they were doing. And I didn't think having an interview by the cops recorded somewhere was a good idea either."

"Good thinking. So you were in Mr. Belton's house when those dreadful people broke in the other night?"

"Strictly speaking they were already in the house when I went in. There were two of them, and one hit me over the head with something heavy. He's got a little bronze statue of a dog on a marble plinth. I think it was that."

"That must have been painful."

"It was, but somehow I remained conscious enough to grab the ankle of one of them as he made a run for it. Caused him to trip and he hit his head on the way down and did himself even more damage than his accomplice did me."

"Do you know who they were?"

"I doubt it'll be a secret for long that the injured one was Percy's PA, but I think the one that hit me was a woman. Tamara mentioned that there was a woman asking questions in the street the day before. She quite probably has nothing to do with it, but I thought it wouldn't hurt to find out if it were somebody I recognised."

"I told the police about her. They didn't seem interested, but Tammy said you wanted a copy of our recordings, so I put it on a datastick for you. I didn't know how to edit it, so I copied the whole week, is that okay?"

"That's perfect thanks a lot." he said taking the proffered thumb drive.

Drew left them and walked across to Percy's house, rang the bell, and waited. There was a long pause before Cassie opened the door. Percy was in his living room. "How are you Percy?"

"I'm okay. More worried about you to be honest. How are you?"

"I'm fine, thanks. Just a few more stitches, and one more scar to add to the list. The hair will grow back, and nobody will be any the wiser."

"I've just been asking Cassie to try and persuade you to leave this business alone. Whoever these people are, they're dangerous and I don't want any of you getting hurt on my account."

"Percy, I appreciate what you say, but this isn't just about you. There are other people caught up in this; Anna, Cassie, and me for example, not to mention two missing children. I can't just walk away now and imagine that the risks to any of us will be reduced. Until we know exactly who's responsible and what it is they hope to achieve, those threats will still be there."

"Are you still investigating the missing girls?"

"Indirectly, yes."

"How do you hope to cover all aspects of this business?"

"Because I'm not working alone, and because I'm not restrained by the same rules as the authorities."

"What if you get caught breaking the law?"

"I'm willing to take the chance to protect my family, but I won't be caught unless someone I trust betrays me. Changing the subject, how did your crime scene clean up go?"

"Not too bad. It just needs a flick of paint on the wall."

"That's good."

On the drive home Drew asked, "How did he seem to you Cassie?"

"A bit strange to be honest. I asked him if there was any CCTV from his own system and he said it hadn't been working for weeks but wouldn't say why he hadn't had it fixed. Then he started pleading with me to get you to stop investigating, not just asking; I mean almost begging."

"I suppose we have to remember he's getting older now. It's not unusual for older people to get a bit paranoid after a shakeup. Remember, in the space of twenty-four hours he's had an attempt on his life, two if you count the bomb in his car, and his house has been the site of an aggravated burglary. Now he's having to come to terms with the fact that his closest work colleague appears to be part of it."

"I didn't know about a bomb."

"In the end it wasn't exactly a bomb, more a device designed to make sure he has a crash, and you know what a fast driver he is."

"These people are crazy. What do they want?"

"Money, in the end it will all be about money. What I don't understand is why whoever is responsible chose to involve us in it?"

At home he grabbed a cup of coffee and went to his study to examine the footage from the Pritchard family's CCTV. His first impression was that the standard of the video film was very high quality. The system was PIR activated so it skipped long periods of time when nothing happened, on the other hand it was very sensitive, so it was often triggered by small things like a bird or a cat.

It took a while to speed scroll through to the point where Tamara appeared walking the dog, and then wind back to the first appearance of the woman. The angle wasn't the best, but he was sure he didn't know her. He scrolled through until the woman no longer appeared. It was clear that her interest had been predominantly in Percy's property.

He clipped the movie to include just the part with the woman, attached the file to an email and sent it to Digits asking him if he could use facial recognition to try and identify her. Then he went in search of his wife. He found her in the laundry room with Jason and Cassie folding sheets.

"Hi, sweetheart."

"Hello, darling. Can you do me a favour? Next time you invite half the population of Berkshire to stay overnight, can you stick around to help with the laundry."

"I'm sorry about that. It didn't occur to me. What can I do now?"

She smiled. "Nothing; it's under control now. There's one more load in the washer at the moment, and when that's dry we'll be up to speed. The only thing is, there's nothing ready for lunch. Can you call in an order for something, but remember Rhian and Tina are still here."

Megan was in the family room with Rhian and Tina.

"Hiya, Drew baby. Did you have a good time with Uncle Perse?"

"Yes thanks. Did you enjoy yourself last night?"

"Yeah, it was cool. Cassie's got some nice friends, and there were loads of hot babes to ogle. If I weren't already hooked up with this gorgeous chick I might have made a play myself."

Tina blushed.

"Is Chinese okay for lunch everybody?"

It was over an hour before their lunch was delivered, but it took less than that to consume. It wasn't long after clearing away before Drew asked Megan to join him in the study.

"Sorry to take you away from Rhian, but I need to run something past you before I go off on a tangent."

"Go for it."

"I've been developing a theory about part of this. I hope I'm wrong so let me explain it all before you say what you think. If I've got this wrong I'm going to upset a lot of people that I really don't want to."

It took him over an hour to make his thoughts clear and tie in all the things they knew, the things they were speculating about, and explain what was making him link them together.

"Jeez Drew. You're right about upsetting people."

"Am I right though?"

"I don't know but now you've planted it in my mind, it'll always be there, unless we can rule it out. I think you have to explore it, for your own peace of mind if nothing else."

"How do you think I should go about it?"

"Safest bet would be to do it at arm's length. You've got access to plenty of resources. Use them until you've exhausted all other means, that way you can claim you didn't know what they were doing if it goes tits up."

"I guess that's best, although I'm not sure how well that excuse will wash if the shit hits the fan."

Megan confessed that she'd essentially been considering the same thing hours earlier. He picked up his phone and began making calls.

"What's happening with Braithwaite, Do you know?"

"Gasowski say they searched his home, and it looked as if he's made a run for the hills."

TWENTY-FOUR

11:00 hours, Second Monday – Pangbourne House

When Drew's phone rang he wasn't expecting it to be Digits with positive news quite so soon.

"Babycham, that woman in the video you sent me yesterday, her name's Brigitte Laurent; she's twenty-eight years old; a French citizen but she appears to have been living in the UK for eighteen months. She rents a flat in Stanton Road, Wokingham."

"That makes sense, Braithwaite comes from near there."

"There's more, she's got a sister name of Natalie."

"Don't tell me, Ariana Georgiou's nanny."

"That's right."

"Ariana told me that Natalie flew home hours after the incident."

"I haven't checked for that yet; she may have done."

"Natalie looks Mediterranean in the photo I've seen, or maybe Middle Eastern, nothing like Brigitte."

"You may have been given a bad photo or even the wrong one, but they could be half or stepsisters."

"I think I need to pay Brigitte a visit."

"Good idea. Do you want me to take a closer look at Natalie?"

"Yes please."

Anna opened the study door holding a cup of coffee. "Have you been busy, sweetheart?"

"Yeah, struggling where to go next. Digits has just given me something that needs looking at, so I'll be going out later."

"Cassie just got back; she wants a word when you're free."

"She's back early; her lessons are supposed to be three hours minimum."

He took the coffee and followed his wife back to the kitchen.

"What's up, sweetheart?"

"We were being followed, so I thought we'd better come back."

"You did the right thing. Tell me about it."

"I think there might have been more than one. When we set out, Dav was driving, and we turned left out of the gate towards Reading and I saw a car stopped in the gateway to the big field. I didn't pay it much attention, except it had a memorable number, it was something like CR15MAS. It made me think of Christmas. Anyway we went back to the housing estate. I took over and we drove around for a while, and I kept seeing the same car in my mirror. I told Dav about it, but when she turned around to look the car had turned off. Then I kept seeing a different car all the time, so she turned around again and wrote the number down, but she thought I might be getting a bit paranoid."

"Was that the end of it?"

"No, because when the second one turned off, the first one came up behind us again and I said I wanted to come home. I told her about being kidnapped before, so she agreed."

"Have you got the number of the second car?"

"Dav gave me the page from her notebook."

"Okay, sweetheart, give it here and I'll deal with that."

"The bastards just won't leave us alone, Drew, will they," Anna said? He wasn't sure if she was more upset or angry. She followed him into the study.

With his phone on speaker, he called Lightfoot, explained what had happened and gave him the car numbers.

"Hold the line, I should be able to give you something right away."

They listened to him tapping away at his keyboard for a minute or two.

"Right," he said. "Car number one should be a grey VW Polo, registered to Christopher Rayner, 25 years old. Address, 4b Vale Court, Kenrick Street, Reading." Then after another spell of tapping, "The second one is supposed to be a Ford Fiesta, registered to Mark Rayner, 22 years old, also of 4b Vale Court, Kenrick Street. Looks like they're brothers. Want me to do a quick CRB check?"

"That would be good, thanks."

The line went quiet apart from the sound of Lightfoot typing into his computer until he said, "Okay, you're dealing with a right pair of master criminals here. They've both been involved in petty crime since before they finished school, assuming they actually went to school, and there isn't a lot of evidence of that. It's mostly theft of and from cars, shoplifting, drug possession, burglary, and street robbery sometimes involving minor violence until about eighteen months ago. Then they graduated to armed robbery involving an unloaded shotgun. They surprised the owner of a small company that runs a fleet of burger stands and ice cream vans while he was counting the day's takings. They only got away with about five hundred quid. They pleaded not guilty in the magistrates court, but it's been shoved up to the crown court. Their case hasn't come for trial yet so they're still on bail."

"How were they caught? Does it say?"

"The CCTV caught their car number, and when they were robbing the guy they called each other by their own Christian names. Then somehow Mark managed to leave his fingerprints on the cashbox."

"They used their own car!? I know you don't have to be a genius to be a crook, but these two must struggle to walk and breathe at the same time. Okay, Lightfoot, that's great thanks. Can you send me the details with photos if you can?"

He ended the call and looked at Anna.

"What are you going to do?"

"I'm going to ask them what interest they have in our daughter and explain that any continued curiosity about her might not be conducive to their continued good health."

"Are you going alone?"

"Yes I think so. I don't want to keep taking Megan away from her primary function of looking after you and Cassie. Anyway Rhian and Tina are still here."

"You shouldn't keep taking risks, darling."

"Risks? With these two? Don't be silly. I was hoping you were going to compliment me for using the word *conducive*. I don't think I even knew that word existed before I met you."

She was forced to smile. "Have some lunch first."

"Good idea."

At six o'clock he pulled up in Kenrick Street and watched the home of the Rayner brothers. It was what the British called a maisonette, in other words a two-storey house with a separate dwelling on each floor. 4a was the ground floor flat with 4b above, and the access doors to the two homes were side by side.

Having already established that both cars were parked in the road outside he thought it likely that they were both home. Holding a clipboard he knocked on the door to 4a.

A woman opened the door and timidly said, "Yes?"

"Excuse me Ma'am, I'm from Reading Borough Council." He quickly showed his SIA licence. "I'm investigating a complaint of noise nuisance locally, and I was wondering if you've experienced any problems."

"Yes but I don't want to talk about it."

"I understand. Do you feel reluctant to speak for fear of reprisals?"

"That's right."

"In which case I won't trouble you any longer. I'm going to speak to your neighbours from upstairs about it to ask if they've had similar problems. I hope our discussions don't disturb you too much. Have a good day."

He knocked on the adjacent door and waited. When nobody answered, he banged on the flimsy timber door so hard it rattled in its frame.

"Fuck off!" a male voice shouted.

Drew sighed and banged again, harder still. This time a small pane of glass fell out of the segmented semi-circular decorative window at the top of the door. He heard steps thundering down wooden stairs, before the door was snatched open.

"What the fu..." Chris Rayner never got to finish what he said before a huge fist flattened his nose and another hand grasped his clothes and pushed him inside.

Drew slammed the door behind him and dragged the semi-conscious man up the stairs.

"What the fuck's going on, Chris?" The second brother shouted, and appeared in the doorway of the main room just as Drew dumped the older brother at the top of the stairs. Before another syllable escaped his lips Drew punched Mark in the stomach. The force of the blow left him huddled on the floor struggling to get air into his lungs.

Having satisfied himself that there was nobody else in the flat, he dragged the two men into the main room and deposited them side by side on the sofa. On the coffee table, in amongst the empty beer cans and an overflowing ashtray, were two cellphones, he put them in his pocket before taking a quick look in the other rooms.

When he returned, he found Chris had recovered enough to stand and was reaching in a drawer of a side unit. He turned unsteadily toward Drew holding a revolver. Drew took three long strides across the room, grabbed the gun, and viciously twisted it out of his hand, breaking the guy's finger in the trigger guard as he did it.

Drew waited for the guy to stop screaming. "Go and sit on the sofa with your brother like a good boy, and don't move until I tell you to."

"Who are you? What do you want?" he asked, spitting blood and broken teeth.

"Shut the fuck up. I'll tell you when to speak. This morning, you two assholes followed my daughter around Reading while she was having a driving lesson. I want to know why, I want to know who paid you to do it, what else you were supposed to do, and how much you got paid. Now you can speak."

"We ain't thnitcheth," he mumbled, attempting to sound defiant.

"You're not informers. That's very admirable, but if you don't tell me, you'll find that talking to anybody won't be an option, because you'll be either so badly injured you won't be able to, or you'll be dead. If you think that's just a threat, you should bear in mind that for twelve years I killed people for a living. So are we going to keep playing this game where you pretend you're a hard man until I have to hurt you again, or are you going to do what we all know you're going to do in the end and just tell me?"

The older of the two replied, but Drew had to make him repeat it twice, eventually guessing he'd been warning him against firing the weapon because people would hear it.

"God you're a fucking dumb bastard. I don't need a gun. I disabled the pair of you with two punches and didn't get out of breath. Imagine what I can do when I make an effort. Just start talking or I'll start by crushing your balls."

His diaphragm was still in spasm, but between gasps Mark managed to explain. "We were just supposed to scare her a bit by making her have a small accident or something, but we could never get close enough."

"Whose idea was this?"

"A guy in a pub gave Chris two hundred notes."

"What guy?"

"Don't know his name, Chris said he was Polish or Russian or something."

"Is that right Chris?"

The older brother had given up articulation but nodded painfully.

"So he just handed over two hundred pounds, told you what to do, then walked away trusting you to do what he asked?"

"Another two hundred later," Mark managed to say one syllable at a time.

"Weren't you supposed to report back when you'd succeeded?"
Mark nodded.

"By phone?"

He nodded again.

"What's his number?"

"It's in my phone. He said his name was Marian."

"What's the PIN number for your phone?"

"It's 220798. Our mum's birthday."

"Is his the same?"

"Yes."

Drew quickly tried the number in both phones, satisfied himself that the number worked, then put them back in his pocket with the gun.

"Has he been in touch since?"

"No. His phone is turned off."

"Okay. I'm going to leave you now, with a little piece of advice. If I see you, hear about you, or learn about either of you again I'll take great pleasure killing you very painfully. Do we understand one another?"

Back in his car he put the confiscated gun in the glove box together with the two cellphones that he doubted would bear much fruit. He was about to drive away when one of them started to ring.

He quickly retrieved it before it went to voicemail, saw that it was 'Marian', and answered in the best approximation of a British accent he could muster, "Yeah."

"You didn't drive bitch off road and shoot at her with gun I give you like I say, you not get rest of money now. If you want rest of money you have to shoot bitch's father. If you do it before end of week, you get thousand-pound bonus. You not have to kill but must at least hurt him bad."

"Okay, we can do that."

Whoever it was ended the call. 'What the fuck is going on?' Drew asked himself, 'What makes me or my family a target?'

Deciding that other than remaining vigilant, he could think of little to do about it until he or the police had identified who was responsible for everything that was happening; he put the car in gear and drove away.

The short journey to Wokingham gave him little opportunity to think about the situation. Stanton Road was a one-way street with parking restrictions, so he turned into a side road to park. After learning nothing from his quick reconnoitre on foot, he went to the communal entrance of the small apartment block expecting to have to press a random bell and hoped to be admitted. In the end he was lucky that his arrival at the door coincided with someone leaving who smiled and held it open for him.

Brigitte's flat was on the second floor, and taking the stairs two at a time he was soon outside her door. He knocked, waited, and listened for any sign of activity. The only noise was the faint sound of a TV news programme from the flat opposite.

After pulling on a pair of nitrite gloves he picked the simple night latch, opening it in less than a minute. A quick look around the tiny apartment established that she'd hurriedly packed and made a run for it. Drawers in the master bedroom had been left open and mostly empty; likewise the bathroom cabinet.

It didn't look as if she'd be returning soon so he began a detailed search. He'd been at it for over an hour and was beginning to think his efforts would be fruitless, when among some magazines by the main bed he discovered a printout from Booking.com. The reservation in Brigitte's name was for a three-bedroom holiday home which by Drew's judgement looked expensive.

The reservation was made four days before the first phone call from Ariana. It was to begin the day after and last a month.

If she'd booked a long expensive holiday, why had she been in Percy's house eight days after it was supposed to start? It didn't make sense until he found something that answered that question and many others.

He began making calls even before he left the flat, and by the time he was home he had the seedlings of a plan in his mind.

As he walked through the door, Anna greeted him, and asked, attempting to sound less anxious than she was. "How did it go, sweetheart?"

"A very successful outing I think."

Cassie joined them. "Did you find those men, Daddy?"

"Yes I did, sweetheart, and they won't be troubling you again, but if Dav doesn't mind I'm going to get Megan to go with you on your lessons for the time being, just to be on the safe side. You don't mind do you?"

"I'll be a bit nervous with someone watching me."

"She won't be watching you; she'll be watching what goes on around you."

In his study he booted up his computer and made a reservation. Then a few more calls.

"Can you stop long enough to have something to eat now? Eli made a fantastic meal and we put some aside for you."

"That's great. I'm going to be leaving early in the morning and I may be away overnight."

"Have you got a lead to what's going on?"

"To part of it, yes. I hope to get confirmation in the next hour or two."

"Can you tell me?"

He explained what he'd uncovered."

Anna was aghast. "Oh my God, do you really believe she'd do that? It's appalling even for Ariana."

"We still can't be sure whether she's victim or perpetrator, so I need to get to the bottom of that first."

Before going to bed he put the gun he'd seized from the Rayner brothers in the underground safe he'd had fitted behind the stables. It would be safe enough there until he needed it.

TWENTY-FIVE

03:30 hours, Second Tuesday – Pangbourne Grange

Anna kissed him goodbye and asked to be kept informed of what was happening, although she knew that he'd only ring if there were any major developments.

As he was about to get in the car Megan stopped him. "Are you sure you don't want me with you Drew?"

"It would be good, but I don't think it'll be necessary, and I think you may be more use here."

It was a two-and-a-half-hour drive to his first stop, which was the Eurotunnel Shuttle terminal just outside Folkestone where he was booked on the 06:00 train to Calais. He hadn't used the service before, but it was certainly impressive. Once boarded he'd be in France in less than forty minutes. Like everybody else he had to go through French Immigration control before being allowed to join the queue, and his American passport prompted a slightly longer stop at the kiosk than those in front. In the end there were no problems and the queue to board began to move almost as soon as he joined it.

With travel time, the short wait to drive off the train, and the one-hour time difference, he'd still be at his destination by 08:00 local time. The holiday home that Brigitte had rented was a generous three-bedroomed gîte in Wissant, a fishing port and farming village about halfway between Calais and Boulogne.

He'd fixed the town map in his mind and had a good idea where the gîte was located and he didn't want to be there too early, so he'd texted his contact to confirm an early meeting and drove to a twenty-four-hour restaurant in the centre of the town.

Drew's language skills were limited, but the waitress spoke enough English for them to understand one another, and he ordered a large coffee with three croque madams.

While he waited for his food he checked his emails. The content of one confirmed that his trip was justified; whether it was to be wasted remained to be seen.

Halfway through his meal a man took the seat opposite him at the table. "Bonjour, Êtes-vous Monsieur Benjamin Franklin?"

"Oui Monsieur, vous devez être Charles de Gaulle? Peut-on parler anglais maintenant?".

"English is good. I have this package for you. I understand it is for rental only, that is good. But if you use it then it cannot be returned; the price remains the same."

"I understand." He handed the guy an envelope containing a thousand Euros, and the man handed him a small but heavy parcel.

"When you've finished with it and want to return it unused, put it back in the package, call the number on the outside and arrange a time to hand it to me at the Eurotunnel terminal in Calais."

"Fine by me, Merci."

The man stood up and walked out of the restaurant. Drew finished his food which by this time was almost cold. After two more cups of coffee and a visit to the toilet he returned to his car.

The gîte was less a traditional rural country cottage; more a large modern chalet bungalow in a quiet residential road. He parked where he could observe the house, hopefully without being too obvious to the occupants or its neighbours. There was a car in the driveway.

He waited for over an hour before there was any sign of activity. Then the front door opened, and a woman and two young girls came out followed by a young man. The four of them walked toward the centre of town. Drew left it until they were almost out of sight before following them.

If the man had been employed as a bodyguard, he clearly wasn't very good at his job. With very few people alive as distinctive as Drew, any protection officer worth his pay would have spotted him within moments even without a specific instruction to look out for him.

The small group continued through the town until they were at the seafront. This wasn't a seaside holiday resort where you'd normally bring children. There were none of the usual shops or amusements. The only thing to keep kids entertained was the sea, but these girls were used to the hot sun and warm waters of the Aegean, not the changeable climate and cool waters of the English Channel. The sun was warm at that moment, but the strong breeze could whip up the surf and bring colder temperatures very quickly if the weather changed. Drew doubted they'd want to stay long if that happened.

He found a seat where he could observe the group from a distance, which was simple enough because they were the only ones on the beach. In theory he could have called Forester and told him what he'd discovered and where, but if he did that now, the NCA would have hordes of French police rounding them up within two hours, and that would prevent him challenging Natalie and getting the truth from her. It wasn't yet time.

From where he sat the body language of the group didn't suggest a bodyguard and his charges, more a case of a girl and her boyfriend with two children in their care. If that were the case it certainly simplified things.

His prediction about the effects of the weather proved correct. The wind changed, clouds gathered, and the temperature dropped eight degrees within just a few minutes. The kids hurried from the surf and Natalie wrapped them in towels. She dried first one and then the other before hiding them from view while they dressed.

The boyfriend sat on a towel watching the ships moving in the Channel, showing no interest in what his girlfriend was doing, nor offering to assist in any way. When the girls were ready they all moved off the beach and headed back the way they'd come. Drew didn't follow, instead he headed in a similar direction along a parallel street, ensuring at each intersection that he was neither overtaking nor falling behind.

Unsurprisingly they stopped in a town centre café, no doubt for a treat like a pain au chocolat, an éclair, or an ice cream, but soon they were on their way again.

When he was confident that their destination was the gîte he hurried ahead, picked the lock, let himself in, and relocked the door before waiting in the ground floor cloakroom for their return.

It wasn't long before he heard the front door opening and Natalie's voice giving instructions to the girls in French.

"Oui Natalie," they parroted and hurried upstairs.

"J'ai besoin de pisser." He heard the boy say.

Drew was no linguist, but he knew that meant the guy wanted to take a leak and he braced himself to be discovered. The gun he'd had delivered to him in the restaurant earlier in the day was in his hand and when the door opened he pointed the gun in the boy's face and began to say, "If you keep quiet, and do what I say, nobody is going to get hurt."

However the boy was so terrified he released an involuntary squeak, and Drew had to repeat himself.

"Qu'est-ce qui ne va pas, Michel?" Natalie called.

"Michel just had a little fright that's all," he said, and nudged Michel backwards toward the living room.

Natalie appeared in the doorway. "What do you want?"

"Just a little talk that's all. Tell Michel to sit down and keep quiet. This doesn't concern him."

"He speaks English."

"That's good. Sit down Michel, and don't speak until I tell you. And you, Natalie, I'm not going to shoot anybody, but neither am I going to allow anybody to leave." He tucked the gun in his belt.

"Who are you, and what do you want?"

"I think you know who I am, but let's pretend that you don't. At the moment you are teetering on the edge of a very long prison sentence for international child trafficking. And, as an accomplice Michel, so are you."

The boy's eyes opened wide, and he looked from Drew to his girlfriend and back.

"I haven't abducted anybody," Natalie protested. "The girls are on holiday with me that's all."

"That's not what Ms Georgiou has told the police in the UK. At the moment there's a massive hunt for them. If you want to avoid that prison sentence, you need to be prepared to tell the police everything you know when they get here which I estimate will be in little more than an hour, perhaps two."

"Ariana told me that they had to be taken away to keep them safe from being kidnapped."

"Unfortunately, I don't believe a single word of that, and I doubt the police will either. On the back of my head is a wound with twenty stitches where your sister Brigitte tried to kill me with a bronze ornament. She's mixed up in a huge conspiracy to steal millions of pounds. I don't know how deep you're involved, but if you're to stand a chance of avoiding eight years in a British prison or fifteen in a French one I suggest complete cooperation."

"Ariana will tell them I'm not guilty."

"I admire your faith, but Ariana Georgiou is the most untrustworthy and duplicitous person I've ever known, and if she thought it was to her advantage she'd throw you under the bus in a heartbeat. Remember, for the last two weeks, she's been telling the British police how terrified she is that the girls will be harmed. You have to understand that whether you go to jail or not is of little interest to me. I wish you personally no ill will, but the people who I believe instigated all this have twice tried to kill me and two days ago sent two

177

armed men to attack my daughter. So I need to know what you know, right now."

She looked torn, and Drew began to think she wouldn't confess, but Michel intervened and angrily told her to reveal whatever she knew.

She started slowly, but eventually she told Drew everything. The children interrupted several times, concerned when they heard her crying, but she sent them back upstairs to play with their iPads.

By the time the police arrived he had a good idea of the sequence of events. Nonetheless he was still unsure whether Ariana was an accomplice of the Russians, being exploited by them, or trying to take advantage of what they'd started.

It was never going to be straightforward, but the French police arrested all three adults, Drew for carrying a firearm, and the others for child abduction. Initially the children were taken into care by French Social Services with the intention of transferring them to the British system as soon as possible, but then a dispute arose whether they were UK or Greek citizens, and then whether the French or British police would deal with any potential trafficking charges.

Drew's European Bodyguard Licence allowed him to carry a firearm, but the cops weren't happy about him using it when he wasn't operating as a personal protection officer. Thankfully after an intervention by Forester, the French Police accepted that in this instance he was acting as de facto bodyguard to the children and released him without charge.

It was too late to catch a return shuttle by the time he was finished at the police station, and the chances of getting a room for the night were close to zero, so he spent the night in the car having reserved a place on the 06:00 shuttle to Folkestone.

He'd called Anna and told that subject to the traffic on the M25 motorway, he hoped to be home by about 9am.

He put the seat back and closed his eyes, but almost immediately his phone rang. "Ariana, what can I do for you?"

"You fucking bastard."

"What's wrong, I found your kids like you asked."

"You've had them taken into care."

"I think you'll find that was your fault for using them as some sort of decoy or distraction from whatever con you're trying to pull with your father's ill-gotten gains. Anyway I'm tired now, we can talk about this another time. And in case you were in any doubt, there definitely will be another time."

He ended the call and closed his eyes again.

TWENTY-SIX

09:45 hours, Third Wednesday – Pangbourne Grange.

"How did it go, darling," Anna asked as he came through the door? "You didn't tell me anything last night."

"Can I get some food first. I've not eaten since 10am yesterday French time."

"Jason, can you try and recreate one of Cassie's breakfasts for him? You're better at it than me. Now sit down, darling and I'll get you a coffee." She poured a cup from the jug she'd started making as soon as the gate alarm sounded. "Can you at least give me the headlines?"

"I found the kids, they're now in the care of the French authorities."

"Thank God for that. Will that be the end of it?"

"Not a chance, but it might help us to focus on the other side of things that I'm not sure the cops give a shit about. That's the bit that directly involves us."

"Is Ariana out of the picture though?"

"That woman is still in this right up to her neck, and I intend to make sure I find out precisely how. When I do I'm going to expose her for the reptilian parasite she is."

"So how was Natalie involved?"

"She claims that Ariana asked her to take them away to keep them safe from some Russians who were threatening her, and the best way to do that was to make out that they'd been kidnapped. Between them they arranged for her sister to rent the gîte and gave her the money to do it. I'd found Brigitte's bank statement with the transfer of five-thousand-pounds from Ariana, along with the booking for a gîte when I searched her flat. Digits discovered a record of tickets on the Eurostar for Natalie and the kids. She'd taken them the to stay at the gîte and used the opportunity to shack up with her boyfriend. Natalie admitted that Ariana stayed in touch with the girls using an iPad that logs on to the Wi-Fi of Ariana's neighbour. I thought that bit was pretty damn clever by the way. That's why my surveillance team wasn't able to see the digital traffic."

"Doesn't all that explain the kidnap though?"

"Not even close. Natalie might have been able to explain her involvement that way, but it doesn't explain Brigitte's connection to Braithwaite, or what she was doing in Percy's house."

"What about this supposed stockpile of millions that her father is alleged to have secreted away?"

"I wouldn't be surprised to find it exists. In fact I'd be more surprised if it didn't now, but it may turn out to be much smaller than these people hope. The other question remains what to do with it, but that's a question for another day."

"If the money exists in the form of shares in a hedge fund that has large holdings in Silico it could be catastrophic."

"Let's find out what the situation is before we start worrying what to do about it."

"What are you goin to do next?"

"I need to corner Braithwaite and get him to tell me how he got involved. Likewise Natalie's sister. But with Natalie in French custody, they're unlikely to let me anywhere near her to question her further. I need to find some way to locate Brigitte on my own."

"Where's Braithwaite now?"

"I don't know that either. He's not been charged with anything yet, and he was released on bail under investigation like I was. As far as I know his bail hasn't been lifted, but I've been too distracted by everything else to keep up to date."

"Could that be what Ariana has been trying to do?"

"It could be. It's the sort of devious move I'd expect from a member of that family. The problem with that theory, is the amount of resources being thrown at it. If you take it all into account, it's huge."

"Is it a conspiracy between Ariana and the Russians then?"

"That's my favorite explanation at the moment, but I think that's only part of it. Given what we know about these Russians, it goes without saying that they can't have unlimited resources, and yet to even get to the point where they approach Ariana they must have spent a million, maybe more. That's why it's my guess that they've thrown in their lot with her and they're now working together."

"If you were bailed on Friday, would that be the same day as Braithwaite?"

"I think so."

"Then he'll be expected to answer to bail on the same day as you were. You could get someone to watch out and then follow him."

"You're a genius, sweetheart. Well done. I'll pull one of the guys off Ariana and get him to do that," He said and bent to kiss her.

She shied away. "Wait until you've cleaned your teeth."

"Was Cassie okay on her lesson yesterday?"

"Yes she was fine, although Dav wasn't wild about having a passenger. It went okay though. Rhian and Tina went home yesterday afternoon. They said to say goodbye."

Later, after a shower he called Digits. "Hi, I gather you had a bit of a result in France," his contact said when he answered.

"Yeah, it worked out quite well I guess."

"I looked at Natalie as we said and at first I thought I was wasting my time. Her call log up to the day of the kidnap was predominantly to and from her employer or her boyfriend whose name is Michel Renault. I guess you knew about him, had a quick look at him, nothing of note to say. Then about a week before the kidnap Natalie started getting calls from unregistered phones; not many, but enough for it to be noticeable against her normal pattern."

"Always the same number?"

"No, but she did get repeat calls a couple of times. So I looked a bit closer at those numbers and guess what? One had received a call from the same phone that set off that little gadget in your alarm system."

"Bingo. And that reminds me, Lightfoot was looking into Wes Fletcher, the crooked engineer. He sent me a report, but I haven't had time to do anything about it."

I may be wrong about this, but I'd hazard a guess that the prime suspect for that would be Braithwaite."

"What makes you say that?"

"Because the call was made from the vicinity of some of the calls that his cell phone made before all this kicked off," Digits explained. "If there's anything else you need, get back to me whenever. I know it's your life and a big problem for you, but this is much more interesting than my usual stuff. I rarely get involved in live investigations. So anything you need pal, just ask."

"Thanks, that's great to know."

Cassie was next to grab Drew's attention. "Hi, Daddy. Mummy said you went to France and found the two little girls. You are so clever, I'm so proud of you."

"I didn't do any of this on my own. Without the help of technical experts I'd just be a dumb guy with a gun for hire."

"Don't keep saying that, Daddy. I know all these people help you gather all the bits of the puzzle but you're the person who puts it all together."

"How was your lesson?"

"It was really good. I went out on the main roads today. Dav thinks I'll be ready for my test by the end of next week. That's not much help though, I checked online, and the waiting time is fifteen weeks."

"It would be if you applied now, but I applied on your behalf as soon as you'd passed the theory test at Easter. Your appointment is in three weeks, unless Dav can get you an earlier cancellation."

"I'm so spoiled, I don't know anybody whose dad would think to do something like that."

"Hopefully, you'll have your licence in time for you to start uni in September. How is Robert finding his new job?"

"He says they all seem very nice people, but they haven't let him do much so far. There are only about eight that work there, but he hasn't met them all yet."

"As long as he likes it."

"They said they might get him to shadow their creative director one day a week, so he can offer artistic ideas."

"That sounds promising. Is he good enough to be able to do that already?"

"I've seen his portfolio. He's really clever. He did a series of things for college where he took well known advertising campaigns, and showed how he might have tried to send the same message differently."

"Maybe he'd show me and your mom one day."

Later he was thinking about everything that had happened, and how his search for the Russians and their accomplices seemed to have stalled, and it occurred to him that he needed to find a way for them to come at him without putting his family at risk.

He was still mulling an idea in his mind when Anna brought him a cup of coffee, so he took the opportunity to share his thoughts.

"Sweetheart, I've had an idea and I need to run it past you. You won't like it but hear me out before you dismiss it."

She listened to what he suggested but didn't agree. "I can't do that, sweetheart, it's too much to ask."

"It's only until this is over; until we've found out who's behind what's going on."

"But on its own it won't tell you that; all it does is put you in harm's way, and there's no guarantee that it won't expose us to greater danger. You're not the only target you know."

"So far, the attacks on our family have all been, either directly or indirectly on me or to attract my attention. They want to draw my attention away from what they're doing."

"I don't agree, and I can't bring myself to tell people that you've left me, so if you're asking my permission, then the answer is no. You'll have to find another way to draw them out of cover. You've said yourself that they must have limited resources. Isn't there any way you can make them use them faster."

"That's it. Why didn't I think of that?"

"What do you mean?"

"If their only remaining significant financial support is Ariana, all I need to do is deny her access to her own money."

"Can you do that?"

"In the short term I think so yes. I'll speak to Digits."

"I'll leave you to it then. Just don't come up with any more stupid ideas like the last one."

When he explained to Digits what he wanted him to do, the man laughed.

"Can you do it?"

"For a limited amount of time yes. As long as I don't just withdraw a big chunk of money in one go. If I can make it look as if she's raiding other people's accounts to boost her own I can create enough suspicious activity for them to freeze her accounts for a week maybe longer. I may need to use some of your money to start the ball rolling though."

"How much do you need?"

"About twelve grand should be enough."

"I'll transfer it right away."

"No need, I'll get her to take it from your business account. It won't appear to have been her that's taken it, but the trail will lead back to her. That will only be part of the story, but if it works as well as last time I did it, then it'll fuck her up for anything up to a fortnight."

"Do I need to do anything?"

"Look out for the deduction and when it happens report it to your bank as suspicious as soon as possible. Then just sit back and wait. Most of the activity won't involve you in any way, and your transaction will be one of dozens so she may not ever become aware that your account was one affected."

"Sounds clever."

"If you really want to fuck with her mind, you should ask her for an advance for the work you've done and when she won't be able to pay, it may send her into a spin."

"I like that."

After ending the call he thought through the people still on his to do list, Giles Braithwaite, Brigitte Laurent, Wes Fletcher, Brian Sturgess, and if he weren't one of the others, the M4 shooter.

Braithwaite and Brigitte had gone to ground, so there was little hope of getting to them for the time being, and so far he had no more information about Sturgess. That left Fletcher. He called Lightfoot.

"Babycham, what can I do for you?"

"I'm going after Fletcher today, so I wondered if you'd had time to get any more gen on him."

"I thought you'd have heard. He was found dead in his home, the day after I sent you his details, so I didn't look any further."

"Shit. No I hadn't heard that. Do you know how he died?"

"I got the impression that it was suspected suicide, but I may be wrong. Have a look at the press reports online. If you want me to look closer, give me a call."

It didn't take long to pull up local paper reports of Wes Fletcher's body being discovered by his visiting mother who lived nearby. The police were quoted as saying that it was an unfortunate death, and they weren't looking for anybody else in connection with the incident.

Drew decided that he'd attempt speaking to Fletcher's mother. The FSB were the World's leading experts on murder by fake suicide, and with Turgenev involved anything was possible

TWENTY-SEVEN

14:30 hours, Third Wednesday – Woking, Surrey

Parked half on and half off the pavement of the narrow road where Wes Fletcher had lived, Drew looked at the poorly kept front garden of the two-storey building that contained the alarm engineer's home. Fletcher had occupied the ground floor flat. He was in two minds whether to pick the lock and have a look around or to try to find the mother who 'lived nearby', when a woman in her late sixties or early seventies crossed the road and let herself in.

He climbed out of the car and approached the open door that the woman had just entered. He knocked and she appeared from what he could see was the living room.

"Mrs. Fletcher?"

"Yes."

"I'm sorry to interrupt at what must be a difficult time for you, but I wonder if I could ask you a few questions about your son."

"Are you another bloody reporter?"

"No. I'm a sort of investigator, and I'm working on something right now that leads me to believe that Wesley may have been dragged into something he didn't understand."

"The police are saying he killed himself."

"I know, but I believe it's possible that he didn't."

"Come in. Who are you?"

"My name is Drew Parker, here's my card."

"This says you're a close body protection officer. What does that mean?"

"Roughly it translates as bodyguard, but I run a recruitment agency that provides people like me to politicians, movie stars, and extremely wealthy people, but I also do investigations."

"What's that got to do with my Wesley?"

"I'm sorry to have to say this, but days before he died, he made illegal alterations to the alarm system in a house, which allowed an arsonist to carry out an attack."

"You're lying."

"I can show you a film of him doing it if you want. The thing is I think he was either tricked or forced into doing it by others, and it's those people that I'm after."

The woman was clearly set to object, and demanded, "Show me."

186

Drew played the video while the woman watched.

"Is that Wesley?"

"Yes, but that could be anywhere, and he could be doing anything. Whose house is that?"

"It's mine Mrs. Fletcher. If you look at my card you'll see that my address is in Berkshire, and Wesley's area was Surrey wasn't it? My security system wasn't due to be serviced for another two months."

"When was that video made?"

"You can see the date at the bottom of the screen."

"He wasn't working for them by then. He got the sack two weeks before."

"Which kind of verifies what I said, doesn't it? How did he die?"

"They said he took an overdose of sleeping pills, but Wesley didn't take sleeping pills. He'd been a bit down after losing his job, but he told me that he'd been offered a new contract. They even paid him a thousand pounds advance."

"Did he say who that was for?"

"No, but he showed me his bank account on his phone."

"I don't suppose you remember which bank do you?"

"No but his bank statement arrived in the post this morning, I haven't got around to cancelling it yet."

"May I see?"

"It's over there by the phone."

The envelope had already been opened. He removed the papers from inside and spotted the thousand-pound entry straight away. He quickly snapped photos of all three pages, making sure he included the account details.

"Listen, Mr. Parker, I don't know what you're going to do with that, but I've got to clear this place before tomorrow or I'll have to pay another month's rent, so I need to get a move on."

"How would you like me to give you a hand?"

"You'd do that?"

"I should confess that I've an ulterior motive. The people who put that money in Wesley's account are almost certainly the same people who were responsible for the arson I mentioned, they've have made three attempts on my life, one on my daughter, and one on a close friend, as well as beating another man almost to death. I'm hoping that I may find something in Wesley's effects that would lead me to them."

"Why aren't the police looking into it then?"

187

"Because, as you indicated, the police don't seem to want to join the dots."

She gratefully accepted the help he offered, which didn't amount to much in the end, just one or two small items of furniture, and some boxes of personal items carried across the road.

"There's all his clothes as well," she said. "They need to go to a charity shop, but I don't drive."

"I can take them for you, if it helps."

"You're being very kind."

"Don't worry about it, but we ought to go through the pockets first, in case there's anything personal in them."

"That's a good idea."

Between the two of them they searched all the clothes before putting them in bags to take away. They found a few coins and little else except a piece of paper with Drew's name and address, with a printout of his security system details from the company that serviced it, including the engineer's access code.

A final search through Wesley's papers revealed nothing, so he loaded the bags for the charity shop into the trunk of his car and said goodbye to Mrs. Fletcher.

"Will you be able to prove that Wesley didn't commit suicide?"

"I doubt it, but if you give me your phone number and I learn anything that will help you understand what happened I'll let you know. Thank you for everything."

"No, thank you, Mr. Parker."

He stopped outside a charity shop in Woking town and quickly unloaded the bags of clothing without getting a parking ticket.

He'd sent the bank statement photos to Lightfoot and asked him if he could find out more about the money trail of the thousand pounds without expecting a reply very quickly. He hadn't been sure if it was his area of expertise because in the past he'd given that sort of work to Digits. However, as he drove through the gates of the Grange his phone rang.

"Well, that was straightforward," Lightfoot said.

"How's that?"

"That thousand pounds came directly from the current account of one Ms Ariana Georgiou, of Lindfield Gardens, Hampstead."

"That's almost too good to be true, thank you, Lightfoot. My bill with you must be building up by now. Do you need me to give you something toward it?"

"No. it's fine. I know you're good for it."

By the time he ended the call, he'd reversed into his garage, and was inside the house. Eli was preparing the evening meal and Jason was chopping vegetables, but Anna, Cassie and Megan were nowhere to be seen. He found them in the living room.

"Hi, darling. What've you been up to? You're covered in dust?"

"I've been helping an old lady move furniture. What does it look like?"

They laughed, not knowing whether to take him seriously.

"There's a package for you in your study. Were you expecting anything?"

"No, I wasn't. Get everybody outside now."

Megan ushered them all from the building, stopping only to get Jason and Eli outside with them.

"Do you want me to call the cops?" Megan called back inside as she went.

"Not yet, I need to take a look first."

When he was sure they were all outside and well away from the building he gingerly approached the study. The package was in the centre of his desk, it was about fifteen inches long, eight inches wide, and six inches thick. It had been carefully wrapped in brown paper and tied with string in the manner of an old-fashioned Christmas parcel.

He moved toward it and lifted his laptop out of the way so he could read the address label. Whoever had posted it had meticulously handwritten the label in large, neat capital letters. The return address was in much reduced lettering and from where he was standing he couldn't read it. He moved around the desk.

Taking a deep breath, he stooped to read the smaller writing and at that moment the cell phone in his breast pocket vibrated and rang. He jumped back and retreated to the door before removing the device and rejecting the call without seeing who'd rung.

His heart was pounding as he retraced his steps towards the desk, it was at that point that he noticed something for the first time, a tracking label. He breathed a sigh but didn't completely relax. He didn't know who the courier had been, but it would be unusual for a bomber to deliberately leave some way to track his package.

This time when he bent to read the return address he could see who the sender was and laughed at himself.

Cutting the string with scissors and tearing the paper revealed the box he'd used to take evidence about Stamelis finances to Dennis Hargreaves.

He walked outside via the kitchen and found the others behind the stables.

"You can come inside again now. It's all safe."

"Was it a bomb, Daddy?"

"No, sweetheart, it was somebody returning something to me that I wasn't expecting back yet, that's all."

"Please don't do that to me again," Anna gasped. "I nearly had a baby, and I'm not even pregnant."

The relief allowed them all to laugh.

"I'd better see if I can rescue your dinner I suppose," Eli told them.

As they walked back to the house, Drew checked his phone to see whose call he had rejected. He smiled again when he saw that it had been Dennis Hargreaves. Returning the call he waited for Dennis to pick up, but it went to voicemail, so he left a message promising to call back.

"So tell me again about your furniture moving expedition."

He explained his encounter with Wes Fletcher's mother and what he'd learned.

"Do you think he was murdered?"

"That would be my guess, but I put my chances of proving it at close to zero, and I've got other things to worry about."

"What can you do with the information about Ariana?"

"Directly, at the moment, I'm not going to do anything, but in the next day or two I'm going to force her into doing something that she really doesn't want to, I may need to use it then."

They were climbing into bed together later that evening when Anna said, "This is so complicated. I don't know how you're keeping it all in your head."

"I guess when your family are being threatened it heightens your senses."

"You're spending so much money on all this. Will you let me give you something towards it?"

"It's not necessary. Every last cent I've spent will be covered by Ariana, including what I would have made on the contract I had to cancel because of her."

TWENTY-EIGHT

07:00 hours, Third Thursday – Pangbourne Grange

"I was really frightened yesterday, Daddy."

"Me too for a while. We need to have a protocol to deal with deliveries. We can talk about it later."

"I mean when you were in there by yourself. What if it had been a bomb?"

"I didn't touch it, Cassie. I just identified what it was from the outside."

"We didn't know what was happening though."

"What did Megan tell you?"

"She said that you'd have been trained how to know whether it might be innocent, and if there were any doubt you'd leave it to experts to deal with."

"There you go then."

"Are you any closer to finding out who's doing all this?" She was talking as she ran today, which normally meant she was just making conversation. He thought that was a good thing.

"I think there's part of it I still don't understand, but think I know who all the main players are, even if I don't know exactly which part they're all playing."

"Are they dangerous?"

"The Russians are, and they're after the money, but I can't give them that, and they must know that by now."

They finished off their morning exercise with a sparring session in the mini dojo extension that Drew had had built on the side of the gym. Cassie's ability to inflict damage to her opponents had grown exponentially since her kidnap two years before, and in spite of the height and weight difference between them he had to stay alert. That morning she managed to catch him with a sharp punch, and he knew he'd have a swollen eye later in the day.

His daughter had learnt not to apologise. The bumps and bruises they each got in their sessions, whilst unintended, were accepted as an unfortunate consequence of the process. They didn't practice any particular martial art or discipline, but most of their moves appeared in one or other of defendu, krav maga, MCMAP, and karate. The end result was closer to MMA than anything.

At breakfast, the morning conversation proceeded much as usual until Cassie casually asked, "Mummy, would it be okay if I moved into the bedroom next to you and Daddy now?"

Anna and Drew looked at each other. "Why's that, sweetheart?"

"Now that Robert stays over it means that we wouldn't have to cross the landing to use the bathroom in the night. We sleep naked so it means we wouldn't have to put on a bathrobe."

Jason choked on his toast and Megan struggled to suppress a grin.

"There may be disadvantages from being so close to each other don't you think?" Anna tried to say without stuttering.

"You mean being able to hear each other when we're... busy? We already can though, can't we?"

"Would anybody mind if we changed the subject?" Jason pleaded.

"Why's that Jason? You already know that Robert and I... you know."

"Yes, but what the eye doesn't see the heart doesn't grieve over."

Cassie smiled. "DH Lawrence said, 'What the eye doesn't see, and the mind doesn't know, doesn't exist'. But you already know it exists."

"Yes, but I try not to think about it over the breakfast table."

At that point Megan started to laugh, and everybody soon joined in.

Immediately after breakfast Drew checked his business account online and spotted a debit of £11,957 by a cosmetics company in Lancashire. He smiled, called his bank's customer service line, and reported it. They promised to look into it, but in the meantime restored the money to his account.

"I have a board meeting this morning, darling," Anna told him. "One of the first items on the agenda is going to be the issues arising out of the attack on Percy. I don't want to put anything on the record yet that will jeopardise your investigations, but I won't be able to hold out much longer. Can you give me a summary of where we stand?"

"From the attack on Oliver Babcock we know for sure that some people believe that Alhambra Capital Management are holding some Silicon stock that used to belong to Stamelis. We don't know how that came to be, how big the holding is, or which of Alhambra's investors have been taking the income. I think from the involvement of Carrington we can assume the theory is correct, and I'd hazard a guess that he's one of the culprits.

"My guess is that when the Russians started poking their noses in, then Carrington et al decided to try and sell the Silicon stock to insulate themselves from involvement, in other words take the money and run. The trouble is you can't dump that much stock all at once without ringing all sorts of alarm bells. That's why they needed the cooperation of Babcock.

"We also suspect that Nevada Foothills Capital Management is holding some of Stamelis' Silico stock. If so, we don't know who, or who's taking the income from that either.

"What we definitely know is that Giles Braithwaite owns Silico shares and is mixed up in whatever is going on somehow although we don't know exactly how. From his connection to Natalie via her sister, it's clear that he's somehow connected to Ariana. But I don't think I should reveal that we know that yet. Just to complicate things further, I suspect the Braithwaite may have had communications with the Ruskies.

"What both you and I need to know - and I suspect the other board members do as well - is what was the purpose of that impromptu meeting at the plant the other day. The police will already have asked that question, and Carrington will have had to have given them some sort of answer, but Alhambra's interests aren't necessarily the same as Silico's.

"I think that you ought to encourage the board to take a closer look at some of the larger investors in funds that hold big chunks of Silico stock. If you can get them to do that then they can legitimately look at Nevada Foothills at the same time without raising suspicion."

"I can't hand over confidential stockholder information to you without breaking the law though, darling."

"I know that, and I don't want you to. But the implications of this aren't just financial. What's happening could have security ramifications as well, and your pals in the MoD will want to know about that. The most important thing is that this conspiracy gets shut down permanently and it doesn't matter who does it; me, the police, the NCA, or the government." Then Drew determinedly added, "I don't know what the official line would be if any assets once deemed to belong to Stamelis are proven to now belong to his heirs. One thing I do know is, that I won't allow her to be further enriched by that asshole if there's any way I can stop it."

"It would probably be the Financial Conduct Authority that decides in the end, and that could take years. None of that is anything to do with you though, Drew."

"Both Ariana and Turgenev have reasons to want to wreak revenge on me, but I think they're using that as a distraction to everything else that's happening. If that's right it was probably Ariana's idea."

"I'm glad I didn't ask for the detailed version, darling. What's next for you though?"

"Top of my agenda is to try to locate the two Russians and this Sturgess character."

"So are you going to forget about Ariana for the time being."

"Absolutely not, I have moves afoot to seriously impede her ability to act, and hopefully impact on her Russian pals as well."

"Is she working for them, with them, or being controlled by them? Do you know?"

"It's my guess that she's thrown her lot in with them and agreed to divide the spoils."

"I'll leave you to it then."

He stood to kiss her goodbye, and when he sat down again his eyes settled on the box that Dennis Hargreaves had sent and he remembered promising to call back.

Dennis picked up on the second ring. "Mr. Parker, thank you for calling back. Did you receive the parcel I sent okay?"

"Yes thanks Dennis. The information I posted was all copies so there was no hurry,"

"Yes I knew that but, something had been niggling at the back of my mind since I finished working on it, so I decided to take a second look. It took a little time to pin it down and I think I found what it was that was troubling me. When I did, I had to do quite a bit of research beyond the material you sent me. I won't charge you for the extra work, I was so intrigued by what I thought I'd found, I needed to take a closer look for my own peace of mind."

"I insist that you get paid for all the time you spent working on my stuff Dennis, whether or not you find anything that's relevant to what I'm working on, but I sense that you've unearthed something else important."

"Yes, I think so. It's a bit obscure. I've put my report on a thumb drive and it's in the box. Some of my conclusions are a bit tenuous and they involved collusion with at least one of my former colleagues at the FCA, so I didn't want to attach it to an email. Anyway read it and see what you think."

"When you send your invoice make sure you include that extra work, if for no other reason than it sounds as if it fits right in with the theories I've been working on."

After closing the call he retrieved the thumb drive from the box, but as soon as he plugged it into his USB, the sophisticated malware protection software on his laptop notified him that something might be wrong and sounded an alert.

After responding to the request to rectify, the file manager showed a single file. He opened it to reveal a fifteen-page document.

Before reading it he called Dennis back. "Dennis, I thought I should let you know that you've some malware on your system. You should get that looked at."

"Oh God, how did I pick that up? I hope I haven't infected you."

"No, my system is clever enough to detect anything that's there and either disinfect or isolate it."

The report was detailed, yet careful to avoid anything libelous. Even so its author left the reader in little doubt about who and what he was talking about. Although Drew was far from any sort of expert in the business of dealing in high finance, he managed to find his way through the jargon, and what he found explained a lot.

He called Dennis again. "Can you spare me an hour or two tomorrow? I need to make sure that I fully understand the implications of what you say."

"Yes of course. Actually, I'm glad you rang again because I found something else that might be important."

Drew was interested to learn about what had happened at Anna's meeting, and when she stood at the study door, he looked up. "Hi, sweetheart, how did it go?"

"The words cat and pigeons spring to mind. If I'd announced the company was about to be taken over by Fisher Price and Disney it couldn't have created a bigger stir."

"Tell me more."

"Steve Boardman suggested that I was overreacting, and that even if some of the investments in hedge funds had been owned by Stamelis then it was nothing to do with Silico, and it didn't matter anyway. Carrington agreed with him.

Then they were both shouted down by all the other members of the board pretty much singing with one voice. They argued that if the market learned that the company was 25% owned by funds potentially infiltrated by a foreign power it could have a catastrophic effect on the share price. They were deeply concerned about the national security implications and the company couldn't afford to be associated with anything like that. They held off bringing in the FCA until they'd had time to make further enquiries."

"What did Carrington say about the ad hoc meeting?"

"He said it was an experimental meeting to canvass opinion of investors that held significant holdings but were still too small to have a voice on the board. Specifically in this case about changing the company name. The board accepted his explanation but decided that in future any such meetings must take place off site."

"Did he say who'd been invited?"

"He gave a list of twenty investors that had been sent invitations, nine responded, but including Percy and Giles, only seven attended."

"What about the NCA? Haven't they been asking questions?"

"Mostly only the same ones as you. They're going to be speaking to all those who were sent invitations but that's all we know."

"Anything else of note?"

"Not really, but they voted to put the whole issue of a name change to bed for the time being, but expressed a preference of dropping NorArm rather than Silico if there were to be any change in the future."

TWENTY-NINE

09:00 hours, Third Friday – Pangbourne Grange

"Bye, Daddy. It's my last driving lesson today. Wish me luck."

"You don't need luck, sweetheart. You'll be great at that, just like you are at everything else."

"Will you be here when I get back? There's something I want to talk about."

"I don't know, darling. I've an appointment this morning and I might have to go into London this afternoon. Is it urgent?"

"Not really. I just need your advice."

The short drive to Dennis Hargreaves' home followed his third cup of coffee and a second reading of the report. An ambulance travelling in the opposite direction passed him as he neared his destination. There were no sirens, so it was clearly not an emergency.

The flashing lights of police vehicles blocking the road as he turned into the street made it obvious that something was very wrong, and as he neared the Hargreaves home, Drew could see that it was the centre of whatever was going on.

He pulled over, walked closer and joined the small crowd of onlookers straining to see what was happening.

"I heard the shots, but I thought it was a car backfiring, and didn't think any more of it," one woman was saying to another.

"Are they dead?" he heard her ask.

A nearby man interrupted. "The ambulance left without any live casualties, so it looks like it."

"Why would anybody want to shoot a lovely old couple like that though?"

"Dunno, but they're a bit weird, aren't they? Fancy still living with your mum at that age."

"She wasn't his mum; she was his wife."

"What really? That old woman? I told you they were weird."

Drew ignored the irrelevant and ignorant speculations and was about to leave when he was spotted by Detective Sergeant Gasowski.

"Mr. Parker, what're you doing here?" he said, summoning him to one side.

"I had an appointment with Mr. Hargreaves."

"Really, what was that about?"

"He's been doing some work for me."

"Would you like to give me some more detail about that?"

"Not here in the street I wouldn't, no."

"Perhaps if I visited you at your home later."

"By all means, but call first, I wouldn't want you to make a wasted journey," He said. "From what I've been overhearing in the crowd, the Hargreaves have been shot and killed, if that's right, I'm assuming it's a double murder. A murder suicide would make little sense."

"That appears to be the case. Could it be connected to other incidents we've spoken about?"

"Quite possibly."

"Then we will definitely speak later."

Back in his car he stopped and thought before driving away, remembering the malware that his system had detected, before calling Digits.

"Hi Drew, I was about to call you."

"Before we talk about that, I've some bad news for you." He went on to explain the events at Dennis's home.

His friend was furious. "He was a good honest man; only ever tried to do the right thing. Did you say that his wife was also killed?"

"It looks that way."

"These bastards need to pay for this."

"The cops spotted me at the crime scene. I didn't try to pretend that my involvement couldn't be connected."

"No, it wouldn't have worked anyway. I've been trying to log on to his computer as we've been speaking but it's either off or disconnected from the network, so I won't be able to locate where that malware came from."

"Will the thumb drive help?"

"I doubt it, not now you've deep cleansed it. Anyway I thought you should know that as of this morning, Ariana Georgiou has now been locked out of every one of her accounts that I'm aware of. Whether she knows about it yet, I don't know.",

"I need to think about this," Drew told him. "I was going to land on her doorstep this morning and confront her with all I know, but they're killing so many people now; this has to stop."

"Let me know if there's anything else you need Drew. I'm going to pull out all the stops to find something on this bitch. If she's tied up with those fucking Russian bastards, she needs to go down with them."

"I agree, let's keep in touch."

Driving back to Pangbourne he made a decision that would change his whole approach to the plan he'd been developing.

When he arrived home Anna was in the library with the door closed on a video conference call, and Cassie hadn't returned from her lesson so he joined Megan and Jason in the kitchen.

"Not with Cassie today Megan?"

"As it's her last lesson, she asked me not to go with her, is that okay?"

"I guess," he replied, noting that Megan looked worried.

He was about to ask if something was wrong when Jason remarked, "You look really pissed off Drew."

He told them about Hargreaves and his wife.

"So you think this has something to do with Stamelis' money," Megan said.

"The timing suggests it, and he'd just discovered something in Stamelis' paperwork that was going to throw a lot of brown stuff into the fan. He's a retired accountant for fucks sake; never done anything but good in his life. He and his wife have been murdered just to cover up someone else's criminality or feed their greed."

"Are you going to tell the cops?"

"I was going to anyway, but I no longer think I have a choice. It's not going to make them happy though because, I think I need to bring in the NCA."

"What did Hargreaves discover?"

The door opened and Cassie came in with a big smile.

"How did it go, sweetheart?"

"Dav wants to give me two or three more lessons to include dual-carriageway and night driving, and she wants me to practice parallel parking before my test which is two weeks today."

"Do you feel confident?"

"I think I feel confident enough to drive on my own, but I know I need lots of practice to be fully competent. Will you take me out in the Audi when you've got time?"

"No problem. I've got to make a couple of calls now, but we can have that chat after if you want."

In the study he found the card that Forrester had left him and called his number.

"Agent Forrester, it's Drew Parker. There have been some developments that I think that you or one of your colleagues need to know about."

"We're aware of the children's recovery, Mr. Parker, and your part in it."

"I guessed you'd have been informed, but that's not why I called. There are wider issues with implications that a local police force may not want to lead on. As you've already been involved I thought it best to let the NCA know so they can to decide if continued involvement is necessary."

"Give me a summary of your concerns."

Drew explained about the audit of Stamelis' affairs that he'd asked Dennis to do, his initial discoveries, and his initial report. Then he summarised his latest findings.

"You were right to call, Mr. Parker. It is something that we'd very likely want to take an interest in. I'll talk to my colleagues in the relevant team. What's the name of the local officer?"

"At the moment, it's Detective Sergeant Gasowski. You met before."

"Okay, thank you. We'll be in touch, but for the moment, can you email me a copy of that report."

When he called Gasowski and told him that the NCA were taking an interest the cop wasn't best pleased.

"This is a straightforward murder enquiry, Mr. Parker. The NCA have better things to do."

"That's the problem, Detective. I don't believe it is straightforward. Dennis Hargreaves had just discovered the possible corrupt involvement of a senior FCA officer in a multi-million-pound-fraud that could have national security implications."

The detective ended the call by saying he wouldn't wait for the so-called elite agents to get their act together and he'd be at the Grange at some point in the afternoon.

Cassie stood at the door waiting for him to finish his call.

"Come in, sweetheart. There was nothing in either of those calls that was particularly confidential. You didn't need to wait. What is it you want to talk about?"

There weren't many secrets among the family members or the household, so he was surprised when she closed the door.

"Is something troubling you?"

"Not really, but I want to ask your advice before I broach the subject with Mummy."

"Is it to do with Robert?"

She smiled. "No, nothing like that. I've been thinking about what to do after uni."

"I thought you wanted to work in an art gallery or museum. Isn't that why you've chosen art and literature for your degree?"

"I am interested in history and in literature, and still want to take that course, but I think about them more as a hobby than a way to earn a living."

"You don't really need to worry about income though do you?"

"I know that, but I want to do something productive with my time, not just get paid pocket money to do my hobby. Neither you nor Mummy need to work for financial reasons, but you do, and you do it because you'd go crazy if you didn't. I know she hated it when she was married to Theo and he stopped her doing anything worthwhile. I feel the same, and I don't want to do something inconsequential."

"So what do you want to do?"

"I've thought about this quite a lot, and I think I'd like to work with you."

"Doing what?"

"I thought as a close protection officer and investigator like you but when the principal specifically asks for a woman."

"That's a bit of a leap isn't it?"

"I know, and I also know that just because I can fight a bit isn't enough for me to even start the training let alone pass it. But I want to be involved and begin the process."

"What about your uni studies?"

"I'm really good at time management and staying focused, so I think I can do both. Most of the other students will be doing a job alongside their studies."

"How do you think you could start; I mean CPOs can't really do ride-a-longs can they?"

"No, but I can help with your online investigative work that you seem to be doing more and more of lately, you know that I've got really good research and IT skills."

"Why are you speaking to me and not your mom? Because you know I won't say no?"

"It's not that at all. I just want you to tell me if I'm being silly for even asking."

"It's a surprise that you asked, and it's not unreasonable that you did, but it would be a complete sea change from what you've been doing."

"Would it though? You always share your work with us as much as you can, so I know what you do. I've watched how you operate under pressure and often thought, 'would I be able to do that?' or even 'I could do that.' You've always encouraged me to go for my goals, as does Mummy, but with you it feels more you're saying, 'Tell me what you want, and I'll do what I can to help you get it.' It's like you take on my ambition. I think it's an American thing. Don't tell Mummy I said that."

"What if it doesn't work out?"

"So what? I know that being a CPO is a tall order, but I could do intelligence work, and if neither works out I'll have my degree to fall back on."

"I'm not going to try to persuade you differently and if you're sure it's what you want I'll do what I can to facilitate it. Perhaps get you to spend some time with Digits if he'll let you. But it's your job to talk about it with your mom."

"You are definitely the best dad in the world. Can we start as soon as I've passed my driving test?"

The gate bell rang before they could further the discussion and Megan came to tell them that Gasowski and Ballard had arrived.

"Good afternoon, detectives, come through to my study. Can we get you a tea or coffee?"

"No thank you. This isn't a social call," Gasowski said.

"I didn't imagine it was, Sergeant. I was trying to be polite, is all."

"Do you mind if I record our conversation?" Ballard asked.

"Not at all."

"Can we start by you explaining what your business with Dennis Hargreaves was."

"You already know that I was asked to look into the abduction of Ariana Georgiou's children. The ransom demand was that she provide access to some hidden resources of her late father. Ms Georgiou said she hoped that I'd have more luck in locating the alleged stash than she would herself."

"Why would she think that?"

"It isn't exactly a secret that Manos Stamelis had spent many years trying to steal my wife's company from her on behalf of the Russian government. Before he died I spent a great deal of time and effort preventing that, and in doing so learned a lot about his illicit financial dealings. She thought I'd have better luck. I hadn't been aware of any secret resources based in this country because I hadn't been looking for them, so I asked Dennis to have a professional look at the records that I'd kept."

"And did he find anything?"

"Yes. He found something that indicated the secret funds could well exist, and that in order for them to exist the arrangement had to have been facilitated by a senior executive of the Financial Conduct Authority."

"Did he name them?"

"Yes, but as the NCA have expressed an interest in this aspect of things I'd rather not go into detail just yet."

"How did he communicate his findings to you?"

"In a report. In fact in two reports, the second being an enhanced version of the first. His first was sent by email, the second on a thumb drive. The purpose of our meeting this morning was to discuss the implications of the second report."

"Mr. Hargreaves computer has been stolen."

"That doesn't surprise me."

"This morning at the crime scene, you suggested that the murders might be connected to your investigations. Would you like to explain how you came to that conclusion."

"It wasn't a conclusion; it was a logical conjecture made from the evidence available and the fact that I'm not a big fan of coincidence. Less than twenty-four hours after forwarding a report to me about criminality involving a puppet of the Russian secret service and/or a senior executive of the FCA, the author of the report gets murdered. If a staid gentleman like Dennis just happened to have two people wanting to execute him, it would be a very big coincidence; don't you think? Not only that, but the thumb drive that the final report was delivered on came complete with spyware that I'm pretty sure he didn't know about."

"Can we have a copy of that report?"

"Of course. Once I've provided one to the NCA, I'll be sure to give a copy to you."

"The NCA and police are all on the same side you know."

"Of course you are, and you all have your own specialties I'm sure. Without wishing to sound patronising, I doubt yours are high finance just as mine aren't."

"Does this mean you've ended your investigations then?"

"Sergeant, these people have made a laundry list of violent and intrusive moves against me and my family. Do you really think I'm going to walk away now?"

"I'll have to re-iterate the warnings given to you by Inspector Jefferies about obstructing a police investigation."

"Thank you Sergeant, but I think you'll find that contrary to hindering or obstructing police investigations, my involvement has been helping to move them along. The discovery of the two children in France for example."

"Can you explain how you achieved that?"

"No. Not least because that was an NCA investigation not yours."

"Can you explain your whereabouts at 06:45 this morning?"

"I was here."

"Can you prove that; did anybody see you?"

"My daughter and I would have been on our second or third lap of the grounds if that helps. Also the exercise app on my phone that links with my watch will be able to give my precise location."

The gate bell rang again and not long after Forester and a woman in her forties were shown into the room by Jason.

"Good afternoon Agent Forester."

"This is my colleague, Elite Agent Vesey. She's more versed in financial crime than myself and works with the Serious Fraud Office, I thought she'd be better placed to look at the things you spoke about."

"Nice to meet you. I'll leave you to introduce each other, I haven't eaten since breakfast, and I need a coffee. Here are two hard copies of the report. I've highlighted the areas of particular concern. Sergeant if you could play the recording of our conversation to the agents, it may save time going over things again." He paused at the door. "Oh and Agent Forester, this isn't an invitation to help yourself to a search through my affairs like you did last time. I'll send some drinks through; call me when you're ready."

Anna and Cassie were in the kitchen with Jason, but there was no sign of Megan.

"We need to send some coffee through to them while they deliberate whose responsibility is whose," he said.

"I'll do that," Jason said. "Sit down and eat. I made you some sandwiches."

"How was your morning, Anna? I heard you going at it with some people when I got back."

"It was Boardman and Carrington thinking they could bully me into changing the company name again. They really haven't got the message yet, that being a woman isn't the same as being weak."

"I don't understand the issue. Why is it so important to them?"

"I don't know either, but in the end I told them that next time they brought the subject up I'd propose changing the name by dropping NorArm, and as I'm effectively the majority shareholder it would go through on the nod. It shut them up."

"It would be my guess that within the next week both of them will be out of work anyway, so it won't be an issue any longer."

"Oh really, what do you know that I don't?"

"I've read Dennis Hargreaves' report."

"I've never met Dennis, but Megan told me what had happened. The poor man. Do you think it's connected to the Ariana thing?"

"There's not a single doubt in my mind that there was a Russian finger on the trigger."

"Cassie's been talking to me about her plans. She tells me that she'd discussed them with you already."

"Yes, while you were having your verbal showdown with Boardman and Carrington."

Cassie offered to leave while they discussed it.

Anna turned to her daughter. "No you don't need to do that, sweetheart. You'll be eighteen in a few months and in charge of most of your own affairs anyway."

"So what do you think of her idea then?"

"I admit I'm not wild about the idea of her being a close protection officer, although I think she'd be a brilliant intelligence analyst, but it's her decision." Anna conceded.

"Robert's coming over tonight, and we're going to London for the day tomorrow."

"Anywhere nice, darling?"

"The Tower of London. Robert's never been."

The gate bell rang again to announce Eli's arrival, Jason let him through, and as he came in through the rear door, Ballard came to ask Drew to join them again.

"Hello Eli, what're you doing here?" the detective asked.

"I work here now."

"Small world, eh? How's your mum?"

"Doing okay now, thanks."

"That's good, give her my regards."

"I will."

"How do you know Eli?"

"I used to go in his dad's pub," Ballard explained. "He's a good kid, but had a few tough breaks, I'm pleased he's found a good place. I was on the team that investigated his dad's murder."

The NCA agents and the detectives spent the next hour going through what had happened with Drew. The four of them left without giving any indication of what they intended to do next, but that was okay with Drew because he'd given them no information about his plans either. He didn't mind being cooperative, but he sure as Hell wasn't going to be feeding them information only for them to decide what or if they were going to use it.

"Have you got a minute, Drew?" Megan asked.

"Sure. What's up?"

"I was wondering if you could manage without me for a few days."

"You got problems?"

"It's Rhian. She and Tina had a bit of a crisis and she's not dealing with it too well."

"No problem. Hopefully we're through the threats against us. Now that the cops are involved in all parts of this investigation, there's nothing for the Russians to gain by going after us again. You go and make sure that Rhian's okay. I'll let you know if I need you again, and if it's a problem I'll get someone else."

"Rhian puts on that brash front, but she's still a pretty fucked up kid inside."

"You send her all our best wishes and tell her it would be great if she could come and stay again some time."

THIRTY

08:00 hours, Third Saturday – Pangbourne Grange

Drew had taken his morning exercise alone after Cassie and Robert left to catch an early train to London,. Megan had left for home the night before straight after dinner, taking with her the good wishes for Rhian from all at Pangbourne Grange.

He was deep in thought as he made himself a cooked breakfast and at first when Jason spoke it didn't register.

"Sorry, what did you say?"

"I said that I hope Rhian is okay."

"Yeah, me too. She's a great kid."

"Megan never told us the whole story, but Rhian let slip a few details to Cassie and I couldn't help overhearing. She was lured from a care home by traffickers when she was eleven, then forced to become a sex slave to some rich bastard in Wales. Megan rescued her, somehow got her a new ID and they've lived together ever since,"

"That's enough to fuck any kid up. Megan probably wouldn't want too many people to know about that though, so best we keep it between ourselves."

"Of course, I shouldn't have said anything. I just get so angry when I hear how some people just destroy other people's lives for their own personal advantage as if they're the only ones that matter. Like the bastards responsible for killing that poor couple you told us about last night."

"Yeah and Lemonis, Stamelis, Ariana Georgiou, and the Russian assholes behind all this latest business; it's greed and self-interest behind all of it."

"I overheard some of the things that were being said in your meeting with those policemen yesterday. They said that Mr. Hargreaves' computer had been stolen so they couldn't look at what he'd been working on."

"That's right."

"I thought that most people saved all their work to the cloud these days, can't the police get access to that?"

"I don't think it's that straightforward. The big tech companies don't like responding to the police. The cops have to get court orders and the tech guys always resist; it can take months."

"Just the three of us for breakfast this morning?" Anna remarked, as she leaned over Drew's shoulder and kissed his cheek.

Jason smiled nostalgically. "It feels strange doesn't it? What're we going to do when Cassie leaves home?"

There was a moment or two of silence before Anna said, "Please don't. I don't want to think about that just yet."

Drew's thoughts were elsewhere. He'd woken after a disturbed night; the Hargreaves' murders had infuriated him. He was the one who had brought Dennis into this business, and he felt obliged to do something about it, but his investigations had stalled. The police and the NCA seemed to be no further ahead. They seemed to have accepted Drew's theory that the most likely prime suspects behind a whole catalogue of crimes were the two Russians, but dismissed the idea that Ariana was a willing participant.

Conscious of the stress that the attacks were having on his whole family, Drew was anxious to bring the business to a close as soon as possible. He had no leads to help him locate the Russians, but something that Jason had just said provoked a thought that might provide him with another thread to pick at. His problem was that he didn't have the necessary tech skills to follow it up. He called Digits, who answered straightaway.

"Hi, I need advice."

"Tell me."

"If I wanted to supplement my cloud with physical storage as a secondary back up, how difficult would it be?"

"Not difficult at all, but if you want the two backups to be synchronised, the software to do it in real time isn't off the shelf in PC World, but it's readily available online if you want me to recommend something."

"Not at the moment. What would the physical storage look like?"

"Just another PC would be good enough as long as the storage capacity and RAM were big enough, and the CPU was sufficiently fast."

"How would you connect them?"

"Any number of ways. Straightforward ethernet cables via a simple hub or server, or via Wi-Fi."

"What if I didn't want anybody to know that something like that existed?"

"Then Wi-Fi is probably the only option, the system would need to be very fast to be efficient though, and most people gaining access to the mother computer could see that the connection exists. It's possible to disguise it, but the person setting it up would need to be quite tech savvy."

"Could Dennis Hargreaves have had something like that?"

"Oh yes, quite possibly. He was a bit of a computer nerd and had almost encyclopaedic knowledge of computer systems; don't ask me why."

"What would he need other than another PC?"

"A pretty good Wi-Fi router. Ideally the client PC or server would be located remotely with its own router, because even the best have limited range."

"I'm going to try and find out if he had anything like that, something that neither the murderers nor the police would have spotted."

"Let me know if there's anything I can do to help."

"Thanks. There was something else I wanted to run past you though, totally unrelated."

"Go on."

"Cassie has expressed an interest in joining the business as a research or intelligence analyst when she finishes her degree. I was wondering if she could spend some time with you time when her studies allow."

"Wow, I wasn't expecting that. An apprentice; what a thought. Yes, I'd be delighted."

"That would be great. Thanks Digits, I'll let you go now."

"Before you go; are you intending to go to look for this supposed alternative backup system yourself?"

"That was the idea, yes."

"If you find it would you, A recognise it, and/or B know what to do with it?"

"Not sure about B, I was planning on sending you a picture and asking you to talk me through it."

"What if I met you there and we do it together?"

"Have you got time?"

"At the moment. I've put everything else on hold and I've been working on your stuff pretty much full time, so I suppose I can say yes."

"That would be great."

"What size overalls do you wear?"

"I've no idea, 58 inch chest and 36 inch inside leg. Does that help?"

"Jesus wept, I heard you were big but for fuck's sake. Your dad must have been massive."

"I've no idea. Why did you ask?"

"Well we can't just turn up, let ourselves into the house and have nobody notice. I'll be in a Ford Transit with Openreach livery and wearing their overalls, but I haven't got anything to fit you. Wear something that makes you look as if you work for a living. Park further down the road until you see me pull up, then join me in the van. I'll see you in about ninety minutes."

Drew had worked with Digits on a number of ops while he was in Delta, and on several occasions since, but they'd never met. Their communications had always been by phone, radio, or Internet.

Dressed in the nearest equivalent to a British working man's clothes that he could muster, Drew waited in his car about a hundred yards from the Hargreaves' home. When the van pulled up behind him, he got out, walked back to the passenger door, and climbed in.

"We finally get to meet eh big guy!" They shook hands.

"Yeah. Where did you borrow this from?"

"I didn't, it's mine. This isn't my first time off the ranch you know. I bought it about two years ago and had the paint job done, comes in handy when I need to get my hands dirty. I've been thinking about this on the way over, if Dennis's setup has actually got this facility and neither the cops nor the intruders have found it, then it won't be in the house. It's probably in the garage or a garden shed, so breaking into the house won't be necessary."

"What about the roof space?"

"With his false leg, I doubt it. Let's go."

He put the van in drive, moved it the short distance and parked across the Hargreaves drive.

Digits got out and confidently walked to the front door carrying a canvas tool bag on a shoulder strap. He ignored the police crime scene tape and knocked. He hadn't expected an answer, and he didn't get one. Meanwhile Drew walked between the house and the garage to the gate that accessed the back garden, which contrary to his expectations was mostly well-kept vegetable beds.

The pedestrian access to the flat-roofed garage had been forced, probably by the police, and Drew looked inside. There was no light switch, the only natural illumination was from the small dirty windows at the top of the hinged wooden doors at the front.

Using the torch on his phone he saw a small collection of garden tools neatly arranged against the rear wall. Then panning around the light fell on a small green estate car from the 60s that didn't look as if it had been driven for twenty years.

"Good God, a Morris Traveller, I haven't seen one of those for years," Digits said from behind him.

"It doesn't look like there's anything in here," Drew observed.

"No, you're right. There's not even an electricity supply by the look of things."

"What about a garden shed?"

"There is one. It's in worse condition than this place, but I suppose we ought to check it out."

Behind the garage was a ramshackle garden shed that looked as if it might collapse at any moment under the weight of its own roof.

Drew reached for the rusty hook and eye door catch.

"Excuse me, are you looking for Dennis's Internet box thing?" a voice said from behind them.

They turned to see a balding man in his sixties peering across the fence from next door.

Digits smiled. "Yes, that's right. The police asked us to take a look."

"It's here behind my pigeon loft."

"Come around, I'll open the gate for you."

They followed the man's directions, and he led them along his garden path past a vegetable patch as immaculately tended as his neighbour's to a comparatively new pigeon loft. Beside the timber structure was a large plastic garden storage box.

"It's in there," The man said pointing. "You're not going to cut it off are you?"

"No, that's not our department."

"Only it provides my internet connection too."

Digits open the doors to the box to reveal a small network server rack with tiny green lights flashing on several modules behind its glass door. He laughed. This is a very elaborate setup for a house, Sir, if you don't mind me saying."

"It was for Dennis, not me. He told me never to tell anybody this, but when everybody thought he'd left the civil service he hadn't really. He was really working undercover to try to find some crooks working in his old department. He said he needed a superfast Internet connection, and he needed to have his equipment where nobody could find it if they broke in.

"I thought it was weird, but he offered to replace my pigeon loft and have this contraption installed at his expense if I'd put it in my name."

"You're very lucky; he's provided you with a Rolls Royce system here."

"Who's going to pay for it now though?"

"If it's in your name, it should be easy enough to have the payments taken from your own account in the future, but that's not our department. I just need to run a few tests and we'll be out of your hair."

"Okay."

"Did you tell the police about this arrangement?"

"I was going to, but after they'd finished asking me if I'd seen anything, they said they'd be in touch if they wanted to know anything else. Then I forgot to mention it."

"Did you see anything?" Drew asked, while Digits plugged a solid-state hard drive into the server via his laptop and begun copying files.

"No, I heard the shots, but I thought it was a motorbike backfiring. Why would anybody do such a horrible thing? They were just a harmless couple; never had a bad word to say about anybody."

"There's no telling the workings of the human mind sometimes."

"Should I tell the police about this do you think?"

"I expect they'll get back to you if it's relevant, but otherwise I wouldn't bother. They'll be too busy looking for the culprits."

"I'll leave you to it then. I'm making a batch of rhubarb and apple jam at the moment. If you could let yourself out when you're finished. Once I've got it on the boil if I let it get too hot it'll spoil."

It took Digits half an hour to finish copying, but then they were on their way back to the van.

"How long will it take to analyse?"

"Difficult to say, because I don't know what I'm looking for. How about I follow you back to your place and we go through it together?"

"That would be great," Drew said. "There's one thing I don't understand though. If Dennis was such a whizz with computers, how come he managed to get himself infected with that virus?"

"He told me a few months ago that he was experimenting with new anti-virus software. It may be that whoever is producing it wasn't keeping their virus definitions up to date. Or alternatively it may just have been bad luck and he picked up a new one. More likely, if these fucking Russians were only looking to steal or corrupt recently created files they'll have used one of their own with only limited functions. It often takes a week or two to identify a new one, so if it hadn't been used before then it could have slipped the net."

THIRTY-ONE

15:00 hours, Third Saturday – Pangbourne Grange

Back at the house Drew introduced Digits to Anna and Jason.

"I've heard you mentioned so many times over the years it's lovely to put a face to a name, but I can't keep calling you Digits. What's your real name."

"People who've been brought up properly call me Michael."

"Well then, Michael; I hope you'll stay for dinner."

"It would be rude not to. Thank you very much."

In the study, the top of Drew's big desk soon became practically invisible under pieces of electronic gadgetry.

"First we've got to figure out his passwords, but thankfully he's helped us out there; the system password was on the door of the server rack. All we need to do now is figure out his software password."

"How the hell do we do that?"

"Most people are simple folk, and I doubt that Dennis was much different. Any idea of his wife's name?"

"No, he called her mother."

He turned to his laptop and tapped away the keys and within a few minutes he announced. "Mildred Beryl Walters born 29 February 1952. Excellent, let's start with that."

He opened another piece of software and used the pieces of information to complete various fields on the screen and then pressed enter.

"Okay now we wait. You couldn't rustle up a sandwich could you, I hadn't had breakfast when you called."

"Why the Hell didn't you say?" He looked at his watch, it was almost one o'clock.

The conversation over the food largely centred on Cassie's kidnapping in Canada and the USA two years earlier.

Digits remarked, "She must be a pretty tough kid to put all that behind her and still be ready to go to uni?"

"After the first business when her sister was taken she asked Drew to teach her self-defence. It turned out she wanted to learn more than mere defence. She's a fast learner and very tenacious. In another life she'd have been good to have around on ops. Losing her sister that way had made her angry and galvanised her into wanting to know how to hurt people who went after her that way again."

They were halfway through their second hot drink when Digit's phone beeped twice. "That was quick, sometimes it can take hours.

They returned to the study and Digits connected a mouse to the computer.

"There we are," he said, pointing at the screen, which displayed a column of sets of seemingly random collections of Alpha numeric characters and letters. '29M!Ldr3DB3r!lO252' was highlighted and flashing.

"How did it come to that?"

"Look at it, 29 that was the day of her birth, then at the end is February fifty-two. In between is Mildred Beril. Beryl has been misspelled to confuse anybody guessing it, but my little programme is too clever for that."

"Did you write that programme then?"

"Well there others available on the dark web, but I like to steer clear of that cess pool, and it was a good little project to work on when I first went private. The MoD have got something similar, but I think mine is better. Totally illegal though, but it's a nice little earner."

"Do you sell it?"

"No way, but using it gets a lot of my bread-and-butter clients out of trouble."

"Does the password work though?"

He copied the number into his RAM, switched screens, and pasted it back in when prompted. Then, opening a hard disk file manager, he asked, "What do you want to look for?"

"I guess we need to see the things he'd been working on in the few days before he died."

Digits changed the display so that the files were displayed in reverse date order and right at the top was a video file. When he opened it the first thing they saw was the wall behind Dennis's chair.

"It's his webcam footage," Drew said.

A few seconds later Dennis's face appeared looking scared.

"Is there sound?"

Digits clicked on an icon, and they heard, "But I don't know what you're looking for."

A voice from out of shot said, "You do work for fucking Parker bastard. We want know what you find out."

"He asked me if I could recover some files off a broken hard drive, but I couldn't."

"You fucking lying bastard. Show me what you did."

They watched Dennis's face as he typed. Then he turned the laptop toward the other speaker and they heard him say, "There you see it was so corrupted that was all you could see."

They saw two other people in the room, one was Turgenev the other was Sokolov.

"You think I fucking stupid. That not from Parker; that from someone else."

"No, it's from Mr. Parker. It's from his son's laptop, I promise you."

"Parker not have son, you lying cunt. Hit him Miron."

They watched Sokolov charge across the room and heard Dennis cry out.

Then Turgenev said, "Now get up and find what Parker wanted you find."

"That's it; you see there was nothing to find, not on a disk anyway. He gave me a pile of papers and asked me to look to see what I could find, but I searched everything line by line. There was nothing there, so I sent the papers back."

"Sokolov, hit him again."

"It won't matter how many times you hit me; I can't show you something that doesn't exist."

Sokolov hit him again and the computer was knocked sideways, still showing them the thug dragging Dennis back onto his chair. His eye was swollen, and blood was pouring down his face.

"Let me bring the old bag in here," another voice said.

"That good idea. How you like we give mother good beating? That help you find what Parker wanted; no?"

Dennis righted the screen turning it back towards the door and Sturgess appeared pushing Dennis's elderly wife in front of him.

"Leave her alone you ignorant cowardly bastards."

Astonished, they watched Mildred turn toward Sturgess and punch him. "What've you done to my Dennis?"

The blow would have been completely ineffective, but it clearly enraged its recipient, who simply lifted his gun and shot her. The watchers couldn't see how she fell, but she made no further sound.

"You stupid English cunt. You know nothing. How can we use her make him give us what we want now?"

"I'll make him talk," Sturgess shouted.

"I not want him to talk. I want him find things on computer, you stupid dumb English asshole."

"Why should I do anything for you now you've killed my wife."

They saw Sturgess stride across the room and point the gun towards where Dennis must have been sitting.

"Give them what they want, or I'll put a bullet between your eyes you dumb old cunt.

"I'll tell you this. What you're looking for is probably somewhere on this computer. If you can find it after you've killed me then you could have made a decent living without resorting to murder. So if you're going to kill me you'd better go ahead and do it. But you're not that clever are you? In fact you're just what that Russian cunt said, *a dumb English arsehole.*"

The rage in Sturgess eyes was obvious. His lips drew back over his clenched teeth, and he went bright red as he pulled the trigger, three times.

There was a momentary quiet before the two Russians began shouting at each other in their own language. Then Turgenev said, "Take fucking computer you dumb asshole. We get someone else to look."

The screen went black and then returned to the file manager.

Neither of them spoke for a few seconds, until Digits said, "Jesus Drew, I knew he was a gutsy bastard, but for fuck's sake..."

"These bastards have to be stopped soon, and I need to be the one to do it."

"I'm right there with you bro."

"What else is there for the previous day or two?"

Other than diary entries, and a few other inconsequential documents, there were only about thirty files that post-dated the report that Dennis had written for Drew. Most of them were business letters alongside one or two quotations for his services and a contract refusal.

Lastly they found an unfinished document where Drew appeared to be the intended recipient. It listed bank accounts for payers and payees of money from accounts in the two hedge funds.

"Bingo," Drew announced.

"It doesn't help us to get those Russian bastards though."

"It seems to me that what the Russians have been after all along is what's in that unfinished memo. In other words what I've suspected for some time."

"Tell me how it works," Glover asked.

"Stamelis had been hiving off a percentage for himself from the profits he was making with Russian money and salting it away. All the time he was working on his scheme to steal Silico from Anna and her first husband. As the astute investor he was, he recognised the company's huge potential and decided to invest what he regarded as his own money in the firm. Of course he couldn't do it directly in his own name, so the hedge fund option was the only way. I'm assuming he corrupted people in the hedge funds to allow him to invest under assumed names, probably by giving them a percentage of the take. I'd already guessed that the assumed name in the Alhambra fund was Percy Belton, and as we can see from that memo, they used it in the Nevada Foothills fund as well.

"But after Stamelis disappeared, the imposters must have thought all their birthdays and Christmases had come at once and begun pocketing all the profits for themselves. At the time, his daughter very likely either didn't know of the secret stash's existence or didn't know where it was, although we can't be sure if she was getting an income or not. Without a death certificate, the will couldn't be executed, so her entitlement to any assets was effectively frozen. Meanwhile the rake off for the hedge fund crooks was mounting.

"Then along comes Turgenev and his pal, who either knew or strongly suspected the existence of Stamelis's little treasure trove, but they themselves had only limited resources and had gone for the Hail Mary approach to find it.

"This is the bit where my speculation becomes influenced by my knowledge of Stamelis's daughter. The Russians first stop was to approach her and try to force her to reveal what she knows. Somehow during that conversation she convinces them that she knows nothing and the only person who might know who's involved is me. That's when they come up with the idea of faking the kidnapping to drag me in to find it on their behalf."

Digits thought about what Drew had told him. "So why all the attempts to kill you?"

"I'm not sure if the first attempts were supposed to kill me or just look that way to make sure I didn't just tell Georgiou to fuck off. I think that when they found out about the existence of the Alhambra fund they thought that was it. But by the time they learned about Foothills, they must have thought that I was getting too close. But remember, this Turgenev is a psychopath. His capacity for rational thought is reduced every time he has what he perceives as a setback."

"If the Georgiou woman didn't know about the hedge fund investments, how come the Russians got onto Babcock and Braithwaite?"

Drew thought for a few seconds. "They could only have found out about them from Ariana. She must have been double dealing with the hedge fund guys and the Russians. She paid Fletcher to fix our alarm system, and I've been working on the assumption that the arson attack at our house was done on behalf of Carrington. If that's the case, do the Russians know that she arranged it? The truth is that all of this is speculation. I doubt that the hedge fund guys are working with Turgenev, but Georgiou is undeniably colluding with him in one way or another."

"They could've had someone like Dennis looking into the finances of the hedge funds and found out about Babcock and Braithwaite that way."

"Good point, but who?"

"There's always the bent FCA executive. How much do we know about this Sokolov guy?"

"You're the one who identified him."

"From what I recall he was just a finance officer. Let me spend a bit of time working on that. If they'd been given some sort of lead to one or both hedge funds, and they had someone with Dennis's kind of skills, they could have found a spoor to follow."

"That sounds great, but there are two things I haven't got the first idea what they mean."

"What are those?"

"What the fuck is it with maroon coloured Land Rovers, and why they recruited Sturgess?"

"I don't think they're connected," Digits told him.

"How do you mean?"

"Think about it. The businesses with your security alarm and with Percy Belton's car could have been done by anyone with a good understanding of electronics. If they'd wanted to be really sure of having an effect and they had an explosives expert at hand they would have blown something up. I think that both of those incidents were instigated by someone in one of the hedge funds. Maybe they're trying to shut you up so they can do a deal with the Russians."

"In that case it must be Carrington."

"On top of that, whatever was planned with the Land Rovers and the minibus is almost certainly dead in the water now because the minibus and most of their fleet of Land Rovers were destroyed in the barn fire. Also they must know by now that we suspect something involving them. Let me look closer at Carrington and Boardman, who from what Dennis was saying in that memo are the prime suspects."

"Do you mind if I interrupt?" Anna asked from the doorway.

"Sure thing, sweetheart."

"I've been listening to what you say, and it all makes perfect sense, except for one thing."

"What's that?"

"At what point and how did Carrington and Boardman discover that the Russians were looking for the money?"

"We haven't figured that out yet."

"It would be my guess that Ariana has been taking a cut from the hedge fund crooks all along, and when the Russians came along she and her two fellow conspirators were spooked. She probably thinks that when her father is finally declared dead, she'll be able to have the will executed and stake her claim to whatever is being held in the two funds."

"Do you think that Boardman and Carrington are aware of each other?"

"Maybe not at first but I'd be surprised if they still aren't. They always seem to be singing the same tune at board meetings, and the way they're colluding over the company name change business is a case in point. Although whether that's got anything to do with what else is happening God only knows."

Thinking aloud, Drew speculated "When this scheme of Stamelis was set up, NorArm and Silico were still separate companies. Maybe they think that if Silico's name were erased it makes it easier to cash the holdings out." .

Anna thought about that. "It wouldn't benefit Boardman or Carrington, but it could quite possibly benefit Ariana after Stamelis death is accepted."

Drew nodded. "If that's the case then she's probably putting the squeeze on them to get the name changed; some sort of blackmail."

"If we get these assholes, what happens to the money?" Digits asked.

"It's not important as long as it doesn't go to Ariana, Turgenev, Boardman or Carrington or anybody else involved, and I'll do whatever I can to see that they don't," Drew said. Those listening knew that he meant every word.

"Anyway chaps, what I originally came to ask was Indian or Chinese?"

Over their meal, Digits revealed what Drew didn't know and would never have guessed. Dennis Hargreaves had never been just a civil servant. He'd been a captain in the SAS and lost his leg in Belfast in the eighties before becoming an SIS agent working undercover in Bosnia in 1994 and had narrowly escaped capture when he was betrayed to Milosevic's forces.

Mildred had been his handler.

THIRTY-TWO

Bocharov Ruchey, a Government dacha on the Black Sea, Sochi, Russia

Sergei Babanin was a former Major in the 3rd Spetnaz Brigade, awarded the Order of Zhukov for his services in the annexation of Crimea 2014, an honour only awarded to the bravest of military unit commanders. He waited to be escorted into a room to meet with a man who terrified almost everyone he met and millions of people whom he hadn't. Nobody offered him a seat and it wouldn't have occurred to him to take one.

Unlike most of his predecessors, he was there at his own request. Acting on his own initiative he'd conducted an operation and wanted to report his success. Babanin wasn't scared, as many of those before him standing on that piece of carpet had been. In fact he was expecting congratulations and hoping for a promotion.

Two years earlier Babanin had been given temporary control of a vast empire of assets to operate for the benefit of the Russian state, and by his own estimation, it had gone well. He'd had certainly had no complaints.

He'd come to this room on several previous occasions to give progress reports, sharing the space with his host's personal security guards and one of his several female secretaries. A wait of at least an hour was normal, so he was mildly surprised when after only five minutes, the silence was broken by a quiet buzzer on the woman's desk. She looked up and nodded to one of the guards.

"We can go in now, Mr. Babanin," the guard said, completing the ritual that had been performed by on thousands of other occasions.

Like all before him, he'd been meticulously searched for weapons on his arrival. Nevertheless he was now frisked again. The guard opened the door and Babanin unevenly but confidently stepped through, followed by the guards, the limp caused by a poorly-fitting artificial leg noticeable to all.

His host, Vladimir Putin, President of Russia, looked up from a document he'd been reading. "Comrade Babanin, I understand you have good news."

"Yes sir, I've been making extensive enquiries and they've at last borne fruit. The traitor Turgenev has been located in England in the company of a Miron Sokolov, a former finance officer in the Turgenev department stores."

"I thought I remember you telling me that they drowned in the Gulf of Finland attempting to flee."

"All the indications were that that's what happened. The body of Turgenev's cousin was washed up on the Finnish coast some days after he vanished."

"I see, but now, all this time later you tell me that they're in the UK. How was this discovered?"

"I was informed by departments of the FSB that there had been renewed interest in Turgenev and Sokolov by an unidentified hacker, suspected of operating somewhere in London."

"And how did you respond to this information?"

"I asked FSB to make a facial recognition search of CCTV cameras in London, and Turgenev was picked up several times in the vicinity of Hampstead, a wealthy area in North London. After several days agents found that the two traitors had called on the London home of Manos Stamelis' daughter."

"What did you do with that information?"

"I authorised our agents to question her about why the traitors had been there. After they'd applied their interrogation techniques, she quickly revealed that Stamelis had for years been systematically stealing undisclosed profits and squirreling them away for himself. She believed it was his escape fund in case things went badly for him as our agent."

"I assume you've made arrangements to recover those assets."

"It's difficult, Sir. Stamelis has been extremely clever in disguising where the money is and made it inaccessible to us at present, but I've devised a plan that I hope will at the very least prevent Turgenev, Sokolov or Stamelis daughter gaining access to them."

"Explain."

"I asked our agents to plant somebody next to Turgenev and act in our interests to sabotage their efforts to recover."

"How?"

"They've chosen a man called Sturgess, a former British soldier with explosives expertise."

"Who's financing this incursion? I'm assuming that the British soldier isn't."

"I authorised an advance of one million pounds, that he's to repay from whatever he can recover from the traitors or the Georgiou woman."

"And how is this Sturgess going to achieve what you plan?"

"His instructions are to ensure whenever they get close to discovering where the money is, he is to disrupt their efforts. He's devised a clever plan to kill the two traitors with explosives at the end using a series of decoy vehicles allowing him to escape discovery."

"Do you know where the money is?"

"Not yet in precise terms, Comrade President. The Georgiou woman says she knows of its existence but not its location or how to access it. She revealed that she'd engaged the services of a specialist to try to learn more. However, the traitors weren't happy with that, told her that they wouldn't need him, and attempted to have him killed. Unfortunately, the attempt failed. The man seemed to be getting closer to discovering the location of this money, so I asked Sturgess to use other methods to discourage him from continuing his investigations, including threatening his family."

"Why?"

"Because I didn't want the UK authorities learning about it."

"What do you know of this specialist?"

"His name is Parker, an American with special forces experience living in the UK."

"Would that be Drew Parker?"

"That's right, Sir. Do you know of him?"

Putin knew a lot about Parker, he was the man responsible for Stamelis disappearance and thereby making the Russian assets that the Greek had been holding available for recovery. He ignored Babanin's question. "How big is this secret fund?"

"At the moment we don't know, but I'm sure it is significant."

"But you don't think we can recover it anyway?"

Babanin was suddenly no longer quite so sure of himself. "No sir, I don't think so."

"To summarise the situation as it stands then. You tell me that Turgenev is dead along with his accomplice Sokolov. Then fifteen months later you discover that you were wrong, and without authority you approved the use of valuable Russian assets on foreign soil. You then develop an unauthorised masterplan to prevent the traitors from recovering assets which you believe to be unrecoverable, and to

225

accomplish this you authorise the gift of a million pounds of Russian money to a foreign national. Is that correct?"

"Yes, Comrade Putin," Babanin admitted, his confidence slipping away fast.

"All this risk, effort and expense over what may turn out to be only a few million pounds. What was the point?"

"To prevent any chance of Turgenev and Sokolov getting hold of the money, Sir."

"We'd normally do that by killing them."

"Yes, Sir, but at this sensitive time I thought assassinations on British soil could cause an international incident."

"And you didn't think that all these other fucking stupid things that you've been doing wouldn't?"

"I'll get somebody to deal with the traitors immediately sir."

"No you won't because it isn't necessary. The only good thing about this is the involvement of Parker, One thing we know about him is that, now that you've threatened his family, he won't rest until Turgenev and Sokolov are dead. That way we can't be accused of it."

"What about the money?"

"Fuck the money; and fuck you. Get this fucking idiot out of here and dispose of him will you, Orlov," the dictator demanded of the senior guard.

"Yes, Sir."

The two guards grabbed Babanin by the arms and dragged him out of the room.

Putin picked up a phone. "Get Gribov in here now."

A few minutes later the door opened and a short man in his sixties wearing camouflage fatigues with the insignia of a Lieutenant General walked through.

Leonid Gribov was a lifetime veteran of the Russian army, and loyal supporter of Putin. He was popular with the President because he never asked for or expected accolades for his consistent performance yet the list of his successes both military and political was very long and continued to grow.

"Gribov, I take it you were listening to that imbecile as I asked."

"Yes Comrade Putin, Sir." He replied, standing rigidly at attention.

"Now is your moment to step out of uniform, at least for a time. I need you to take over from Babanin with immediate effect. Your first job is to look into everything that that fucking, gibbering baboon has done in the last two years and put a stop to it until we find out what it is. First on your list is to deal with the disaster in London and salvage anything you can from it. Be sure to commit no more than the minimum resources."

"Comrade President, as you instructed, I've been examining the records of Babanin's actions so far, and I think it might be worth approaching the two crooks, Boardman and Carrington and persuading them to handover what is rightfully ours."

"Can that be done without any assassinations? They're not important enough to make the trouble worthwhile?"

"It'll depend on whether, they've already been made aware of the Russian interest."

"Very well, if you think you can recover a significant sum, then go ahead, but at the first sign that you think our involvement could become exposed, pull out. I don't want anything being traced back to us."

THIRTY-THREE

06:45 hours, Third Sunday – Pangbourne Grange

Cassie and Robert returned from London in time to be introduced to Digits before he left for home.

"Mummy told me about what happened to that poor man and his wife. Robert had already read about it and pointed it out to me because it was so close to us. I didn't know he'd been working for you."

"He was a really brave and decent man who didn't deserve to die like that, and neither did his wife."

"Mr. Glover seems really nice; I'm looking forward to learning from him."

"There's an awful lot to learn, Digits has had the advantage of military training at the expense of the UK state, that sort of training isn't available in civilian life. Not only that, ten years as an analyst in the UK Strategic Command Defence Intelligence, specialising in SIGINT. During that time he'll have made dozens if not hundreds of contacts, learned who to trust and who not to, and conversely they'll have got to know him. You set yourself a tough mountain to climb, sweetheart."

"But you're not saying don't do it?"

"When I was your age, people were always telling me not to do something, or that I wasn't capable of doing them, and it only made me want to do them more. My trouble was that I hadn't been taught right from wrong, so I didn't always take notice of the right people or choose the right path. You don't need to overcome that hurdle."

"Do you think I could be any good at it, Dad?"

"I think that if it's possible for you to do it, then you will, but it's a tall order, and lot will depend on how much people take you seriously, so working under a pseudonym might be best until you've built a reputation."

"I was thinking it might be best to do that anyway, for security reasons."

"Good thinking. Are you going to the cricket this afternoon?"

"The match has been called off. The other side can't get enough players."

"Have you got anything else planned, sweetheart?"

"Robert wants to have lunch with his mum and dad then work on something to take into the office tomorrow, so I'm free."

"I'm planning on going to see Percy, and I'd like for you to come along."

"With Mummy as well?"

"No, just you."

He stopped at the oak tree, indicating that he wanted to talk.

"Is there something wrong?"

"I hope not, sweetheart, but if there is, I'm hoping it's not, but the business with the investments in Silico could be very serious, and it's very strange. I think it's possible that Percy knows more than he's been prepared to admit. The thing is, I know he's a good man, and he'd never knowingly do anything that he thought for one moment would harm either of you. I suspect though, that he may have been drawn into something he didn't understand the full ramifications of, and he doesn't know what to do about it."

"What can I do though?"

"I don't want to compromise your mom's professional position, and if she learns something that impacts on the company, she'll feel obliged to repeat it to the board. I don't think that Percy could lie to either you or your mom directly so I'm hoping that he might reveal something that he hasn't already."

"I couldn't lie to Mummy though Dad."

"I know that. Neither could I, and I wouldn't want you to. I've told her why I'm going and that I might ask you to go along. She understands and will try not to ask us too many penetrating questions afterwards. If she asks us a direct question though, then we'll just have to answer it or tell her why we can't."

"Okay, I suppose. I hate this."

"Me too, but we need to rid these assholes from our lives. I think we're getting close now, and I'm hoping that if Percy can give us a lead it might be over in a day or two."

It was two o'clock when Drew and Cassie turned up at Percy's door unannounced. His car was on the drive, so they were confident he'd be at home. Drew rang the bell, but when there was no reply he rang again.

"I'm going to look around the back. Go across and wait in front of Tammy's house for the moment, but if I don't let you in within three minutes, or if someone else other than me or Percy opens the door, call the police."

The only way to the rear of the property was via the gate at the side of the attached garage or by climbing the fence into the back garden. He grabbed the wrecking bar that had found its way from Megan's trunk into his own. But before clambering over the six-foot timber barrier, he tried the gate that he knew was normally kept bolted. It opened.

The gate wasn't in great condition, and neither were its hinges, they creaked noisily but he hoped it was too far from the house to be heard inside. He crept along the back of the garage toward the house and peeped into a utility room window but there was nothing unusual to see. Another few steps brought him to the back door. That lock, however, was damaged and had obviously been forced.

He sent a quick text to Cassie, 'There's been a break-in Call 999, and tell them there's an elderly man who may be in trouble. RSVP'

Seconds later his silenced phone vibrated in his hand as Cassie acknowledged.

He pushed the door and to his relief it noiselessly opened into the rear lobby. He moved silently across the tiled floor into the vacant kitchen. Now he could hear voices but at first he couldn't make out what they were saying.

Moving into the hall he recognised Turgenev's voice. "You think we not shoot people eh, English cunt."

Percy weakly replied. "It wasn't me. Iit was my secretary pretending to be me."

"Shoot him, Miron. Kill that useless English piece shit."

"No...!"

The deafening sound of two gunshots rang through the house. Drew burst into the rear living room where Sokolov stood over Sturgess' still twitching body, and Turgenev waited ready to hit the badly beaten Percy with a wooden rolling pin.

Drew's assessment of the situation was instant and in a single motion he viciously swung the crowbar with all the strength he could muster.

Sokolov barely had time to register the big man's presence in the room before the swinging steel bar hit him in the side of the head, shattering his skull. The momentum of Drew's action threw him off balance and he staggered against the wall, and by the time he'd recovered Turgenev had escaped into the garden through an open patio door.

Percy was seated in an armchair, obviously in a bad way, so Drew had to fight the instinct to chase the fleeing Russian and stay to assist his family friend. The elderly man's face was swollen and distorted. His right arm was twisted at an unnatural angle and his breathing was irregular.

Taking out his phone he called 999 and asked for an ambulance for the severely beaten man, wfo was now evidencing breathing difficulties. Next he called Cassie. There was no reply, and it went to voicemail. He repeated the action three more times before she breathlessly answered.

"I'm here, Daddy."

"Where were you? I've been going crazy?"

"I chased that Russian man, but he got away. I hurt him though. Are you alright? What about Uncle Percy?"

"Percy's in a bad way, but I'm fine. I've already called an ambulance, but can you call them again; we need them here in a hurry. Did you call the cops?"

"Yes."

"I'll call them again anyway. Call your mom and tell them I'm likely to be needing that solicitor again."

After telling the police control room who he was, and that he was calling from the scene of a previous call, where there had been an armed home invasion. One of the invaders had shot another and subsequently been killed; another had escaped. He told them Sergeant Gasowski had been in charge of a related enquiry and the NCA were involved.

The ambulance arrived and were reluctant to enter a building where there had been shooting. Their protocols required them to wait for clearance from the police.

Drew stood at the door arguing with them. "Look you were here at this house only a week or two ago and drove me away in the back of a meat wagon after one of those dead assholes in there tried to kill me. If you don't get in there soon you'll be taking the poor old man that lives here to the morgue not the hospital." He knew that not all of that statement was strictly true but at that moment he didn't think it mattered.

Cassie rushed to join her father. "What's wrong with you?" she shouted at the paramedics. "My uncle's in there dying, and you're standing out here arguing over rules and regulations. Let me get in there. Daddy, I need to see Uncle Percy."

Ignoring the protests of a paramedic and snatching her sleeve from his grasp, she pushed past her father. She was inside for less than twenty seconds before coming back to scream at the paramedics, "Get in there now you stupid bastards, he's dying!"

The female paramedic pushed through and immediately returned. "Jess get in here quick, bring a gurney."

Cassie rushed back inside with the medic. The other medic leapt into action, hurrying back to the ambulance before returning with the stretcher. Drew stepped out of his way and waited for the police. First to arrive was a patrol car with a single very young cop. He was one of those who'd come to the house on the previous occasion.

Drew turned around and put his hands behind him. "I'm guessing you'll want to cuff me?"

No sooner had the second cop car arrived than the paramedics came hurrying out pushing a wheeled stretcher with Percy on it, an oxygen mask clamped to his face. Cassie came to stand by her handcuffed father.

"How is he, sweetheart?"

"I don't know, Daddy, he's still alive but he isn't conscious."

"Okay, Mr. Parker let's have you in the back of my car 'till CID get here eh?" the young cop said and left him under the observation of another officer.

Next on the scene were Anna and Jason. She marched up to the cop standing outside the car with Drew sat inside and stood right in front of it. "I hope you're not arresting my husband again, just for attempting to save the life of a dear family friend from homicidal maniacs."

"Ma'am, your husband isn't under arrest at the moment. He volunteered to come to the station to help with our enquiries."

"Why is he in handcuffs then?"

"He offered his hands for restraint. My colleague thought it would be impolite not to oblige."

She looked at Drew through the closed window. He just smiled and shrugged.

Gasowski and Ballard were next to arrive. The sergeant glanced at Drew, and walked to the front door of the house to talk to the other cops. One of them was clearly struggling to describe the situation, pointing variously at the house, Drew, and Cassie who was now standing with Jason and her mother.

Cassie abandoned Jason and in a perfect imitation of her mother stormed up the drive to the detectives and blasted them with her own version of what she thought should happen next.

Gasowski listened to what she said, and then gestured to Ballard. She was obviously being asked to give a preliminary statement in a fashion that indicated the junior detective should take notes.

Finally Gasowski instructed two of the patrol cops to take Drew back to the station where he was booked in, uncuffed, and taken to a holding cell, which he thought odd because he hadn't even been arrested. He was asked to give them his clothes for forensic examination, and once again there were no suitable overalls to fit him.

He lay down on the crude bed in his underwear, closed his eyes and waited.

THIRTY-FOUR

17:00 hours, Third Sunday – Thames Valley Police Station, Reading, Berkshire

It was well over an hour before someone brought him something to wear, a grey training suit that, as before, was way too small. Then nearly another hour before he was taken to an interview room where his wheelchair bound solicitor was waiting.

"We meet again, Mr. Parker, and so soon."

"Afternoon, Alli."

"Let's try and get this over as quickly as possible shall we? I got a pretty good overview of events before the shooting and immediately after from your daughter's interview, but if you can talk me through the whole thing from start to finish. I'm proposing we do the same as before, refuse to answer questions and just give them a prepared statement, if that's okay with you."

"It's fine but I haven't been arrested, so I guess I could just walk straight out of here."

"Legally yes, but I wouldn't advise it. There are two dead people back at the crime scene and they're rightly taking this seriously. Let's not mention the young constable's faux pas about the lack of a formal arrest unless it becomes necessary. It looks good that you're cooperating. Tell me what happened."

It took nearly an hour to bring the lawyer up to date and prepare a statement. Alli looked at it and said. "That is completely consistent with your daughter's statement and the evidence the police have given me so far so that's great. I can't see any reason why you both can't be released without charge."

"Are you telling me that they've got Cassie locked up in here too?"

"She's in another interview room. They arrested her for assaulting an elderly man, who I believe must have been your Mr. Turgenev."

He knocked on the door to tell them he was ready, but the cop outside said they weren't yet; they'd been asked to wait for the NCA. "We'll take you back to your cell in a few minutes. I can let you out, Ms Scrivens."

"My client has been cooperative and patient and has prepared a statement. As he isn't under arrest he chooses to leave now and make himself available for interview by the National Crime Agency's representatives should they care to make an appointment."

"Not under arrest. I don't understand," the cop said, taking the pieces of paper. He left them, returning ten minutes later with Gasowski.

"Okay, you can go," the detective said.

"Mr. Parker would like his personal possessions returned. You can hold on to his clothes if you think it's worth the trouble."

Gasowski turned away, leaving the junior cop to deal with the formalities.

Alli stopped him. "Please make sure that Miss Parker-West is allowed to leave with him."

In the entrance lobby Anna and Jason were waiting, both wearing worried frowns.

"Where's Cassie?" Anna asked.

"I think she'll be out in a minute," Alli told her.

"What was all that about me not being arrested do you think?"

"It's a first in my experience, but my guess is that the NCA had a tag on your name, and they cleared waiving the arrest without direct evidence of your guilt. Unfortunately, you put yourself in the frame by asking to be handcuffed."

"You Brits are a weird lot sometimes."

Anna knocked on the window to the reception and asked the weary looking clerk, "Haven't you got anything else for my husband to wear. He looks ridiculous in that outfit."

"I'm sorry Ma'am we don't cater for the BFGs of this world. Try M&S."

Anna couldn't resist a smile.

The door beside the desk opened and Cassie walked through.

The first words out of her mouth were, "How's Uncle Percy? They won't tell me?"

"We don't know yet, sweetheart. They won't tell us either. Let's go home and get your father some decent clothes. Then we can go to the hospital to see if we can learn more."

When they thanked Alli; she replied that the case of Prosecco that Drew had sent last time was thanks enough.

"Were you frightened, darling?" Anna asked her daughter when they were in the car.

"Not really. I was too worried about Uncle Percy."

"Why did they arrest you? I don't understand."

"I'd called the police, but while I was calling you I saw this man run out of the gate. I recognised him from the photos so I chased after him. He was limping and couldn't run very fast, and I easily caught him up. I wrestled with him and managed to get him in an armlock, but another old man came out of his house, started hitting me and telling me to leave the Russian man alone. I tried to explain the Russian was an escaping criminal, but he wouldn't believe me and grabbed my tit. That surprised me so much that the Russian broke free and hit me in the eye. Before I could catch him again he jumped in a car and drove away. The old man made a big fuss to one of the policeman, so they arrested me."

"Were you hurt?"

"No more than when I spar with Dad sometimes."

"Perverted old git," Jason remarked. "What's that blood on your top?"

"It's off Turgenev's shoulder. It must be from where Dad shot him last time."

"Let's grab a sandwich and get your father some respectable clothes to go back to the hospital in. We don't know how long we'll be," Anna said.

Jason dropped them off at Percy's house to collect Drew's car.

When they got to the hospital A&E Department they had to argue that Anna and Cassie ought to be given information about him because they were Percy's godchildren, and he didn't have any close family. Eventually they were told that Percy had been sent for surgery and was likely to be moved to intensive care later.

It was two hours before anybody could tell them how their injured friend was, and the news wasn't encouraging. The doctor told them that Percy was stable but not out of the woods. During the beating he'd sustained a collapsed lung, ruptured spleen, broken rib, nose, and arm, as well as a cracked eye socket which might require further surgery. It would be at least twenty-four hours before he could receive visitors and the police had asked to speak to him as soon as he regained consciousness.

Both Anna and Cassie were deeply shocked by what had happened and spoke very little on the way back to the Grange. They left it to Drew to update Jason with the latest on Percy.

It was gone nine-thirty when Drew's phone rang.

"Agent Forester, I've been expecting your call."

"We need to talk."

"I agree. How soon can you get here?"

"I propose nine-thirty tomorrow. We'll come to you. I expect the locals will want to be there."

"That suits me perfectly. I've an important meeting later on in the day."

THIRTY-FIVE

06:00 hours, Third Monday – Pangbourne Grange

Drew and Cassie met on the landing as usual, and both were surprised when Anna joined them. She was still in a bathrobe.

"I couldn't sleep. I'm going to call the hospital, then have a swim to try and clear my head."

On their exercise, Cassie was clearly out to push herself, and their pace was considerably faster than usual, which suited Drew. There was no conversation between them until they reached the tree on their tenth lap when Cassie stopped with her hands on her knees to catch her breath. When she'd got it close to normal, Drew asked, "How are you, sweetheart?"

"Angry, fucking angry. Those bastards aren't human. Torturing an old man like that, to try to get their hands on something that may not even exist, and behaving as if they had some right to it. If it belongs to anybody at all, it belongs to the Russian people. It was stolen from them, or at least the seed money was. Putin and his henchmen stole it, gave it to ruthless assholes like Stamelis to exploit whoever they could, who stole some for himself. Now others are fighting to claim it as theirs. It's like a Chaucerian tale."

"I don't know what that is, but if it means a story with a moral then you're right. There has to be some sort of lesson in there somewhere."

"Don't the police have any idea where Turgenev is? He keeps appearing out of nowhere and then disappearing again."

"He's clearly got somewhere to hole up, but I've no idea how we find out where it is."

"Do you think that Ariana's helping him out?"

"Probably; if not her then someone else, but that's not what's most worrying me at the moment. Now all his accomplices have been killed, I'm concerned that if he's caught, the Secret Service might try to give him some sort of break, in return for information about Putin."

"Would they do that?"

"Without a second thought, but I'm also worried how he's managed to recruit all the minor league crooks. They're a disparate bunch, from different areas and different backgrounds. Turgenev can't just have gone into a pub and asked around for crims looking for work. They've had help in that respect. My guess would be a bent copper."

"I'm so scared about Percy though, Dad. He's been there for me all my life. He was the one that recruited you and got us through all that business with Theo."

"I understand, I really do. I felt the same about my grandma. She was a tough old bird, always there putting me in my place and trying to pick up the pieces after I fucked up. When she passed it was like losing part of me. If it hadn't been for Lina, I'd have gone right back where I was before. People like that leave a big piece of them behind when they're not there; sometimes it's a hole, sometimes it's memories, sometimes a piece of their goodness."

"Do you think that Percy is going to die?"

"I hope not but I think it's possible. It's a long way back for a man of his age, and he wasn't in the best of health."

"I hope I'm not around when Turgenev shows up again, because I might kill him."

"If someone puts you in a position that you've no choice but to kill them, it's okay, but doing it in any other circumstances would leave a black stain on your conscience for the rest of your life. Let's go in now."

She followed him inside, thinking his words might not be hypothetical.

Thirty minutes in the gym, and another thirty in the pool finished their daily regime.

They hadn't finished eating breakfast when the gate bell rang. Jason went to the security screen and pressed the button to admit Forester, Pelham, and Vesey.

"Good morning agents, you're early," Drew greeted them, clutching his last piece of toast.

"We wanted a quick word before the bobbies get here."

"That suits me as well. Go through. I'll bring coffee."

Drew brought the promised coffee and told them there'd be more when necessary.

Forester kicked off. "We've read your statement, and we've accepted it as a full and accurate account of what happened, and we will be encouraging the locals to do the same. There has been some resistance to that I understand. Can you throw any light on that?"

"Only that it's consistent with some speculation on my part."

"Care to share."

Drew outlined the detail of his suspicions regarding Turgenev having assistance from someone in the police.

"Thank you, Mr. Parker. We weren't aware that a person responsible for the interference with your system might have been identified. So you believe this Wes Fletcher's suicide was actually a murder?"

"That's right, although I doubt you'll be able to prove it. My suspicion is that he was identified to Turgenev as someone who could interfere with my alarm, and I believe that only someone in the police would have been able to do that. I guess you could speak to the company."

"Any speculations as to which copper might be involved?"

"This would be pure guesswork, but the only cop that has shown any hostility toward me throughout this business has been Detective Inspector Jefferies from High Wycombe. There's no logical reason for his aggression. My actions have been self-explanatory, and I've been fully cooperative throughout. Furthermore he keeps cropping up in different aspects of the case outside his area."

"That's interesting."

"I won't ask you to expand on that, Agent Pelham."

"Best not," he replied.

"I think we've got a handle on most of this now, Mr. Parker, but just so we're singing from the same hymn sheet would you care to give us a summary of how you think that things have panned out the way they have."

Drew proceeded to lay things out to the NCA agents in much the same way as he had to Digits the last time he saw him, only omitting details of the internal operations of Silico, and direct incriminating evidence against Boardman and Carrington.

"I think we're on the same page now, Mr. Parker. We've gone over the head of Sergeant Gasowski and asked for him to restrict his current investigations into yesterday's events. Thames Valley didn't like it, but they understood."

"I'm going to take a wild guess here and say that MI6 are now involved."

"I couldn't possibly comment, Mr. Parker."

"That would be a yes then."

That was when Agent Vesey spoke for the first time. "I noticed that you've been a little short on detail about the connection of these crimes to NorArm Silico, Mr. Parker."

"Agent Vesey, just so you understand, my wife is as strict a stickler for protocol when it comes to running her company as she is to operating this family. We don't discuss things that don't concern us. My wife doesn't tell me things about her work that I'm not supposed to know, and I don't ask. The same applies in reverse. If you want to know something about Silico I suggest you speak to her." All that wasn't strictly true, but they didn't need to know that.

"I will, thank you."

The two cops Gasowski and Ballard had been waiting for some time when they were eventually invited in, and they didn't appear very happy about it.

"Sorry to keep you waiting, Sergeant," Drew apologised. "Would you like my daughter to join us?"

"Yes please, it might save time as it seems that the scope of our investigation is to be limited."

"It's in all our interests, Sergeant, take my word for it," Forester told him.

Vesey stood and walked to the door. "I'll leave you to it and speak to your wife, Mr. Parker, if that's okay."

"Go ahead. I'm sure she'll be happy to help."

Cassie joined them and sat on the desk.

"Is there anything you want to add to your statement from last night, Mr. Parker."

"No, I don't think so."

"Miss Parker-West?"

"Me neither. I just want to know how Mr. Belton is. Do you know?"

"We're told he's awake and stable."

Drew interrupted. "Has he been able to give you any more information about yesterday?"

"Not yet. He's still not well enough to be interviewed."

"I'm concerned for his safety. Turgenev is crazy, I wouldn't put it past him to have another go at Percy in the hospital. Have you put a guard on him?"

"We've had a cop on his door since he came out of surgery."

"Thank you."

"If Turgenev is caught, is that the end of it for you?"

"Absolutely not. If the money exists, and now I'm pretty certain it does, there are other people who've had control of it before and since Stamelis disappeared. They need to be caught and punished."

"What makes you so certain that it exists?"

"The attack on Oliver Babcock could only have been prompted by someone who had inside knowledge of something, and the same applies to the M4 attack on Percy Belton. If you are still claiming to have any doubt then you are either not very good at your job or being particularly obtuse; and I don't think you're a poor copper."

Gasowski smirked.

Drew then added, "But one thing has crossed my mind and that is why after such a long catalogue of connected murders, attempted murders, brutal assaults, and arson attacks has the police investigation been left in the charge of a mere sergeant, no offence intended you understand."

"None taken. That very question has crossed my own mind, Mr. Parker, but I can assure you I am being supervised."

"Far be it for me to tell you your job, but if I were you I'd keep asking the question."

Gasowski changed the subject. "If I were to ask you to speculate about who we should speak to next about all the attacks you mentioned, what would you say?"

"I'd say that the world of high finance is way beyond the expertise of a simple soldier."

"There are a lot of words I could think of to describe you but simple isn't one of them. Thank you for your time, and you Miss Parker-West. We'll leave you to get on with your day. I believe you have an appointment."

"Indeed I do, Sergeant. I need to visit Ms Georgiou to terminate our contract," he replied. "That is if she hasn't already skipped the country."

"Do you think that's a possibility? What about her daughters?"

"I'm sure she believes she loves them, but would you risk your children in that bat-shit crazy kidnap venture? A better question would be, 'Does she love them more than money?' My own view; I doubt it."

THIRTY-SIX

12:15 hours, Third Monday – Home of Ariana Georgiou, Hampstead, North London

The lunchtime traffic had been light, and he was outside Ariana's house not long after midday. When she came to the door and saw it was him, her lip curled in a sneer. "What the fuck do you want. Haven't you done enough damage?"

"You asked me to find your daughters, and that was what I did. What's the problem?"

"You were supposed to bring them home. You've had them taken into care."

"If you hadn't been using them and me in some sort of warped Machiavellian plot, finding them was all I'd have needed to do. To put you straight though, I didn't have them taken into care; the French police did that, on the evidence of their nanny."

"She lied."

"Oh really? Explain it to me, because I can't think of a single reason why a young woman without a criminal record would want to lie with the threat of fifteen years in prison hanging over her. On the other hand, very little of what you've told either me or the UK police has been true."

"Natalie must be in it with the Russians."

"So you're suggesting that the Russians have paid her to take your children to another country in order to make it look as if they'd been kidnapped. Why would they do that? Why not just kidnap them?"

"Because they thought they'd be more difficult to find I suppose."

"That would be much more convincing if you hadn't been in contact with your children the whole time."

"Don't be ridiculous. Of course I haven't. I've been going out of my mind wondering where they are."

"So Natalie has coached the girls to tell the police that they'd been speaking to you every night?"

"They haven't said that."

"I happen to know that they have." His contact in France had given him an outline of the French police's investigation.

"They wouldn't say that."

He ignored her denial. "If Natalie is being paid by the Russians without your approval, why did her sister pay for an overpriced gîte for them to stay in? And why did you send her the money to do it? Is she getting paid by the Russians as well?"

"How do you know...? Yes, I expect she is."

"Perhaps you can also explain why she broke into the home of my daughter's godfather?"

"What?"

"And what connection does she have to Giles Braithwaite, personal assistant to my daughter's godfather?"

"How should I know?"

"I don't believe you, so you can consider my contract with you cancelled." He handed her an envelope. "This is my itemised invoice. It includes all my expenses and costs incurred to date."

"How much is it for?"

"Twelve million, one hundred thousand, three hundred and forty-seven pounds. I'll accept Twelve million one hundred thousand for prompt payment. It is due now and I expect you to transfer the full amount before I leave. If there are any further costs incurred, I'll bill you separately."

"Twelve million pounds! How can it possibly be as much as that?"

"It includes a two-million-pound bad faith charge for lying to me. There's a late payment surcharge of five hundred thousand pounds per day weekends included, so you need to transfer the money today. I could waive that if I were of a mind. I don't choose to."

"I didn't agree to that."

"It was in my contract, that I served on you by email on the day you engaged me, which you accepted by return. I've incurred a lot of costs."

"What costs?"

"I've received two personal injuries involving hospital treatment as a direct result of my investigations; there are charges for each of those."

"They're not my fault."

"Once again I refer you to our contract. I've had to employ a number of specialist technical experts who don't come cheap. One of them, along with his wife was murdered this morning and I've obtained video footage that proves that they were killed by your Russian friends so there's a further million-pound surcharge to compensate the victims' family."

"Murdered?!"

"Three cars and two computers have had to be replaced."

"Three cars!"

"One that I was travelling in was written off when people employed by your Russian friends tried to kill me, two were set alight on my driveway by people operating under your instructions. They sent a warning to lay off the investigation or the next time a member of my family would be in one." He was sure that the arson attack on the cars was by someone acting for Boardman and Carrington, nonetheless it wouldn't have happened if he hadn't been dragged into this by her.

"I didn't have any control over that."

"When you tossed your lot in with a former member of the Russian Secret Service, what did you expect? And why the fuck did you go out of your way to involve me, and worse still, drag your children into it?"

"But I didn't..."

"I'm not interested in any more of your lies Ariana. Are you going to pay or not?"

"I can't."

"Why not?"

"My accounts have all been hacked."

"That's probably your Russian friends. If it was, you'll be lucky to get out of this with a penny."

"Stop calling them my Russian friends. They're not my friends."

"Are you going to keep pretending that you've not been working with them?"

That was when her rigid porcelain-like façade cracked, and tears began to flow down her cheeks.

"I didn't want to do it. They forced me."

"Tell me everything Ariana, and I mean everything."

"There were two of them, Russians. I'd been to a friend's house with the children. It was Natalie's day off, and they were here when we returned. They knew about my father, more than I ever knew. One of them told me that he'd been my father's handler, and how he'd helped him accumulate all his wealth. Then Daddy came to him with the plan to gain control of your wife's company which would enrich both of them and also give the Russian state access to a lot of military secrets."

"That plan involved the murder of Anna's first husband, and the murder and rape of her eldest daughter."

"I didn't know anything about that for years."

"Maybe not, but you certainly knew about them when our daughter Cassie was kidnapped four years later, so you can forget any claim to be an innocent party."

"They told me that my father had hidden away tens of millions of pounds that the Russian State knew nothing about, and they would share it with me if I helped them get it back."

"How were you supposed to help them get it back if you didn't already know about it?"

"I knew it existed, but I didn't know where it was, or how to get to it."

"So what was the plan?"

"One of the Russians, the one that spoke the best English said that you'd murdered my father, and you should be made to pay by helping to get the money."

"I didn't kill your father. I was a thousand miles away when he died. It was the FSB that killed him. If he'd stayed where he was, and accepted his fate, he'd still be alive."

"Where was he?"

"In a refugee processing facility on Leros, reduced to the worthless piece of scum he was."

"You bastard."

"Yeah, I thought we'd already established that. How was I supposed to get hold of this money if I didn't know where it was either?"

"I'd already told him that you know people and were capable of doing things that most people couldn't. That was how you got my father."

"So you decided to collude with these murderous assholes out of pure greed."

"No, they threatened to take the girls if I didn't agree."

"It didn't occur to you to agree to their demands and then tell the cops later?"

"They frightened me."

"Explain how Natalie's sister got to be involved with Giles Braithwaite."

"They knew that Braithwaite was mixed up with Daddy's money somehow and they wanted me to contact him, but I suggested that Brigitte do it."

"So what purpose was my involvement supposed to serve?"

"A distraction mostly, but they hoped that you might have records of his finances that could show something."

"That's bullshit, They've made two attempts on my life, one on my daughter's, and started a fire that could have killed my whole family, That's not a distraction. None of it would have helped me locate your father's secret funds."

"I told you; I had nothing to do with those attempts on your life. They must be doing it for revenge."

"Their revenge; or yours?"

She didn't reply.

"Why would you think they would get access to the money, then split it with you?"

"Because as my father's heir, it would be me that had to be given it in the first place."

"You're still lying."

"I'm not. Stop saying that."

"Have you heard of the Omega Blue Chip Greek Equity Fund?"

"Wha...?"

"To refresh your memory, that's the fund that has been receiving your cut of the dividends from the two funds where Stamelis put his money. When your father disappeared those dividends suddenly stopped and there was absolutely nothing you could do about it because you didn't know the precise source. Somehow you must have discovered that the people responsible for directing the dividends to your Omega account were Steve Boardman and Jared Carrington. But this money was all dirty and everyone associated with it was contaminated by it and you came to an agreement with the conspirators to share the spoils. Only after that did your Omega fund begin to grow again. You've known about it all along."

"I didn't know..."

"What makes me so sick is that you greed is so imbedded that even when your own life and that of your children were under threat from a psychopath, you still couldn't bring yourself to reveal what you knew. Even then you were scheming, trying to find ways to hold on to something that doesn't belong to you, and that you don't need. Instead you concoct a crazy scheme involving me, probably in the hope that I'll kill either the Russians or the two hedge fund crooks and you'll end up keeping at least some of it. Maybe even that I'd be killed as well."

"I didn't want anybody to get hurt," she claimed, too ashamed to look him in the eye.

"That's bullshit. You'd love it if I were killed, and you don't give a fuck who else dies either. But there's a big hole in your plot."

She looked up.

"The only way that the investments in Nevada Foothills or Alhambra funds could be inherited by you, would have been if they were in your father's name. If that were the case the Russians would have found them and taken control of them years ago. Well, I've got news for you. I know whose name they're in, and if he dies they'll go to his heirs, whoever they are."

"Who is it?"

"I'm hardly likely to share that with you am I? The National Crime Agency know most of this. What they don't know yet, is precisely who the sources are."

"How can you know all this?"

"Because the expert that I hired, the one your Russian friends murdered alongside his wife when he refused to tell them what he'd discovered, found a way to make sure that he didn't die in vain."

"Why tell me? Are you just trying to taunt me?"

"I'm giving you an opportunity to call up the NCA and confess before Dmitri Turgenev or Martin Leppik or Marian Bronski, or whatever he calls himself today, gets to you. All his accomplices are dead, so he's completely on his own now with no money and no friends. Wounded animals are most dangerous when they're cornered, and he thinks that you're now his only potential source of cash. If he thinks you can't help him, he'll kill you without a second thought."

"But if I confess, I'll go to prison, I'll never see my children again."

"I doubt you're ever going to see them again anyway Ariana; the French are a very unforgiving race when it comes to the safety of children. Your daughters will remain in care; maybe they'll even be adopted. If they remember you when they're old enough they may visit you in prison or find you if you're out."

"You're an evil piece of shit, separating a mother from her children."

"Like I said earlier, I didn't do that, you did when you gambled them in your crazy plot. You're an obscenely wealthy woman, living off stolen money, you deliberately put my family in harm's way just to get your hands on yet more stolen money and you gambled your kids to do it. What was it you called me that day you engaged me, ruthless, merciless? Well that's exactly what I am, but only when it comes to the safety of the people I love. That's the difference between us."

"You don't understand, it wasn't my idea to try and have you killed. That was the Russian, Bronski."

"If you hadn't dragged me into it in the first place, they wouldn't have had a reason."

"Last week, two men from the Russian government came here. They did unspeakable things to me to get me to tell them everything. If I don't find out where the money is they'll come back."

"You made your bed; don't come crying to me. By the way, that twelve million pounds has already left your accounts."

As he climbed back in his car, his phone vibrated for the fourth or fifth time. He'd put it on silent while he spoke to Ariana. Lifting it he saw that he'd had four missed calls and a voicemail, all from Cassie.

'Daddy, you have to come back right now! It's Percy he's asking for us. He says that he won't speak to the police until he's seen us, all of us. We're at the hospital ITU.'

He quickly tapped a text reply.

On way 90 min max.

He was scared now, for more than one reason, the urgency of the message, that he might not get there in time, and most of all about what it was that Percy wanted to say. He feared he already knew.

The GPS in his car was programmed to redirect him around road closures and traffic snarl ups, and it predicted a seventy-minute drive. In the event he managed it in sixty-five, probably collecting more than one speeding ticket along the way.

THIRTY-SEVEN

16:45 hours, Third Monday – Royal Berkshire Hospital, Reading.

His speed may have been high, but by the time he'd found somewhere to park, and made his way through the labyrinthine corridors of the huge building, ninety minutes had been about right. When he burst through the door into the ITU waiting room Anna and Cassie turned to him with frightened expressions etched onto their faces. "What've the docs told you?" he asked.

"They say he's stable but very weak," Anna replied. "They don't want him to have any visitors at all, but he's insistent."

Jason appeared from behind him. "I'll let them know you're here Drew."

Drew hugged his wife. "Does he think he's dying?"

"I don't know. The doctors say that given time he should make a good recovery, but there will be ongoing consequences."

"So what's the goddamned emergency?"

"He won't say, but he insists on seeing us."

Jason returned with a nurse.

"Thank you for coming all of you. My name is Huma Abadi, I'm the senior sister on duty today," she said, "I know you all want to see Mr. Belton. He wants to see you all as well. In these circumstances we'd normally much prefer he waited at least another twenty-four hours for visits. However, he's becoming quite agitated, so the doctor has agreed that you spend some time with him, but no longer than an hour. If he becomes distressed or his condition deteriorates I'll have to ask you to leave."

"We understand," Anna said.

"I'll go and wait at home. Give him my love," Jason told them as the nurse led them out of the room.

In the visitor prep room to the ITU they were asked to sterilise their hands with antibacterial gel, and don sterile gowns, hats and masks before being shown through. With some difficulty they managed to accommodate Drew's huge body. After punching a four-figure code into a digital entry lock she led them into the busy ward where heart and blood monitors beeped from all corners of the room, and gown-clad medics tended to seriously ill patients.

Outside the half-glazed private room where Percy was being treated they found Gasowski and Ballard waiting looking as absurd in caps and gowns as they did themselves.

Gasowski stood and greeted them. "Can you try to keep your visit as brief as possible. We really need to speak to him about what happened."

They could see their friend through the open door, and the sight was truly shocking. One arm was in plaster from his shoulder to his wrist and supported in a sling suspended from a bracket attached to his bed, while the bandages around his head and across his nose made his face appear distorted behind an oxygen mask.

The nurse ushered them into the room and touched her patient on the shoulder. The swelling around one eye was so severe it was completely closed, but he opened the other. "Your visitors are here Mr. Belton."

"Thank you, nurse. Can you leave us please, and close the door?" His voice was weak and muffled by the mask. "Come closer."

"Oh my dear, dear Percy, what have they done to you?" Anna Wa tearful, while an equally weepy Cassie stroked his unbroken arm.

"Hush. Let me say what I need to. The painkillers make me drowsy and there's a lot I have to say."

"Two years ago Giles confessed that he'd been working for Stamelis to manage the income from some secret investments he'd made in two different hedge funds with holdings in Silico. Giles had learned from me about Manos's death. He explained that in theory when the death was confirmed the ownership and income revert to Ariana..." He was interrupted by a coughing fit which was obviously very painful.

"Please don't do this Uncle Percy. It's not important," Cassie pleaded.

Percy lifted his hand and reached to her. "My darling Cassie, this is the most important thing I've ever done in my life. Please allow me to finish."

"The holdings that Giles was managing hadn't been made in his name, they'd originally been made in mine without my knowledge, and they'd begun years before when Lemonis first became involved with you, Anna. Giles job was to distribute the income between Stamelis and the people that he'd nominated, who included Ariana. The people inside the hedge funds who helped him set it up, and a percentage for himself."

Another brief spell of coughing interrupted him, before he continued. "I told him it was highly illegal let alone immoral that Ariana was still profiting from Stamelis's ill-gotten gains, and we should report it. Giles said if we did that, the money would end up back in Russia just as the rest of his funds had. He said he was concerned that now the accounts that Manos had set up to receive his own shares had effectively been frozen, my supposed involvement would be exposed. He persuaded me that I should allow the holdings to continue to operate in my name and take Stamelis's share of income in his stead."

Drew speaking for the first time, stopped him. "How much is involved?"

"The funds invest in many companies other than Silico, and the total figure of his investment at the moment is in the region of £325 million. Manos was taking 50% of the income, Ariana 25%, the two enablers inside the funds 10% each and Giles 5%."

"So he was proposing to hand over a hundred and sixty million pounds to you?"

"He didn't feel he had any choice."

"What did the other conspirators have to say about it?"

"At first I don't think they knew. They hadn't had Stamelis's death confirmed and were assuming that his share would pass into his estate once it was. I don't think they found out until Ariana told the two Russians and they came looking for it. He told me that she never knew the detail of how it all operated. She'd just been only too happy to keep taking the money until her father's death had been officially confirmed. Giles told me that he never revealed to any of them that it was my name that they'd used when they set it all up on behalf of Stamelis, but the more I think about it the more I think they must have known. He confessed that Manos had been responsible for putting him in place when I first gave him the job. It was such a betrayal."

"So Braithwaite decided to quit while he was ahead."

"After Oliver Babcock was abducted he must have thought it was getting too dangerous."

"What were Giles and his girlfriend looking for in your house that night they attacked me?"

"She isn't his girlfriend. Before he died Manos arranged that Natalie and her sister would act as middlemen between Giles and Ariana. They get very well rewarded, although I doubt they know what it is they're being used to hide. Giles was probably looking for the laptop where he recorded all the transactions."

"Where is it now, do you know?"

"I took it and hid it in the tack room at Pangbourne Grange. When things started to get violent, I decided I didn't want anything more to do with it."

"What's been happening to the income since you became involved?"

"I haven't taken any, I've just allowed them to be reinvested in the funds."

"Do you know the passwords for the laptop?"

"Under threat of exposure to the police, I forced Giles to tell me. I've since changed the password on the computer and all the relevant accounts so he wouldn't ever be able to access them again. Now they're all *isoldeandcassie121168*'."

"Why have you chosen to tell us all this now though, Uncle Percy? Why put yourself through the pain. It could have waited."

"No it couldn't. People have been dying. If I'd gone to the police when Giles first confessed, they might still be alive. I should have told you about the laptop when you came to my house, but I was too ashamed. Things have now degenerated so badly that I believe that Drew is the only person who can put an end to it."

"Who're the operators inside the funds?"

"I expect it's all on the laptop, if you haven't already worked it out."

"Are you going to tell the police now?"

"Not yet. I don't think it'll help for them to know until after you've brought things to a close. I think you know what I mean."

"I understand," Drew said with a steely expression on his face.

"Will you leave me now. I'm so tired. Before you go I wanted to say that you three are my dearest friends and I'm so ashamed that I've let you all down so badly. I love you all so much and hope that you'll forgive me."

"Percy, you've done nothing to be ashamed of. You've prevented any more of that dirty money getting back into Putin or Ariana's hands. That's a good thing," Anna told him. "We all love you, and we want you to come and stay with us while you recover."

Cassie kissed his cheek. "I love you too, Uncle Percy. Please get better soon."

"You're a tough old codger Percy Belton, many people I've served with would have given over that laptop after half the treatment they gave you."

"They would have killed me anyway, Drew."

"Maybe," he replied and gripped the man's uninjured hand.

"Tell the policemen that I'm too tired to answer questions now. Ask them to come back tomorrow."

None of them spoke until they were inside Drew's car.

"I'm so frightened that he'll die, Mummy. I know he's not my real uncle, but after you and Daddy, he and Jason are the only family I've got."

"It's a wonderful hospital, darling, I'm sure they'll give him the very best treatment, and, he's a tough old codger. He'll come through this."

Jason was asking after Percy almost as soon as they stepped inside. Anna and Cassie were still too upset to say much, but Drew gave him a brief summary of how their friend was faring.

"What did you do about Eli?"

"I told him to take the day off, so we'll need to order in, unless you want me to put something together."

"Thanks, Jason, but no. Get something delivered; your choice. The girls aren't in the mood to think about it at the moment."

Drew left him to go to the stable in search of the laptop. The timber structure had been built at the same time as the house, less than twenty-four years before. It had been well maintained, and Toby was meticulous with his housekeeping, so Drew was curious how it could have gone unnoticed. There were no obvious places to hide something the size and shape of a laptop, so he began a careful search.

Looking around him, the walls were hung with saddle racks and hooks for bridles or helmets, there were open shelves with grooming equipment, leather, and tack treatment products but no unoccupied shelves, and no drawers. He couldn't see anywhere it would be possible to hide a computer.

He called the groom. "Hi Toby, sorry to call you at home but I'm wondering if you could help me out. Percy is in hospital, and he tells me that he hid something in the tack room, but I've looked, and I can't see anything."

"Is he talking about the computer?"

"That's right."

"He came to see me at home a week or two ago and gave me the laptop and asked me to put it in the tack room and look after it. He said if anybody other than a member of the family asked about it I was to deny all knowledge. I thought it was a bit weird, but I took it. You're right though, there isn't anywhere in the tack room to hide it, so I put it in the groom's sleeping quarters. You just tip the wardrobe against the wall and it's underneath."

"Thanks Toby, that's a great help."

"Is Percy alright? What happened?"

"He got quite badly beaten up, and he'll be in the hospital a while yet, I expect. I can't tell you much more at the moment."

With little difficulty, he located what he'd been searching for and took it back to the house. Fortunately, it used the same charging cable as one of the other laptops in the house. The computer required a pin number rather than a password, so he tried the last six digits of the keyword that Percy had given him. They didn't work. He went to Anna and asked if the numbers meant anything to her.

"It's my birthdate written in the American format with the last two numbers reversed," she said straightaway. Are you looking at it now?"

"Yes, I don't think we can afford to waste time."

She followed him through to the study.

It was a very modern expensive piece of equipment with a specification far in excess of what was needed for what it was being used for, but then money had never been an obstacle to people who got it by stealing it from others.

Between them using various six-digit formats they attempted to open the computer. Using Anna's actual birthdate in YY/MM/DD format was the combination that eventually gave him access.

Percy had created a document which opened with the Start programme. It set out the money trail in layman's terms. He'd listed the names of those involved, their pseudonyms and account numbers, he recognised some of the names from the draft memo that Dennis Hargreaves had created.

In Percy's document he'd included screen shots of the balances on a day that must have been about the time he'd handed the laptop to Toby. He explained that most of the accounts would record when they were last accessed and who by, and all accounts had 'view only' access permissions for fellow conspirators.

Braithwaite was still missing, and he had to assume that the others would all be aware of that by now. Opening any of the accounts would alert the others that Braithwaite still had access or that someone else had taken control, and that was something that Drew wanted to avoid for the time being.

Percy went on to explain the paper trail (or in this case, the paperless trail) They had a number of dead letter email accounts - active email addresses to which more than one person had access. If one password holder wanted to leave a message for another, they would create a draft email and leave it unposted. When the intended recipient had read it, they could reply by editing the draft.

Percy had learned from Braithwaite that the password Stamelis had created for all the various email accounts was *Xenia&Elektra'*. Just opening the draft emails in the accounts wouldn't leave a trail so that's what they did. They all had unrecognizable random names, meaningless to anybody else.

Drew and Anna had to assume that there was one email account for each pair of conspirators - Ariana and Giles, Giles and Carrington, Carrington and Boardman, Boardman, and Giles - with a fifth account between Giles and an unknown person.

"Braithwaite has obviously been in contact with all of them, and it looks like they've all been in contact with each other, but we don't know for how long," Drew observed.

"Whose is the fifth account?" Anna asked.

"Dollars to donuts it's Turgenev."

When Drew went to open it he found that like all the other accounts, the computer had saved the password. He doubted it was the same as the other email accounts, but as it only appeared as a series of dots he would never know what it was.

Drew was only able to make assumptions as to the ownership of each of the accounts based on the content of the last edit of the draft email, but the one between Ariana and Giles was obvious. It read:

I've heard nothing from you about dealing with these Russian bastards, so I've made my own arrangements. I've set that bastard Parker loose on them, hopefully they'll kill each other, but if not we'll need to get someone to kill the survivors.

"What a bitch!" Anna exclaimed.

"Yeah, well; that's not news."

They read each of the draft emails in turn and one thing was obvious above all, and that was that the only considerations any of them had were for their own security and how much money each could make, save, or steal.

"I'm surprised that there are no accounts between the two sisters," Anna remarked.

"Maybe there are, but Braithwaite was out of the loop."

"What now though?"

"Until I've dealt with Turgenev, I'm not going to do anything."

"How are you going to deal with him though? You've no idea where he is."

"I'm going to give him something that he thinks he wants."

He explained his plan, which he thought had perhaps an 80% chance of success.

Anna was dubious, worried that somebody else would get hurt.

He opened the fifth account and typed.

The names you are looking for are Stephen Boardman of Nevada Foothills and Jared Carrington of Alhambra, they've arranged a meeting to discuss how to satisfy your requirements. They won't expect you to be there. I won't attend, so it's up to you to sort it out with them. Once you've agreed between you what you want to do, I'll hand over the access codes. After that I'm out, I want nothing more to do with the whole affair. The meeting is 08:30 this Wednesday on the 9th hole of the Cotswold and Berkshire Golf Club, Goring.

He saved the draft and closed the page.

"Are you going to put drafts on Boardman and Carrington's emails as well? So they know to turn up?"

"I don't want them to turn up. I'm just going to tell Gasowski, but not yet."

THIRTY-EIGHT

06:30 hours, Third Tuesday – Pangbourne Grange.

"Can we go and see Uncle Percy today, Dad?"

"If we call first and they say it's okay, I don't see why not. Other than that I was hoping we can have a day off from villain hunting."

"Is it almost over then?"

"The main players will all have been dealt with one way or another in the next few days. There may be one or two minor walk on parts who slip the net, but they won't be in a position to cause us any more trouble."

"What about the woman who hit you over the head?"

"She and her sister will have done quite well out of this plot, but I doubt her motive was to do me harm. More a case of not wanting to get caught."

"And Giles?"

"He's probably done very well out of it too, but thanks to Percy he's lost all future access to the money, and to be frank I can't be bothered to go after him and it's up to the police to deal with the main players, Turgenev, Ariana, Boardman, and Carrington."

"What about the money?"

"It's all in Percy's name so it's up to him to decide what happens to it I guess."

"What about Ariana though? What if she wants revenge."

"This is speculation, but her passport won't allow her out of the country at the moment. None of her liquid assets are accessible to her and she's on the brink of being extradited to France for trafficking her own children. It's my guess she'll face a list of fraud charges here, and her children will likely be adopted. By the time she gets out of prison much of her wealth will have disappeared one way or the other and I think that thoughts about revenge against me will be the last thing on her mind."

Where will her money have gone? I don't understand."

"I expect Putin will have taken it when he finds out that it belonged to Russia in the first place."

"Who'll tell him?"

"I will."

"It's all been so complicated though. Every time I try to get it all in my head, I think of new questions."

"I doubt that anybody will ever know the full story, and no doubt there are a few people involved who we don't even know exist, but they don't need to trouble us. Do you want to go for the full ten today?"

"Yes, I need to work off some of the rage I've been building up."

They both pushed themselves in all three sections of their exercise routine, and after they'd showered and dressed they smiled at each other across the breakfast table.

"Why're you two looking so pleased with yourselves this morning?" Jason asked.

"Dad and I had a really good exercise session this morning. It's the endorphins; they help relieve pain, reduce stress, and improve your sense of well-being."

"I think you're both nuts. I like to ease myself gently into the day. And what's this *Dad* thing, what happened to *Daddy*. I thought that was kind of cute."

"Robert said he thought it sounded a bit babyish, and he's probably right, but that's not why I changed. If I'm going to be working with Dad, talking about my Daddy, wouldn't do my cred any good. You don't mind, do you, Dad?"

Drew had sat silently through that part of the conversation. "Sweetheart, you can call me Dad, Daddy, or Drew. I'm just happy that you think of me like that."

Anna joined them a few minutes later, looking as if she hadn't slept at all.

"How are you this morning, sweetheart?"

"Not brilliant, I'm so worried about Percy. I've just called the hospital. They said he'd had quite a disturbed night, but he's resting now. I asked if we could visit later and they said we could try at three when afternoon visiting began, but not to be upset if he wasn't up to it."

"We'll go on the off chance. If it turns out that he's not up to it we'll go again tomorrow. We've nothing else planned."

"What about Turgenev?"

"The police can handle him."

While Cassie practiced reversing the Audi at the front of the house, Drew spent the next hour or so composing a report for Gasowski to explain the whole series of events from when Turgenev fled Russia up to date.

At about twelve-thirty Anna's phone rang. "What! When how... Good god! What are the police saying?... No of course not... Let me know if you hear anything else."

Drew overheard her half of the conversation as he came to the kitchen to refresh his coffee.

"Everything okay, sweetheart?"

"Steve Boardman's been murdered. His wife found him in his car with his throat cut yesterday evening."

"Fuck! That must have been Turgenev."

"There was another dead man in the car with him who hasn't been identified."

He hurried back to the study and booted up Braithwaite's computer to log into to the email account that he had assumed to be his contact with Turgenev. The draft email had been edited, it now said:

I be there, and you be there too, I kill people who betray me. I need you to change passwords then you never have access again. If you not there I come for you and kill you. I know where you and little French bitch hide out.

Drew sighed. "Turgenev's gone over the edge," he said. "I suppose he thinks that if he gets Braithwaite, he no longer needs Boardman and Carrington."

"Should we warn Carrington?"

"Not directly. I'll call Gasowski." He sighed again and picked up his phone just as it started to ring. "Sergeant. What can I do for you?" He pressed the speaker button.

"I'm in Ashampstead, not far from you."

"That's nice. Did you want to drop in for coffee or something?"

"I was wondering if you know anyone who lives here?"

"Not as far as I know. Why do you ask? Just a minute, my wife is writing something down for me." He waited until she'd finished. "Anna says that a member of her company board lives there, a guy called Jared Carrington."

"He's a member of the Silico board? Oh Jesus!"

"Sergeant, much as I enjoy guessing games, do you want to give me a clue where this conversation is going so I can join in."

"Jared Carrington was murdered in his bed last night and amongst the things found in his room was a piece of paper with your name written on it."

"If you're asking me if I had anything to do with his murder, then this is the weirdest way I ever heard for a cop to do it."

"I'm not suggesting that, because a neighbour saw the man who did it as he escaped, and it definitely wasn't you. It was the man you say was called Turgenev. That was the other reason I rang."

"Sergeant there's something else you should know unless you've already been told."

"What's that?"

"Anna had a call from the company chief security officer about twenty minutes ago. He told her that another member of the board was murdered last night. It may be outside your area though. Where did Boardman live, sweetheart?"

"I don't know the address, but it was somewhere in Surrey."

"Did you catch that, Sergeant?"

"Yes, thanks. Is this connected to all the other shit?"

"I'd be surprised if it weren't."

"We're going to have another long talk about this, Mr. Parker, I'll call you. I need to get back on to this."

"No wait. Turgenev has clearly gone crazy now. That being the case, you need to double up with the guard on Percy Belton."

"Oh Christ you're right, thanks."

"Sorry to be the bearer of bad news, but the Braithwaite guy is also at risk. I've no idea where he is but that doesn't mean that Turgenev doesn't."

"This is getting worse by the minute."

"Are you still being starved of resources by your superiors?"

"Yes."

"It might be worthwhile asking why, in case you're being set up to take the fall when this all goes to shit."

"No kidding. Thanks for your help, I'll call you tomorrow."

"This is crazy, Gasowski is running around like is ass is on fire and the assholes aren't giving him any help."

"What's going on?"

"It's my guess they don't want Turgenev caught by the cops."

"Who doesn't?"

"The spooks. Turgenev could be a treasure trove of data about Putin, his finances, and the hierarchy of his immediate organisation. They want him in their clutches."

"Do you mean they're expecting to let him go in exchange for information?"

"New ID, little bungalow in Ruislip, nice little job in B&Q, small pension. I wouldn't be surprised."

"That's disgusting. He's a multiple murderer."

"He's a former member of the FSB. He was a multiple murderer before he ever set foot in the country."

Having been told that Percy was awake although still tired and they might have to wait, they called Eli and gave him a second day off and had a late lunch.

They'd left themselves plenty of time to get to the hospital before three.

THIRTY-NINE

15:00 hours, Third Tuesday – Royal Berkshire Hospital, Reading, Berkshire

Tuesday was always a busy day at the hospital. It was when many departments had their out-patient clinics, so parking was difficult, meaning they had to park further afield and walk. It was nearly three fifteen before they arrived in the antechamber to get into the sterile clothing as they had the day before.

Anna buzzed to be allowed admission into the third floor ITU's sterile environment, and a voice asked who they were to visit and how many of them there were as patients were limited to four visitors and Mr. Belton already had one. After confirming there were only three of them the buzzer sounded, and the door lock clunked. They were no more than three paces inside the ward when Cassie pointed. "That's him, Daddy. That's Turgenev!"

The gait, size and profile of the masked man dressed in blue surgical scrubs leaving Percy's room had made him instantly recognisable to Cassie. Without questioning her judgement, Drew broke into a run, his daughter chasing after him, almost knocking the policeman over as he came out of a toilet.

"Cassie, Drew! Please don't!" Anna shouted after them. If either of them heard they gave no indication, and she watched her husband disappear through a door at the other end of the ward with their daughter close behind. Astonished medics turned to see what the commotion was about.

Barely a pace behind, Cassie followed her father through the door into a service corridor just as the Russian disappeared into a fire escape stairway. Drew threw the escape door open to see a group of medics on their break gathering on the half landing one flight of stairs below.

Drew shouted at them, "Where did he go?!" Moments of astonished silence followed. "The guy in scrubs, he's a killer, where did he go?" Finally one pointed upwards.

Father and daughter followed the sound of echoing footsteps through two more floors ripping off their gowns as they went. Doors to other floors were all locked to prevent entry from the stairway. Approaching the top they heard a voice shout, "Hey you can't go out there!" followed by a scream of pain.

More flights of stairs brought them to an injured man in overalls sitting beside a door propped open by a toolbox that led onto the flat roof.

"What's going on," the workman asked, clutching a wound in his arm?

"Is there another way down from here?" Drew asked, as Cassie ran past onto the roof.

"Only the far staircase, but you can't open the door without a key."

"Are you well enough to call for help?"

"I've got my radio."

"Get them to call the police up here as well," he said and followed his daughter onto the roof.

Large pipes and galvanised steel ducts criss-crossed the roof between air conditioning units enclosed in white metal cabinets. There were two big brick-built lift motor rooms and at the far end of the building was the door into the enclosure of the other stairway, but there was no sign of his daughter.

"Cassie!" he called.

"I'm here, Dad."

She appeared from behind one of the motor rooms with Turgenev holding her around the waist from behind with his left arm. He was holding a knife to her neck with his right.

"There's nowhere off this roof except past me, Turgenev, and nowhere to go even if you did get past. In a few minutes, this hospital will be crawling with police. The bodies of Boardman and Carrington have been discovered, and the cops know that you're responsible."

"If you not get out of way I kill this bitch."

"How do you think that will improve your chances of escape?"

"You think I make idle threat?"

"Okay then, let me move out of the way. Cassie, don't panic everything will be okay if you remember your training."

Drew began to make sideway steps away from the stairway door, all the time watching the other two move closer to it. Then, as Cassie lifted her right foot to step across a thick pipe wrapped in silver-coloured insulation she burst into action. Her right hand grasped his left wrist loosening his grip enough for her to spin on her left foot and viciously hit him in the side of his head with her left elbow. The series of well-practised moves took microseconds and Turgenev staggered and fell.

Cassie wasn't finished though. She stepped toward him and kicked him under the chin, knocking him flat, before stamping on his wrist to make him release the knife. The man lay stunned as she kicked the weapon out of his reach.

"Fuck you!" she shouted as she stood over the man on the floor, "and fuck everything about you. You're a worthless piece of shit. I hope you die a long and painful death."

Drew moved to stand by her side and put his arm around her shoulder. They watched as the Russian pushed himself to his feet and limped as fast as he were able to the far stairway.

"There's nowhere to go Turgenev," Drew shouted after him, but the man continued until he reached what he hoped was a way to escape. Twisting and pulling at the handle had no effect and he glanced back at the two pursuers casually walking toward him.

"You need to give up. You've reached the end of your murderous road. Now it's time to take your punishment."

He ignored Drew's advice and crept to the side of the stairway housing where a tray of armoured cables disappeared over the edge of the building, and knelt beside them. He obviously intended to attempt to climb down using them.

The cables were secured in the tray by steel bands about three feet apart and the tray stood away from the brickwork by about an inch. To an experience climber in the right footwear it would have provided an easy way down to the flat roof of a building extension below, but to the elderly Turgenev in street shoes it was a fool's venture. Reaching down for his first foothold he slipped and was left hanging by his fingertips. His flailing feet scrambled to find somewhere to gain purchase but hanging by only his hands he had no chance.

"Help me," he pleaded. "Please."

Drew went to the buildings edge and looked down.

"I begging you, help me up."

Any obser might have seen Drew bend and reach out a hand for the Russian to grab, but after two futile attempts the Russian lost his grip on the cable rack. The scream as he fell abruptly ended as he hit the roof of the projecting building below.

Drew looked down to see the murderer's motionless body sprawled unnaturally across a service pipe, turned and looked at Cassie. Her expression revealed nothing, and neither did his.

They walked back toward the open stairway door where someone was treating the injured workman and arrived at the same moment as two breathless policemen.

"He fell," Drew succinctly informed them.

"I saw what happened," the workman said. "This guy tried to save him, but it was too late."

Handing one of the cops his card, Drewsaid, "We've got a real sick family member in the ITU. We need to be with him."

Silently, the two descended the stairs, both anxious about what they'd find. A hospital security guard was standing by the open door, so they had no difficulty recognising which floor they wanted or in gaining entry after a brief explanation of who they were and what had happened.

The care of patients was continuing as if nothing had happened, but there were two more police officers standing at the door to Percy's room. They weren't allowed in, but they could see their friend lying bandaged, lifeless, and alone, his monitoring systems silent and their screens black.

Suddenly Drew heard Cassie began to wail. He turned and caught her as her knees gave way, her chest heaving as painful sobs wracked her body. A policewoman led them out of the unit to a relatives' room where a tearful Anna was waiting with a nurse and another policewoman.

Drew set Cassie on her feet, gathered his wife in his free arm, and the three silently shared their grief.

"The fucking piece of shit murdered that dear sweet harmless old man," Anna eventually said.

"Turgenev's dead now, darling. That's the end of the whole fucking saga."

"Is it really?"

"They're all dead now, except Ariana Georgiou, and she's probably wishing she was."

FORTY
The Aftermath

The next few days were spent in endless interviews of members of the Pangbourne household by the police and members of the NCA including Elite Agent Vesey and a colleague who Drew suspected was really from MI6.

What had been remarkable about the questions from Vesey and her friend wasn't so much what was asked, but what wasn't. There were few questions about the money that Turgenev had been chasing, and very little about the original source of Ariana's wealth.

A post-mortem revealed that Percy had died from a narrow knife wound into his heart, but not before receiving further injuries from Turgenev. The funeral took place three weeks after his death, with a small number of attendees. Anna read a moving eulogy and in accordance with his wishes, he was buried in the local authority cemetery with a simple headstone.

Several days later, the Parker-West family were invited to attend the reading of the will by his solicitor, Patricia Spenser, of Ruskin and Firth, the same firm which represented both Drew and Anna. Patricia revealed that Percy had only rewritten his will a matter of weeks before he passed away. While they waited for her to begin they reflected on the events since their friend's death.

When they talked about it later Drew suggested that whoever it was who had power over these things had decided not to expose the details of the conspiracy. If it became known that so much crooked Russian money had been invested in one of NATO's most important defence companies, albeit indirectly, it could cause huge problems. So as it stood they were leaving well alone.

When the will reading commenced it transpired that they were they only attendees because other than a few minor bequests, there was only one beneficiary.

After reciting the formal introductory paragraphs and listing a few minor bequests, the solicitor read the rest of the document.

I have only one deep regret in my life, and that is that I was never able to father a child as wonderful as the one I have grown to have the greatest possible paternal love, my goddaughter Cassandra Parker-West. So in recognition of all the pleasure she has given me whilst watching her grow into the beautiful, brave, and intelligent woman she is, I leave in trust until she is twenty-four, the entire residue of my estate.

Cassie gasped in shock at what her uncle had both said and done, without realising at the time that the inheritance would include everything that had been invested in Percy's name by Manos Stamelis.

As they left the solicitor's office she said in tears, I don't want it Mummy."

"I know," her mother said, but there's time enough for you to decide what you'd like to happen to it."

The ongoing consequences were that the two hedge funds would continue to operate unaffected, and the heirs of Boardman and Carrington would retain their illegal gains as did Babcock and Braithwaite.

Much of Ariana's wealth had already been sequestered by the UK authorities after she was arrested at a small airfield in Oxfordshire attempting to board a light aircraft to Holland. It would likely be years before she regained control of any of it, if ever. She was on bail awaiting trial on a long list of offences, and her children remained in care in France.

Natalie was facing French charges of conspiracy to traffic children.

The whereabouts of Giles Braithwaite and Brigette Laurent were unknown.

EPILOGUE

Office of the President of Russian Federation, Kremlin, Moscow

Leonid Gribov stepped into the huge room where Vladimir Putin sat at his desk.

"Comrade Gribov, what have you to report?"

"The traitor Turgenev is dead, but I regret to admit that before dying he killed the last two known conspirators in the plot to steal Russian resources conceived by Manos Stamelis. It is believed he also murdered the man I sent to attempt recovery of the Russian money."

"Who was this man?"

"His name was Helmut Kruger, a German citizen who was a minor asset of ours in the German embassy."

"Will his loss be missed?"

"No, Sir."

"Can any connection be made between him and Russia?"

"No, Sir."

"How is life outside the military suiting you?"

"It has been a big change, Sir, but okay."

"Would you be happy if it were made permanent?"

"It would be an honour, Comrade President."

"Then that is what will happen. You've done well Comrade Leonid."

It was high praise indeed.

CRIME FICTION FROM APS BOOKS
(www.andrewsparke.com)

Printed in Great Britain
by Amazon

39628220R00155